THE LABOURS O.

Agatha Christie was born in Torquay and encouraged
to write by Eden Philpotts, the Devonshire play-
wright. In her first book, *The Mysterious Affair at
Styles*, she created the now famous Belgian detective,
Hercule Poirot, who is as popular as Conan Doyle's
Sherlock Holmes. This was published in 1920 and her
acknowledged masterpiece, *The Murder of Roger
Ackroyd*, was published in 1926. She has now written
some 75 detective novels, romantic novels under the
pseudonym of Mary Westmacott and many short
stories and plays – including *The Mousetrap*, still
running in London after nineteen years. MGM have
filmed many of her stories, including *Ten Little
Niggers* and *Witness for the Prosecution*. She is the
most widely read English author today and has made
more money out of 'murder' than any woman since
Lucrezia Borgia! Agatha Christie, now in her eighties,
is married to Sir Max Mallowan, well-known archaeo-
logist and is a Commander of the Order of the British
Empire. They live in Devon.

# AGATHA CHRISTIE

# THE LABOURS OF HERCULES

UNABRIDGED

PAN BOOKS LTD : LONDON

First published 1947 by William Collins Sons and Co Ltd
This edition published 1971 by Pan Books Ltd,
33 Tothill Street, London SW1

ISBN 0 330 02780 8

*2nd Printing 1973*
*3rd Printing 1973*

*Made and printed in Great Britain by*
*Cox & Wyman Ltd, London, Reading and Fakenham*

# CONTENTS

# FOREWORD

HERCULE POIROT's flat was essentially modern in its furnishings. It gleamed with chromium. Its easy-chairs, though comfortably padded, were square and uncompromising in outline.

On one of these chairs sat Hercule Poirot, neatly—in the middle of the chair. Opposite him, in another chair, sat Dr. Burton, Fellow of All Souls, sipping appreciatively at a glass of Poirot's Château Mouton Rothschild. There was no neatness about Dr. Burton. He was plump, untidy, and beneath his thatch of white hair beamed a rubicund and benign countenance. He had a deep wheezy chuckle and the habit of covering himself and everything round him with tobacco ash. In vain did Poirot surround him with ash-trays.

Dr. Burton was asking a question.

" Tell me," he said. " Why Hercule ? "

" You mean, my Christian name ? "

" Hardly a *Christian* name," the other demurred. " Definitely pagan. But why ? That's what I want to know. Father's fancy ? Mother's whim ? Family reasons ? If I remember rightly—though my memory isn't what it was— you had a brother called Achille, did you not ? "

Poirot's mind raced back over the details of Achille Poirot's career. Had all that really happened ?

" Only for a short space of time," he replied.

Dr. Burton passed tactfully from the subject of Achille Poirot.

" People should be more careful how they name their children," he ruminated. " I've got godchildren. I know. Blanche, one of 'em is called—dark as a gipsy ! Then there's Deirdre, Deirdre of the Sorrows—she's turned out merry as a grig. As for young Patience, she might as well have been named Impatience and be done with it ! And Diana—well, Diana——" the old Classical scholar shuddered. " Weighs twelve stone *now*—and she's only fifteen ! They *say* it's puppy fat—but it doesn't look that way to me. *Diana !* They

9

wanted to call her Helen, but I did put my foot down there. Knowing what her father and mother looked like ! And her grandmother for that matter ! I tried hard for Martha or Dorcas or something sensible—but it was no good—waste of breath. Rum people, parents. . . ."

He began to wheeze gently—his small fat face crinkled up. Poirot looked at him inquiringly.

" Thinking of an imaginary conversation. Your mother and the late Mrs. Holmes, sitting sewing little garments or knitting : ' Achille, Hercule, Sherlock, Mycroft. . . .' "

Poirot failed to share his friend's amusement.

" What I understand you to mean is, that in physical appearance *I* do not resemble a Hercules ? "

Dr. Burton's eyes swept over Hercule Poirot, over his small neat person attired in striped trousers, correct black jacket and natty bow tie, swept up from his patent leather shoes to his egg-shaped head and the immense moustache that adorned his upper lip.

" Frankly, Poirot," said Dr. Burton, " you don't ! I gather," he added, " that you've never had much time to study the Classics ? "

" That is so."

" Pity. Pity. You've missed a lot. Everyone should be made to study the Classics if I had my way."

Poirot shrugged his shoulders.

" *Eh bien*, I have got on very well without them."

" Got on ! *Got on !* It's not a question of getting on. That's the wrong view altogether. The Classics aren't a ladder leading to quick success like a modern correspondence course ! It's not a man's working hours that are important—it's his leisure hours. That's the mistake we all make. Take yourself now, you're getting on, you'll be wanting to get out of things, to take things easy—what are you going to do then with *your* leisure hours ? "

Poirot was ready with his reply.

" I am going to attend—seriously—to the cultivation of vegetable marrows."

Dr. Burton was taken aback.

" Vegetable marrows ? What d'yer mean ? Those great swollen green things that taste of water ? "

"Ah," Poirot spoke enthusiastically. "But that is the whole point of it. They need *not* taste of water."

"Oh! I know—sprinkle 'em with cheese, or minced onion or white sauce."

"No, no—you are in error. It is my idea that the actual flavour of the marrow itself can be improved. It can be given," he screwed up his eyes, "a bouquet——"

"Good God, man, it's not a claret." The word *bouquet* reminded Dr. Burton of the glass at his elbow. He sipped and savoured. "Very good wine, this. Very sound. Yes." His head nodded in approbation. "But this vegetable marrow business—you're not *serious*? You don't mean "—he spoke in lively horror—"that you're actually going to *stoop* "—his hands descended in sympathetic horror on his own plump stomach—"stoop, and fork dung on the things, and feed 'em with strands of wool dipped in water and all the rest of it? "

"You seem," Poirot said, "to be well acquainted with the culture of the marrow? "

"Seen gardeners doing it when I've been staying in the country. But seriously, Poirot, what a hobby! Compare that to "—his voice sank to an appreciative purr—"an easy-chair in front of a wood fire in a long, low room lined with books— must be a *long* room—not a square one. Books all round one. A glass of port—and a book open in your hand. Time rolls back as you read: " he quoted sonorously:

"' Μήτι δ᾿ αὖτε κυβερνήτης ἐνὶ οἴνοπι πόντῳ
νῆα θοὴν ἰθύνει ἐρεχθομένην ἀνέμοισι '"

He translated:

"' By skill again, the pilot on the wine-dark sea straightens The swift ship buffeted by the winds.'

Of course you can never really get the spirit of the original."

For the moment, in his enthusiasm, he had forgotten Poirot. And Poirot, watching him, felt suddenly a doubt—an uncomfortable twinge. Was there, here, something that he had missed? Some richness of the spirit? Sadness crept over him. Yes, he should have become acquainted with the Classics . . . Long ago . . . Now, alas, it was too late. . . .

Dr. Burton interrupted his melancholy.

" Do you mean that you really are thinking of retiring ? "

" Yes."

The other chuckled.

" You won't ! "

" But I assure you——"

" You won't be able to do it, man. You're too interested in your work."

" No—indeed—I make all the arrangements. A few more cases—specially selected ones—not, you understand, everything that presents itself—just problems that have a personal appeal."

Dr. Burton grinned.

" That's the way of it. Just a case or two, just one case more—and so on. The Prima Donna's farewell performance won't be in it with yours, Poirot ! "

He chuckled and rose slowly to his feet, an amiable white-haired gnome.

" Yours aren't the Labours of Hercules," he said. " Yours are labours of love. You'll see if I'm not right. Bet you that in twelve months' time you'll still be here, and vegetable marrows will still be "—he shuddered—" merely marrows."

Taking leave of his host, Dr. Burton left the severe rectangular room.

He passes out of these pages not to return to them. We are concerned only with what he left behind him, which was an Idea.

For after his departure Hercule Poirot sat down again slowly like a man in a dream and murmured :

" The Labours of Hercules . . . Mais oui, c'est une idée, ça. . . ."

The following day saw Hercule Poirot perusing a large calf-bound volume and other slimmer works, with occasional harried glances at various typewritten slips of paper.

His secretary, Miss Lemon, had been detailed to collect information on the subject of Hercules and to place same before him.

Without interest (hers not the type to wonder why !) but with perfect efficiency, Miss Lemon had fulfilled her task.

Hercule Poirot was plunged head first in a bewildering sea

of classical lore with particular reference to " Hercules, a celebrated hero who, after death, was ranked among the gods, and received divine honours."

So far, so good—but thereafter it was far from plain sailing. For two hours Poirot read diligently, making notes, frowning, consulting his slips of paper and his other books of reference. Finally he sank back in his chair and shook his head. His mood of the previous evening was dispelled. What people ! Take this Hercules—this hero ! Hero, indeed ! What was he but a large muscular creature of low intelligence and criminal tendencies ! Poirot was reminded of one Adolfe Durand, a butcher, who had been tried at Lyon in 1895—a creature of oxlike strength who had killed several children. The defence had been epilepsy—from which he undoubtedly suffered—though whether *grand mal* or *petit mal* had been an argument of several days' discussion. This ancient Hercules probably suffered from *grand mal*. No, Poirot shook his head, if *that* was the Greeks' idea of a hero, then measured by modern standards it certainly would not do. The whole classical pattern shocked him. These gods and goddesses—they seemed to have as many different *aliases* as a modern criminal. Indeed they seemed to be definitely criminal types. Drink, debauchery, incest, rape, loot, homicide and chicanery—enough to keep a *juge d'Instruction* constantly busy. No decent family life. No order, no method. Even in their crimes, no order or method !

" Hercules indeed ! " said Hercule Poirot, rising to his feet, disillusioned.

He looked round him with approval. A square room, with good square modern furniture—even a piece of good modern sculpture representing one cube placed on another cube and above it a geometrical arrangement of copper wire. And in the midst of this shining and orderly room, *himself*. He looked at himself in the glass. Here, then, was a *modern* Hercules— very distinct from that unpleasant sketch of a naked figure with bulging muscles, brandishing a club. Instead, a small compact figure attired in correct urban wear with a moustache —such a moustache as Hercules never dreamed of cultivating —a moustache magnificent yet sophisticated.

Yet there was between this Hercule Poirot and the Hercules

of Classical lore one point of resemblance. Both of them, undoubtedly, had been instrumental in ridding the world of
certain pests . . . Each of them could be described as a bene-
factor to the Society he lived in. . . .

What had Dr. Burton said last night as he left: " Yours
are not the Labours of Hercules. . . ."

Ah, but there he was wrong, the old fossil. There should be,
once again, the Labours of Hercules—a modern Hercules.
An ingenious and amusing conceit! In the period before his
final retirement he would accept twelve cases, no more, no
less. And those twelve cases should be selected with special
reference to the twelve labours of ancient Hercules. Yes, that
would not only be amusing, it would be artistic, it would be
*spiritual*.

Poirot picked up the Classical Dictionary and immersed
himself once more in classical lore. He did not intend to
follow his prototype too closely. There should be no women,
no shirt of Nessus . . . The Labours and the Labours only.

The first Labour, then, would be that of the Nemean Lion.
" The Nemean Lion," he repeated, trying it over on his
tongue.

Naturally he did not expect a case to present itself actually
involving a flesh and blood lion. It would be too much of a
coincidence should he be approached by the Directors of the
Zoological Gardens to solve a problem for them involving a
real lion.

No, here symbolism must be involved. The first case must
concern some celebrated public figure, it must be sensational
and of the first importance! Some master criminal—or
alternately someone who was a lion in the public eye. Some
well-known writer, or politician, or painter—or even Royalty ?

He liked the idea of Royalty. . . .

He would not be in a hurry. He would wait—wait for that
case of high importance that should be the first of his self-
imposed Labours.

# I

## THE NEMEAN LION

" ANYTHING of interest this morning, Miss Lemon ? " he asked as he entered the room the following morning.

He trusted Miss Lemon. She was a woman without imagination, but she had an instinct. Anything that she mentioned as worth consideration usually was worth consideration. She was a born secretary.

" Nothing much, M. Poirot. There is just one letter that I thought might interest you. I have put it on the top of the pile."

" And what is that ? " he took an interested step forward.

" It's from a man who wants you to investigate the disappearance of his wife's Pekinese dog."

Poirot paused with his foot still in the air. He threw a glance of deep reproach at Miss Lemon. She did not notice it. She had begun to type. She typed with the speed and precision of a quick-firing tank.

Poirot was shaken ; shaken and embittered. Miss Lemon, the efficient Miss Lemon, had let him down ! A Pekinese *dog*. A *Pekinese* dog ! And after the dream he had had last night. He had been leaving Buckingham Palace after being personally thanked when his valet had come in with his morning chocolate !

Words trembled on his lips—witty caustic words. He did not utter them because Miss Lemon, owing to the speed and efficiency of her typing, would not have heard them.

With a grunt of disgust he picked up the topmost letter from the little pile on the side of his desk.

Yes, it was exactly as Miss Lemon had said. A city address —a curt business-like unrefined demand. The subject—the kidnapping of a Pekinese dog. One of those bulging-eyed, overpampered pets of a rich woman. Hercule Poirot's lip curled as he read it.

Nothing unusual about this. Nothing out of the way or—
But yes, yes, in one small detail, Miss Lemon was right. In
one small detail there *was* something unusual.

Hercule Poirot sat down. He read the letter slowly and
carefully. It was not the kind of case he wanted, it was not
the kind of case he had promised himself. It was not in any
sense an important case, it was supremely unimportant. It
was not—and here was the crux of his objection—it was not
a proper Labour of Hercules.

But unfortunately he was curious. . . .

Yes, he was curious. . . .

He raised his voice so as to be heard by Miss Lemon above
the noise of her typing.

" Ring up this Sir Joseph Hoggin," he ordered, " and make
an appointment for me to see him at his office as he suggests."

As usual, Miss Lemon had been right.

" I'm a plain man, M. Poirot," said Sir Joseph Hoggin.

Hercule Poirot made a noncommittal gesture with his right
hand. It expressed (if you chose to take it so) admiration for
the solid worth of Sir Joseph's career and an appreciation of
his modesty in so describing himself. It could also have conveyed a graceful deprecation of the statement. In any case
it gave no clue to the thought then uppermost in Hercule
Poirot's mind, which was that Sir Joseph certainly was (using
the term in its more colloquial sense) a very plain man indeed.
Hercule Poirot's eyes rested critically on the swelling jowl,
the small pig eyes, the bulbous nose and the close-lipped
mouth. The whole general effect reminded him of someone
or something—but for the moment he could not recollect who
or what it was. A memory stirred dimly. A long time ago
. . . in Belgium . . . something, surely, to do with *soap*. . . .

Sir Joseph was continuing.

" No frills about me. I don't beat about the bush. Most
people, M. Poirot, would let this business go. Write it off as
a bad debt and forget about it. But that's not Joseph Hoggin's
way. I'm a rich man—and in a manner of speaking two
hundred pounds is neither here nor there to me——"

Poirot interpolated swiftly :

" I congratulate you."

" Eh ? "

Sir Joseph paused a minute. His small eyes narrowed themselves still more. He said sharply :

" That's not to say that I'm in the habit of throwing my money about. What I want I pay for. But I pay the market price—no more."

Hercule Poirot said :

" You realise that my fees are high ? "

" Yes, yes. But this," Sir Joseph looked at him cunningly, " is a very small matter."

Hercule Poirot shrugged his shoulders. He said :

" I do not bargain. I am an expert. For the services of an expert you have to pay."

Sir Joseph said frankly :

" I know you're a tip-top man at this sort of thing. I made inquiries and I was told that you were the best man available. I mean to get to the bottom of this business and I don't grudge the expense. That's why I got you to come here."

" You were fortunate," said Hercule Poirot.

Sir Joseph said " Eh ? " again.

" Exceedingly fortunate," said Hercule Poirot firmly. " I am, I may say so without undue modesty, at the apex of my career. Very shortly I intend to retire—to live in the country, to travel occasionally to see the world—also, it may be, to cultivate my garden—with particular attention to improving the strain of vegetable marrows. Magnificent vegetables— but they lack flavour. That, however, is not the point. I wished merely to explain that before retiring I had imposed upon myself a certain task. I have decided to accept twelve cases—no more, no less. A self-imposed ' Labours of Hercules ' if I may so describe it. Your case, Sir Joseph, is the first of the twelve. I was attracted to it," he sighed, " by its striking unimportance."

" Importance ? " said Sir Joseph.

" *Un*importance was what I said. I have been called in for varying causes—to investigate murders, unexplained deaths, robberies, thefts of jewellery. This is the first time that I have been asked to turn my talents to elucidate the kidnapping of a Pekinese dog."

Sir Joseph grunted. He said :

L.O.H.

"You surprise me! I should have said you'd have had no end of women pestering you about their pet dogs."

"That, certainly. *But it is the first time that I am summoned by the husband in the case.*"

Sir Joseph's little eyes narrowed appreciatively.

He said:

"I begin to see why they recommended you to me. You're a shrewd fellow, Mr. Poirot."

Poirot murmured:

"If you will now tell me the facts of the case. The dog disappeared, when?"

"Exactly a week ago."

"And your wife is by now quite frantic, I presume?"

Sir Joseph stared. He said:

"You don't understand. The dog has been returned."

"Returned? Then, permit me to ask, where do *I* enter the matter?"

Sir Joseph went crimson in the face.

"Because I'm damned if I'll be swindled! Now then, Mr. Poirot, I'm going to tell you the whole thing. The dog was stolen a week ago—nipped in Kensington Gardens where he was out with my wife's companion. The next day my wife got a demand for two hundred pounds. I ask you—two hundred pounds! For a damned yapping little brute that's always getting under your feet anyway!"

Poirot murmured:

"You did not approve of paying such a sum, naturally?"

"Of course I didn't—or wouldn't have if I'd known anything about it! Milly (my wife) knew that well enough. She didn't say anything to *me*. Just sent off the money—in one pound notes as stipulated—to the address given."

"And the dog was returned?"

"Yes. That evening the bell rang and there was the little brute sitting on the doorstep. And not a soul to be seen."

"Perfectly. Continue."

"Then, of course, Milly confessed what she'd done and I lost my temper a bit. However, I calmed down after a while—after all, the thing was done and you can't expect a woman to behave with any sense—and I daresay I should have let the whole thing go if it hadn't been for meeting old Samuelson at the Club."

" Yes ? "

" Damn it all, this thing must be a positive racket ! Exactly the same thing had happened to him. *Three* hundred pounds they'd rooked *his* wife of ! Well, that was a bit *too* much. I decided the thing had got to be stopped. I sent for you."

" But surely, Sir Joseph, the proper thing (and a very much more inexpensive thing) would have been to send for the police ? "

Sir Joseph rubbed his nose.

He said :

" Are you married, Mr. Poirot ? "

" Alas," said Poirot, " I have not that felicity."

" H'm," said Sir Joseph. " Don't know about felicity, but if you were, you'd know that women are funny creatures. My wife went into hysterics at the mere mention of the police —she'd got it into her head that something would happen to her precious Shan Tung if I went to them. She wouldn't hear of the idea—and I may say she doesn't take very kindly to the idea of *your* being called in. But I stood firm there and at last she gave way. But, mind you, she doesn't *like* it."

Hercule Poirot murmured :

" The position is, I perceive, a delicate one. It would be as well, perhaps, if I were to interview Madame your wife and gain further particulars from her whilst at the same time reassuring her as to the future safety of her dog ? "

Sir Joseph nodded and rose to his feet. He said :

" I'll take you along in the car right away."

II

In a large, hot, ornately-furnished drawing-room two women were sitting.

As Sir Joseph and Hercule Poirot entered, a small Pekinese dog rushed forward, barking furiously, and circling dangerously round Poirot's ankles.

" Shan—Shan, come here. Come here to mother, lovey— Pick him up, Miss Carnaby."

The second woman hurried forward and Hercule Poirot murmured :

" A veritable lion, indeed."

Rather breathlessly Shan Tung's captor agreed.

" Yes, indeed, he's such a *good* watch dog. He's not frightened of anything or any one. There's a lovely boy, then."

Having performed the necessary introduction, Sir Joseph said :

" Well, Mr. Poirot, I'll leave you to get on with it," and with a short nod he left the room.

Lady Hoggin was a stout, petulant-looking woman with dyed henna red hair. Her companion, the fluttering Miss Carnaby, was a plump, amiable-looking creature between forty and fifty. She treated Lady Hoggin with great deference and was clearly frightened to death of her.

Poirot said :

" Now tell me, Lady Hoggin, the full circumstances of this abominable crime."

Lady Hoggin flushed.

" I'm very glad to hear you say *that*, Mr. Poirot. For it *was* a crime. Pekinese are terribly sensitive—just as sensitive as children. Poor Shan Tung might have died of fright if of nothing else."

Miss Carnaby chimed in breathlessly :

" Yes, it was wicked—*wicked !* "

" Please tell me the facts."

" Well, it was like this. Shan Tung was out for his walk in the Park with Miss Carnaby——"

" Oh dear me, yes, it was all my fault," chimed in the companion. " How could I have been so stupid—so care-less——"

Lady Hoggin said acidly :

" I don't want to reproach you, Miss Carnaby, but I do think you might have been more *alert*."

Poirot transferred his gaze to the companion.

" What happened ? "

Miss Carnaby burst into voluble and slightly flustered speech.

" Well, it was the most extraordinary thing ! We had just

been along the flower walk—Shan Tung was on the lead, of course—he'd had his little run on the grass—and I was just about to turn and go home when my attention was caught by a baby in a pram—such a lovely baby—it smiled at me—lovely rosy cheeks and such *curls*. I couldn't just resist speaking to the nurse in charge and asking how old it was—seventeen months, she said—and I'm sure I was only speaking to her for about a minute or two, and then suddenly I looked down and Shan wasn't there any more. The lead had been cut right through——"

Lady Hoggin said:

" If you'd been paying proper attention to your duties, nobody could have sneaked up and cut that lead."

Miss Carnaby seemed inclined to burst into tears. Poirot said hastily:

" And what happened next ? "

" Well, of course I looked *everywhere*. And *called !* And I asked the Park attendant if he'd seen a man carrying a Pekinese dog but he hadn't noticed anything of the kind—and I didn't know what to do—and I went on searching, but at last, of course, I *had* to come home——"

Miss Carnaby stopped dead. Poirot could imagine the scene that followed well enough. He asked:

" And then you received a letter ? "

Lady Hoggin took up the tale.

" By the first post the following morning. It said that if I wanted to see Shan Tung alive I was to send £200 in one pound notes in an unregistered packet to Captain Curtis, 38 Blooms-bury Road Square. It said that if the money were marked or the police informed then—then—*Shan Tung's ears and tail would be—cut off !* "

Miss Carnaby began to sniff.

" So *awful*," she murmured. " How people can be such *fiends* ! "

Lady Hoggin went on:

" It said that if I sent the money at once, Shan Tung would be returned the same evening alive and well, but that if—if afterwards I went to the police, it would be Shan Tung who would suffer for it——"

Miss Carnaby murmured tearfully:

"Oh dear, I'm so afraid that even now—of course, M. Poirot isn't exactly the police——"

Lady Hoggin said anxiously :

"So you see, Mr. Poirot, you will have to be *very* careful."

Hercule Poirot was quick to allay her anxiety.

"But I, I am not of the police. My inquiries, they will be conducted very discreetly, very quietly. You can be assured, Lady Hoggin, that Shan Tung will be perfectly safe. That I will *guarantee*."

Both ladies seemed relieved by the magic word. Poirot went on :  "You have here the letter ? "

Lady Hoggin shook her head.

"No, I was instructed to enclose it with the money."

"And you did so ? "

"Yes."

"H'm, that is a pity."

Miss Carnaby said brightly :

"But I have the dog lead still. Shall I get it ? "

She left the room. Hercule Poirot profited by her absence to ask a few pertinent questions.

"Amy Carnaby ? Oh ! *she's* quite all right. A good soul, though foolish, of course. I have had several companions and they have *all* been complete fools. But Amy was devoted to Shan Tung and she was terribly upset over the whole thing— as well she might be—hanging over perambulators and neglecting my little sweetheart ! These old maids are all the same, idiotic over babies ! No, I'm quite sure she had nothing whatever to do with it."

"It does not seem likely," Poirot agreed. "But as the dog disappeared when in her charge one must make quite certain of her honesty. She has been with you long ? "

"Nearly a year. I had excellent references with her. She was with old Lady Hartingfield until she died—ten years, I believe. After that she looked after an invalid sister for a while. She is really an excellent creature—but a complete fool, as I said."

Amy Carnaby returned at this minute, slightly more out of breath, and produced the cut dog lead which she handed to Poirot with the utmost solemnity, looking at him with hopeful expectancy.

Poirot surveyed it carefully.

" *Mais oui,*" he said.  " This has undoubtedly been cut."

The two women still waited expectantly.  He said :

" I will keep this."

Solemnly he put it in his pocket.  The two women breathed a sigh of relief.  He had clearly done what was expected of him.

### III

It was the habit of Hercule Poirot to leave nothing untested.

Though on the face of it it seemed unlikely that Miss Carnaby was anything but the foolish and rather muddle-headed woman that she appeared to be, Poirot nevertheless managed to interview a somewhat forbidding lady who was the niece of the late Lady Hartingfield.

" Amy Carnaby ? " said Miss Maltravers.  " Of course, remember her perfectly.  She was a good soul and suited Aunt Julia down to the ground.  Devoted to dogs and excellent at reading aloud.  Tactful, too, never contradicted an invalid.  What's happened to her ?  Not in distress of any kind, I hope.  I gave her a reference about a year ago to some woman— name began with H——"

Poirot explained hastily that Miss Carnaby was still in her post.  There had been, he said, a little trouble over a lost dog.

" Amy Carnaby is devoted to dogs.  My aunt had a Pekinese.  She left it to Miss Carnaby when she died and Miss Carnaby was devoted to it.  I believe she was quite heart-broken when it died.  Oh yes, she's a good soul.  Not, of course, precisely *intellectual.*"

Hercule Poirot agreed that Miss Carnaby could not, perhaps, be described as intellectual.

His next proceeding was to discover the Park Keeper to whom Miss Carnaby had spoken on the fateful afternoon.  This he did without much difficulty.  The man remembered the incident in question.

" Middle-aged lady, rather stout—in a regular state she was —lost her Pekinese dog.  I knew her well by sight—brings the dog along most afternoons.  I saw her come in with it.  She was in a rare taking when she lost it.  Came running to me to know if I'd seen any one with a Pekinese dog ! Well, I ask you ! I can tell you, the Gardens is full of dogs—every kind—terriers, Pekes, German sausage-dogs—even them Borzois—all kinds we have. Not likely as I'd notice one Peke more than another."

Hercule Poirot nodded his head thoughtfully.

He went to 38 Bloomsbury Road Square.

Nos. 38, 39 and 40 were incorporated together as the Balaclava Private Hotel. Poirot walked up the steps and pushed open the door. He was greeted inside by gloom and a smell of cooking cabbage with a reminiscence of breakfast kippers. On his left was a mahogany table with a sad-looking chrysanthemum plant on it. Above the table was a big baize-covered rack into which letters were stuck. Poirot stared at the board thoughtfully for some minutes. He pushed open a door on his right. It led into a kind of lounge with small tables and some so-called easy-chairs covered with a depressing pattern of cretonne. Three old ladies and one fierce-looking old gentleman raised their heads and gazed at the intruder with deadly venom. Hercule Poirot blushed and withdrew.

He walked farther along the passage and came to a stair-case. On his right a passage branched at right angles to what was evidently the dining-room.

A little way along this passage was a door marked " OFFICE."

On this Poirot tapped. Receiving no response, he opened the door and looked in. There was a large desk in the room covered with papers but there was no one to be seen. He withdrew, closing the door again. He penetrated to the dining-room.

A sad-looking girl in a dirty apron was shuffling about with a basket of knives and forks with which she was laying the tables.

Hercule Poirot said apologetically :

" Excuse me, but could I see the Manageress ? "

The girl looked at him with lack-lustre eyes.

She said :

" I don't know, I'm sure."

Hercule Poirot said :

" There is no one in the office."

" Well, I don't know where she'd be, I'm sure."

" Perhaps," Hercule Poirot said, patient and persistent, " you could find out ? "

The girl sighed. Dreary as her day's round was, it had now been made additionally so by this new burden laid upon her. She said sadly :

" Well, I'll see what I can do."

Poirot thanked her and removed himself once more to the hall, not daring to face the malevolent glare of the occupants of the lounge. He was staring up at the baize-covered letter rack when a rustle and a strong smell of Devonshire violets proclaimed the arrival of the Manageress.

Mrs. Harte was full of graciousness. She exclaimed :

" So sorry I was not in my office. You were requiring rooms ? "

Hercule Poirot murmured :

" Not precisely. I was wondering if a friend of mine had been staying here lately. A Captain Curtis."

" Curtis," exclaimed Mrs. Harte. " Captain Curtis ? Now where have I heard that name ? "

Poirot did not help her. She shook her head vexedly.

He said :

" You have not, then, had a Captain Curtis staying here ? "

" Well, not lately, certainly. And yet, you know, the name is certainly familiar to me. Can you describe your friend at all ? "

" That," said Hercule Poirot, " would be difficult." He went on : " I suppose it sometimes happens that letters arrive for people when in actual fact no one of that name is staying here ? "

" That does happen, of course."

" What do you do with such letters ? "

" Well, we keep them for a time. You see, it probably means that the person in question will arrive shortly. Of course, if letters or parcels are a long time here unclaimed, they are returned to the post office."

Hercule Poirot nodded thoughtfully.

He said :

" I comprehend." He added : " It is like this, you see. I wrote a letter to my friend here."

Mrs. Harte's face cleared.

" That explains it. I must have noticed the name on an envelope. But really we have so many ex-Army gentlemen staying here or passing through—Let me see now."

She peered up at the board.

Hercule Poirot said :

" It is not there now."

" It must have been returned to the postman, I suppose. I am *so* sorry. Nothing *important*, I hope ? "

" No, no, it was of no importance."

As he moved towards the door, Mrs. Harte, enveloped in her pungent odour of violets, pursued him.

" If your friend should come——"

" It is most unlikely. I must have made a mistake. . . ."

" Our terms," said Mrs. Harte, " are very moderate. Coffee after dinner is included. I would like you to see one or two of our bed-sitting-rooms. . . ."

With difficulty Hercule Poirot escaped.


IV


The drawing-room of Mrs. Samuelson was larger, more lavishly furnished, and enjoyed an even more stifling amount of central heating than that of Lady Hoggin. Hercule Poirot picked his way giddily amongst gilded console tables and large groups of statuary.

Mrs. Samuelson was taller than Lady Hoggin and her hair was dyed with peroxide. Her Pekinese was called Nanki Poo. His bulging eyes surveyed Hercule Poirot with arrogance. Miss Keble, Mrs. Samuelson's companion, was thin and scraggy where Miss Carnaby had been plump, but she also was voluble and slightly breathless. She, too, had been blamed for Nanki Poo's disappearance.

" But really, Mr. Poirot, it was the most amazing thing. It all happened in a second. Outside Harrods it was. A nurse there asked me the time——"

Poirot interrupted her.

" A nurse ? A hospital nurse ? "

" No, no—a children's nurse. Such a sweet baby it was,

too ! A dear little mite. Such lovely rosy cheeks. They say children don't look healthy in London, but I'm sure——"

" Ellen," said Mrs. Samuelson.

Miss Keble blushed, stammered, and subsided into silence.

Mrs. Samuelson said acidly :

" And while Miss Keble was bending over a perambulator that had nothing to do with her, this audacious villain cut Nanki Poo's lead and made off with him."

Miss Keble murmured tearfully :

" It all happened in a second. I looked round and the darling boy was gone—there was just the dangling lead in my hand. Perhaps you'd like to see the lead, Mr. Poirot ? "

" By no means," said Poirot hastily. He had no wish to make a collection of cut dog leads. " I understand," he went on, " that shortly afterwards you received a letter ? "

The story followed the same course exactly—the letter— the threats of violence to Nanki Poo's ears and tail. Only two things were different—the sum of money demanded—£300— and the address to which it was to be sent ; this time it was to Commander Blackleigh, Harrington Hotel, 76 Clonmel Gardens, Kensington.

Mrs. Samuelson went on :

" When Nanki Poo was safely back again, I went to the place *myself*, Mr. Poirot. After all, three hundred pounds is three hundred pounds."

" Certainly it is."

" The very first thing I saw was my letter enclosing the money in a kind of rack in the hall. Whilst I was waiting for the proprietress I slipped it into my bag. Unfortunately——"

Poirot said : " Unfortunately, when you opened it it contained only blank sheets of paper."

" How did you know ? " Mrs. Samuelson turned on him with awe.

Poirot shrugged his shoulders.

" Obviously, *chère Madame*, the thief would take care to recover the money before he returned the dog. He would then replace the notes with blank paper and return the letter to the rack in case its absence should be noticed."

" No such person as Commander Blackleigh had ever stayed there."

Poirot smiled.

" And of course, my husband was extremely annoyed about the whole thing. In fact, he was livid—absolutely *livid* ! "

Poirot murmured cautiously :

" You did not—er—consult him before dispatching the money ? "

" Certainly not," said Mrs. Samuelson with decision.

Poirot looked a question. The lady explained.

" I wouldn't have risked it for a moment. Men are so extraordinary when it's a question of *money*. Jacob would have insisted on going to the police. I couldn't risk that. My poor darling Nanki Poo. *Anything* might have happened to him ! Of course, I *had* to tell my husband *afterwards*, because I had to explain why I was overdrawn at the Bank."

Poirot murmured :

" Quite so—quite so."

" And I have really never seen him so angry. Men," said Mrs. Samuelson, rearranging her handsome diamond bracelet and turning her rings on her fingers, " think of nothing but money."

v

Hercule Poirot went up in the lift to Sir Joseph Hoggin's office. He sent in his card and was told that Sir Joseph was engaged at the moment but would see him presently. A haughty blonde sailed out of Sir Joseph's room at last with her hands full of papers. She gave the quaint little man a disdainful glance in passing.

Sir Joseph was seated behind his immense mahogany desk. There was a trace of lipstick on his chin.

" Well, Mr. Poirot ? Sit down. Got any news for me ? "

Hercule Poirot said :

" The whole affair is of a pleasing simplicity. In each case the money was sent to one of those boarding houses or private hotels where there is no porter or hall attendant and where a large number of guests are always coming and going, including a fairly large preponderance of ex-Service men. Nothing would be easier than for any one to walk in, abstract a letter from the rack, either take it away, or else remove the money and replace it with blank paper. Therefore, in every case, the trail ends abruptly in a blank wall."

" You mean you've no idea who the fellow is ? "

" I have certain ideas, yes. It will take a few days to follow them up."

Sir Joseph looked at him curiously.

" Good work. Then, when you have got anything to report——"

" I will report to you at your house."

Sir Joseph said :

" If you get to the bottom of this business, it will be a pretty good piece of work."

Hercule Poirot said :

" There is no question of failure. Hercule Poirot does not fail."

Sir Joseph Hoggin looked at the little man and grinned.

" Sure of yourself, aren't you ? " he demanded.

" Entirely with reason."

" Oh well." Sir Joseph Hoggin leaned back in his chair. " Pride goes before a fall, you know."

## VI

Hercule Poirot, sitting in front of his electric radiator (and feeling a quiet satisfaction in its neat geometrical pattern) was giving instructions to his valet and general factotum.

" You understand, Georges ? "

" Perfectly, sir."

" More probably a flat or maisonette. And it will definitely be within certain limits. South of the Park, east of Kensington Church, west of Knightsbridge Barracks and north of Fulham Road."

" I understand perfectly, sir."

Poirot murmured :

" A curious little case. There is evidence here of a very definite talent for organisation. And there is, of course, the surprising invisibility of the star performer—the Nemean Lion himself, if I may so style him. Yes, an interesting little

case. I could wish that I felt more attracted to my client—
but he bears an unfortunate resemblance to a soap manufacturer of Liège who poisoned his wife in order to marry a
blonde secretary. One of my early successes."

George shook his head. He said gravely :

" These blondes, sir, they're responsible for a lot of trouble."


### VII

It was three days later when the invaluable George said :
" This is the address, sir."

Hercule Poirot took the piece of paper handed to him.

" Excellent, my good Georges. And what day of the week ? "

" Thursdays, sir."

" Thursdays. And to-day, most fortunately, is a Thursday.
So there need be no delay."

Twenty minutes later Hercule Poirot was climbing the
stairs of an obscure block of flats tucked away in a little street
leading off a more fashionable one. No. 10 Rosholm Mansions
was on the third and top floor and there was no lift. Poirot
toiled upwards round and round the narrow corkscrew
staircase.

He paused to regain his breath on the top landing and from
behind the door of No. 10 a new sound broke the silence—the
sharp bark of a dog.

Hercule Poirot nodded his head with a slight smile. He
pressed the bell of No. 10.

The barking redoubled—footsteps came to the door, it was
opened . . .

Miss Amy Carnaby fell back, her hand went to her ample
breast.

" You permit that I enter ? " said Hercule Poirot, and
entered without waiting for the reply.

There was a sitting-room door open on the right and he
walked in. Behind him Miss Carnaby followed as though in a
dream.

The room was very small and much overcrowded. Amongst
the furniture a human being could be discovered, an elderly
woman lying on a sofa drawn up to the gas fire. As Poirot

came in, a Pekinese dog jumped off the sofa and came forward uttering a few sharp suspicious barks.

"Aha," said Poirot. "The chief actor! I salute you, my little friend."

He bent forward, extending his hand. The dog sniffed at it, his intelligent eyes fixed on the man's face.

Miss Carnaby murmured faintly:

"*So you know?*"

Hercule Poirot nodded.

"Yes, I know." He looked at the woman on the sofa. "Your sister, I think?"

Miss Carnaby said mechanically: "Yes, Emily, this—this is Mr. Poirot."

Emily Carnaby gave a gasp. She said: "Oh!"

Amy Carnaby said:

"Augustus. . . ."

The Pekinese looked towards her—his tail moved—then he resumed his scrutiny of Poirot's hand. Again his tail moved faintly.

Gently, Poirot picked the little dog up and sat down with Augustus on his knee. He said:

"So I have captured the Nemean Lion. My task is completed."

Amy Carnaby said in a hard dry voice:

"Do you really know everything?"

Poirot nodded.

"I think so. You organised this business—with Augustus to help you. You took your employer's dog out for his usual walk, brought him here and went on to the Park with Augustus. The Park Keeper saw you with a Pekinese as usual. The nurse girl, if we had ever found her, would also have agreed that you had a Pekinese with you when you spoke to her. Then, while you were talking, you cut the lead and Augustus, trained by you, slipped off at once and made a bee-line back home. A few minutes later you gave the alarm that the dog had been stolen."

There was a pause. Then Miss Carnaby drew herself up with a certain pathetic dignity. She said:

"Yes. It is all quite true. I—I have nothing to say."

The invalid woman on the sofa began to cry softly.

Poirot said :

" Nothing at all, Mademoiselle ? "

Miss Carnaby said :

" Nothing. I have been a thief—and now I am found out."

Poirot murmured :

" You have nothing to say—in your own defence ? "

A spot of red showed suddenly in Amy Carnaby's white cheeks. She said :

" I—I don't regret what I did. I think that you are a kind man, Mr. Poirot, and that possibly you might understand. You see, I've been so terribly *afraid*."

" Afraid ? "

" Yes, it's difficult for a gentleman to understand, I expect. But you see, I'm not a clever woman at all, and I've no training and I'm getting older—and I'm so terrified for the future. I've not been able to save anything—how could I with Emily to be cared for ?—and as I get older and more incompetent there won't be any one who wants me. They'll want somebody young and brisk. I've—I've known so many people like I am—nobody wants you and you live in one room and you can't have a fire or any warmth and not very much to eat, and at last you can't even pay the rent of your room . . . There are Institutions, of course, but it's not very easy to get into them unless you have influential friends, and I haven't. There are a good many others situated like I am—poor companions—untrained useless women with nothing to look forward to but a deadly fear . . ."

Her voice shook. She said :

" And so—some of us—got together and—and I thought of this. It was really having Augustus that put it into my mind. You see, to most people, one Pekinese is very much like another. (Just as we think the Chinese are.) Really, of course, it's ridiculous. No one who knew could mistake Augustus for Nanki Poo or Shan Tung or any of the other Pekes. He's *far* more intelligent for one thing, and he's *much* handsomer, but, as I say, to most people a Peke is just a Peke. Augustus put it into my head—that, combined with the fact that so many rich women have Pekinese dogs."

Poirot said with a faint smile :

" It must have been a profitable—racket ! How many are

there in the—the gang ? Or perhaps I had better ask how
often operations have been successfully carried out ? "

Miss Carnaby said simply :

" Shan Tung was the sixteenth."

Hercule Poirot raised his eyebrows.

" I congratulate you. Your organisation must have been
indeed excellent."

Emily Carnaby said :

" Amy was always good at organisation. Our father—he
was the Vicar of Kellington in Essex—always said that Amy
had quite a genius for planning. She always made all the
arrangements for the Socials and the Bazaars and all that."

Poirot said with a little bow :

" I agree. As a criminal, Mademoiselle, you are quite in
the first rank."

Amy Carnaby cried :

" A criminal. Oh dear, I suppose I am. But—but it never
felt like that."

" How did it feel ? "

" Of course, you are quite right. It was breaking the law.
But you see—how can I explain it ? Nearly all these women
who employ us are so very rude and unpleasant. Lady
Hoggin, for instance, doesn't mind *what* she says to me. She
said her tonic tasted unpleasant the other day and practically
accused me of *tampering* with it. All that sort of thing." Miss
Carnaby flushed. " It's really very unpleasant. And not being
able to say anything or answer back makes it *rankle* more, if
you know what I mean."

" I know what you mean," said Hercule Poirot.

" And then seeing money frittered away so wastefully—
that is upsetting. And Sir Joseph, occasionally he used to
describe a *coup* he had made in the City—sometimes something that seemed to me (of course, I know I've only got a
woman's brain and don't understand finance) downright
*dishonest*. Well, you know, M. Poirot, it all—it all *unsettled*
me, and I felt that to take a little money away from these
people who really wouldn't miss it and hadn't been too
scrupulous in acquiring it—well, really it hardly seemed wrong
at all."

Poirot murmured :

" A modern Robin Hood ! Tell me, Miss Carnaby, did you ever have to carry out the threats you used in your letters ? "

" Threats ? "

" Were you ever compelled to mutilate the animals in the way you specified ? "

Miss Carnaby regarded him in horror.

" Of course, I would never have dreamed of doing such a thing ! That was just—just an artistic touch."

" Very artistic. It worked."

" Well, of course I knew it would. I know how I should have felt about Augustus, and of course I had to make sure these women never told their husbands until afterwards. The plan worked beautifully every time. In nine cases out of ten the companion was given the letter with the money to post. We usually steamed it open, took out the notes, and replaced them with paper. Once or twice the woman posted it herself. Then, of course, the companion had to go to the hotel and take the letter out of the rack. But that was quite easy, too."

" And the nursemaid touch ? Was it always a nursemaid ? "

" Well, you see, M. Poirot, old maids are known to be foolishly sentimental about babies. So it seemed quite *natural* that they should be absorbed over a baby and not notice anything."

Hercule Poirot sighed. He said :

" Your psychology is excellent, your organisation is first class, and you are also a very fine actress. Your performance the other day when I interviewed Lady Hoggin was irreproachable. Never think of yourself disparagingly, Miss Carnaby. You may be what is termed an untrained woman but there is nothing wrong with your brains or with your courage."

Miss Carnaby said with a faint smile :

" And yet I have been found out, M. Poirot."

" Only by Me. That was inevitable ! When I had interviewed Mrs. Samuelson I realised that the kidnapping of Shan Tung was one of a series. I had already learned that you had once been left a Pekinese dog and had an invalid sister. I had only to ask my invaluable servant to look for a small flat within a certain radius occupied by an invalid lady who had a Pekinese dog and a sister who visited her once a week on her day out. It was simple."

Amy Carnaby drew herself up. She said :

" You have been very kind. It emboldens me to ask you a favour. I cannot, I know, escape the penalty for what I have done. I shall be sent to prison, I suppose. But if you could, M. Poirot, avert some of the *publicity*. So distressing for Emily—and for those few who knew us in the old days. I could not, I suppose, go to prison under a *false name* ? Or is that a *very* wrong thing to ask ? "

Hercule Poirot said :

" I think I can do more than that. But first of all I must make one thing quite clear. This ramp has got to *stop*. There must be no more disappearing dogs. All that is finished ! "

" Yes ! Oh yes ! "

" And the money you extracted from Lady Hoggin must be returned."

Amy Carnaby crossed the room, opened the drawer of a bureau and returned with a packet of notes which she handed to Poirot.

" I was going to pay it into the pool to-day."

Poirot took the notes and counted them. He got up.

" I think it possible, Miss Carnaby, that I may be able to persuade Sir Joseph not to prosecute."

" Oh, M. Poirot ! "

Amy Carnaby clasped her hands. Emily gave a cry of joy. Augustus barked and wagged his tail.

" As for you, *mon ami*," said Poirot addressing him. " There is one thing that I wish you would give me. It is your mantle of invisibility that I need. In all these cases nobody for a moment suspected that there was a *second* dog involved. Augustus possessed the lion's skin of invisibility."

" Of course, M. Poirot, according to the legend, Pekinese *were* lions once. And they still have the *hearts* of lions ! "

" Augustus is, I suppose, the dog that was left to you by Lady Hartingfield and who is reported to have died ? Were you never afraid of him coming home alone through the traffic ? "

" Oh no, M. Poirot, Augustus is very clever about traffic. I have trained him most carefully. He has even grasped the principle of One Way Streets."

" In that case," said Hercule Poirot, " he is superior to most human beings ! "

## VIII

Sir Joseph received Hercule Poirot in his study. He said : " Well, Mr. Poirot ? Made your boast good ? "

" Let me first ask you a question," said Poirot as he seated himself. " I know who the criminal is and I think it possible that I can produce sufficient evidence to convict this person. But in that case I doubt if you will ever recover your money."

" Not get back my *money* ? "

Sir Joseph turned purple.

Hercule Poirot went on :

" But I am not a policeman. I am acting in this case solely in your interests. I could, I think, recover your money intact, if no proceedings were taken."

" Eh ? " said Sir Joseph. " That needs a bit of thinking about."

" It is entirely for you to decide. Strictly speaking, I suppose you ought to prosecute in the public interest. Most people would say so."

" I dare say they would," said Sir Joseph sharply. " It wouldn't be *their* money that had gone west. If there's one thing I hate it's to be swindled. Nobody's ever swindled me and got away with it."

" Well then, what do you decide ? "

Sir Joseph hit the table with his fist.

" I'll have the brass ! Nobody's going to say they got away with two hundred pounds of my money."

Hercule Poirot rose, crossed to the writing-table, wrote out a cheque for two hundred pounds and handed it to the other man.

Sir Joseph said in a weak voice :

" Well, I'm damned ! Who the devil *is* this fellow ? "

Poirot shook his head.

" If you accept the money, there must be no questions asked."

Sir Joseph folded up the cheque and put it in his pocket.

"That's a pity. But the money's the thing. And what do I owe you, Mr. Poirot ? "

" My fees will not be high. This was, as I said, a very *unimportant* matter." He paused—and added, " Nowadays nearly all my cases are murder cases. . . ."

Sir Joseph started slightly.

" Must be interesting ? " he said.

" Sometimes. Curiously enough, you recall to me one of my early cases in Belgium, many years ago—the chief protagonist was very like you in appearance. He was a wealthy soap manufacturer. He poisoned his wife in order to be free to marry his secretary . . . Yes—the resemblance is very remarkable. . . ."

A faint sound came from Sir Joseph's lips—they had gone a queer blue colour. All the ruddy hue had faded from his cheeks. His eyes, starting out of his head, stared at Poirot. He slipped down a little in his chair.

Then, with a shaking hand, he fumbled in his pocket. He drew out the cheque and tore it into pieces.

" That's washed out—see ? Consider it as your fee."

" Oh but, Sir Joseph, my fee would not have been as large as that."

" That's all right. You keep it."

" I shall send it to a deserving charity."

" Send it anywhere you damn well like."

Poirot leaned forward. He said :

" I think I need hardly point out, Sir Joseph, that in your position, you would do well to be exceedingly careful."

Sir Joseph said, his voice almost inaudible :

" You needn't worry. I shall be careful all right."

Hercule Poirot left the house. As he went down the steps he said to himself :

" So—*I was right.*"


IX


Lady Hoggin said to her husband :

" Funny, this tonic tastes quite different. It hasn't got that bitter taste any more. I wonder why ? "

Sir Joseph growled :

" Chemist. Careless fellows. Make things up differently different times."

Lady Hoggin said doubtfully :

" I suppose that must be it."

" Of course it is. What else could it be ? "

" Has the man found out anything about Shan Tung ? "

" Yes. He got me my money back all right."

" Who was it ? "

" He didn't say. Very close fellow, Hercule Poirot. But you needn't worry."

" He's a funny little man, isn't he ? "

Sir Joseph gave a slight shiver and threw a sideways glance upwards as though he felt the invisible presence of Hercule Poirot behind his right shoulder. He had an idea that he would always feel it there.

He said :

" He's a damned clever little devil ! "

And he thought to himself :

" Greta can go hang ! *I'm* not going to risk my neck for *any* damned platinum blonde ! "

## X

" *Oh !* "

Amy Carnaby gazed down incredulously at the cheque for two hundred pounds. She cried :

" Emily ! *Emily !* Listen to this.

' *Dear Miss Carnaby,*

   *Allow me to enclose a contribution to your very deserving Fund before it is finally wound up.*

     *Yours very truly,*

      *Hercule Poirot.*' "

" Amy," said Emily Carnaby, " you've been incredibly lucky. Think where you might be now."

" Wormwood Scrubbs—or is it Holloway ? " murmured Amy Carnaby. " But that's all over now—isn't it, Augustus ?

No more walks to the Park with mother or mother's friends and a little pair of scissors."

A far away wistfulness came into her eyes. She sighed.

" Dear Augustus ! It seems a pity. He's so clever . . . One can teach him anything. . . ."

# II

# THE LERNEAN HYDRA

## I

HERCULE POIROT looked encouragingly at the man seated opposite him.

Dr. Charles Oldfield was a man of perhaps forty. He had fair hair slightly grey at the temples and blue eyes that held a worried expression. He stooped a little and his manner was a trifle hesitant. Moreover, he seemed to find difficulty in coming to the point.

He said, stammering slightly :

" I've come to you, M. Poirot, with rather an odd request. And now that I'm here, I'm inclined to funk the whole thing. Because, as I see very well now, it's the sort of thing that no one can possibly do anything about."

Hercule Poirot murmured :

" As to that, you must let me judge."

Oldfield muttered :

" I don't know why I thought that perhaps——"

He broke off.

Hercule Poirot finished the sentence.

" That perhaps I could help you ? *Eh bien*, perhaps I can. Tell me your problem."

Oldfield straightened himself. Poirot noted anew how haggard the man looked.

Oldfield said, and his voice had a note of hopelessness in it :

" You see, it isn't any good going to the police . . . They can't do anything. And yet—every day it's getting worse and worse. I—I don't know what to do. . . ."

" *What* is getting worse ? "

" The rumours . . . Oh, it's quite simple, M. Poirot. Just a little over a year ago, my wife died. She had been an invalid for some years. They are saying, everyone is saying, *that I killed her*—that I poisoned her ! "

"Aha," said Poirot. "And did you poison her?"

"M. Poirot!" Dr. Oldfield sprang to his feet.

"Calm yourself," said Hercule Poirot. "And sit down again. We will take it, then, that you did *not* poison your wife. But your practice, I imagine, is situated in a country district——"

"Yes. Market Loughborough—in Berkshire. I have always realised that it was the kind of place where people gossiped a good deal, but I never imagined that it could reach the lengths it has done." He drew his chair a little forward. "M. Poirot, you have no idea of what I have gone through. At first I had no inkling of what was going on. I did notice that people seemed less friendly, that there was a tendency to avoid me— but I put it down to—to the fact of my recent bereavement. Then it became more marked. In the street, even, people will cross the road to avoid speaking to me. My practice is falling off. Wherever I go I am conscious of lowered voices, of un-friendly eyes that watch me whilst malicious tongues whisper their deadly poison. I have had one or two letters—vile things."

He paused—and then went on:

"And—and *I don't know what to do about it*. I don't know how to fight this—this vile network of lies and suspicion. How can one refute what is never said openly to your face? I am powerless—trapped—and slowly and mercilessly being destroyed."

Poirot nodded his head thoughtfully. He said:

"Yes. Rumour is indeed the nine-headed Hydra of Lernea which cannot be exterminated because as fast as one head is cropped off two grow in its place."

Dr. Oldfield said: "That's just it. There's nothing I can do—*nothing!* I came to you as a last resort—but I don't suppose for a minute that there is anything you can do either."

Hercule Poirot was silent for a minute or two. Then he said:

"I am not so sure. Your problem interests me, Doctor Oldfield. I should like to try my hand at destroying the many-headed monster. First of all, tell me a little more about the circumstances which gave rise to this malicious gossip. Your wife died, you say, just over a year ago. What was the cause of death?"

" Gastric ulcer."

" Was there an autopsy ? "

" No. She had been suffering from gastric trouble over a considerable period."

Poirot nodded.

" And the symptoms of gastric inflammation and of arsenical poisoning are closely alike—a fact which everybody knows nowadays. Within the last ten years there have been at least four sensational murder cases in each of which the victim has been buried without suspicion with a certificate of gastric disorder. Was your wife older or younger than yourself ? "

" She was five years older."

" How long had you been married ? "

" Fifteen years."

" Did she leave any property ? "

" Yes. She was a fairly well-to-do woman. She left, roughly, about thirty thousand pounds."

" A very useful sum. It was left to you ? "

" Yes."

" Were you and your wife on good terms ? "

" Certainly."

" No quarrels ? No scenes ? "

" Well——" Charles Oldfield hesitated. " My wife was what might be termed a difficult woman. She was an invalid and very concerned over her health and inclined, therefore, to be fretful and difficult to please. There were days when nothing I could do was right."

Poirot nodded. He said :

" Ah yes, I know the type. She would complain, possibly, that she was neglected, unappreciated—that her husband was tired of her and would be glad when she was dead."

Oldfield's face registered the truth of Poirot's surmise. He said with a wry smile :

" You've got it exactly ! "

Poirot went on :

" Did she have a hospital nurse to attend on her ? Or a companion ? Or a devoted maid ? "

" A nurse-companion. A very sensible and competent woman. I really don't think she would talk."

" Even the sensible and the competent have been given

tongues by *le bon Dieu*—and they do not always employ their tongues wisely. I have no doubt that the nurse-companion talked, that the servants talked, that everyone talked! You have all the materials there for the starting of a very enjoyable village scandal. Now I will ask you one thing more. *Who is the lady?*"

"I don't understand." Dr. Oldfield flushed angrily.

Poirot said gently:

"I think you do. I am asking you who the lady is with whom your name has been coupled."

Dr. Oldfield rose to his feet. His face was stiff and cold. He said:

"There is no 'lady in the case.' I'm sorry, M. Poirot, to have taken up so much of your time."

He went towards the door.

Hercule Poirot said:

"I regret it also. Your case interests me. I would like to have helped you. But I cannot do anything unless I am told the whole truth."

"I have told you the truth."

"No. . . ."

Dr. Oldfield stopped. He wheeled round.

"Why do you insist that there is a woman concerned in this?"

"*Mon cher docteur!* Do you not think I know the female mentality? The village gossip, it is based always, always on the relations of the sexes. If a man poisons his wife in order to travel to the North Pole or to enjoy the peace of a bachelor existence—it would not interest his fellow-villagers for a minute! It is because they are convinced that the murder has been committed in order *that the man may marry another woman* that the talk grows and spreads. That is elemental psychology."

Oldfield said irritably:

"I'm not responsible for what a pack of damned gossiping busybodies think!"

"Of course you are not."

Poirot went on:

"So you might as well come back and sit down and give me the answer to the question I asked you just now."

Slowly, almost reluctantly, Oldfield came back and resumed his seat.

He said, colouring up to his eyebrows :

" I suppose it's possible that they've been saying things about Miss Moncrieffe. Jean Moncrieffe is my dispenser, a very fine girl indeed."

" How long has she worked for you ? "

" For three years."

" Did your wife like her ? "

" Er—well, no, not exactly."

" She was jealous ? "

" It was absurd ! "

Poirot smiled.

He said :

" The jealousy of wives is proverbial. But I will tell you something. In my experience jealousy, however far-fetched and extravagant it may seem, is nearly always based on *reality*. There is a saying, is there not, that the customer is always right ? Well, the same is true of the jealous husband or wife. However little *concrete* evidence there may be, *fundamentally* they are always right."

Dr. Oldfield said robustly :

" Nonsense. I've never said anything to Jean Moncrieffe that my wife couldn't have overheard."

" That, perhaps. But it does not alter the truth of what I said." Hercule Poirot leaned forward. His voice was urgent, compelling. " Doctor Oldfield, I am going to do my utmost in this case. But I must have from you the most absolute frankness without regard to conventional appearances or to your own feelings. It is true, is it not, that you had ceased to care for your wife for some time before she died ? "

Oldfield was silent for a minute or two. Then he said :

" This business is killing me. I must have hope. Somehow or other I feel that you will be able to do something for me. I will be honest with you, M. Poirot. I did not care deeply for my wife. I made her, I think, a good husband, but I was never really in love with her."

" And this girl, Jean ? "

The perspiration came out in a fine dew on the doctor's forehead. He said :

" I—I should have asked her to marry me before now if it weren't for all this scandal and talk."

Poirot sat back in his chair. He said :

" Now at last we have come to the true facts ! *Eh bien*, Doctor Oldfield, I will take up your case. But remember this —it is the *truth* that I shall seek out."

Oldfield said bitterly :

" It isn't the truth that's going to hurt me ! "

He hesitated and said :

" You know, I've contemplated the possibility of an action for slander ! If I could pin any one down to a definite accusation—surely then I should be vindicated ? At least, sometimes I think so ... At other times I think it would only make things worse—give bigger publicity to the whole thing and have people saying : ' *It mayn't have been proved but there's no smoke without fire.* ' "

He looked at Poirot.

" Tell me, honestly, is there *any* way out of this nightmare ? "

" There is always a way," said Hercule Poirot.


## II


" We are going into the country, Georges," said Hercule Poirot to his valet.

" Indeed, sir ? " said the imperturbable George.

" And the purpose of our journey is to destroy a monster with nine heads."

" Really, sir ? Something after the style of the Loch Ness Monster ? "

" Less tangible than that. I did not refer to a flesh and blood animal, Georges."

" I misunderstood you, sir."

" It would be easier if it were one. There is nothing so intangible, so difficult to pin down, as the source of a rumour."

" Oh yes, indeed, sir. It's difficult to know how a thing starts sometimes."

" Exactly."

Hercule Poirot did not put up at Dr. Oldfield's house. He

went instead to the local inn. The morning after his arrival, he had his first interview with Jean Moncrieffe.

She was a tall girl with copper-coloured hair and steady blue eyes. She had about her a watchful look, as of one who is upon her guard.

She said :

" So Doctor Oldfield did go to you . . . I knew he was thinking about it."

There was a lack of enthusiasm in her tone.

Poirot said :

" And you did not approve ? "

Her eyes met his. She said coldly :

" What can you do ? "

Poirot said quietly :

" There might be a way of tackling the situation."

" What way ? " She threw the words at him scornfully. " Do you mean to go round to all the whispering old women and say ' *Really, please, you must stop talking like this. It's so bad for poor Doctor Oldfield.*' And they'd answer you and say : ' Of course, *I* have never believed the story ! ' That's the worst of the whole thing—they don't say : ' My dear, has it ever occurred to you that perhaps Mrs. Oldfield's death wasn't quite what it seemed ? ' No, they say : ' My dear, of course I *don't* believe that story about Doctor Oldfield and his wife. I'm *sure* he wouldn't do such a thing, though it's true that he *did* neglect her just a little perhaps and I don't think, really, it's quite *wise* to have quite a young girl as his dispenser— of course, I'm not saying for a minute that there was anything *wrong* between them. Oh no, I'm sure it was *quite* all right. . . .' " She stopped. Her face was flushed and her breath came rather fast.

Hercule Poirot said :

" You seem to know very well just what is being said."

Her mouth closed sharply. She said bitterly :

" I know all right ! "

" And what is your own solution ? "

Jean Moncrieffe said :

" The best thing for him to do is to sell his practice and start again somewhere else."

" Don't you think the story might follow him ? "

She shrugged her shoulders.

" He must risk that."

Poirot was silent for a minute or two. Then he said :

" Are you going to marry Doctor Oldfield, Miss Moncrieffe ? "

She displayed no surprise at the question. She said shortly :

" He hasn't asked me to marry him."

" Why not ? "

Her blue eyes met his and flickered for a second. Then she said :

" Because I've choked him off."

" Ah, what a blessing to find someone who can be frank ! "

" I will be as frank as you please. When I realised that people were saying that Charles had got rid of his wife in order to marry me, it seemed to me that if we *did* marry it would just put the lid on things. I hoped that if there appeared to be no question of marriage between us, the silly scandal might die down."

" But it hasn't ? "

" No it hasn't."

" Surely," said Hercule Poirot, " that is a little odd ? "

Jean said bitterly :

" They haven't got much to amuse them down here."

Poirot asked :

" Do you *want* to marry Charles Oldfield ? "

The girl answered coolly enough.

" Yes, I do. I wanted to almost as soon as I met him."

" Then his wife's death was very convenient for you ? "

Jean Moncrieffe said :

" Mrs. Oldfield was a singularly unpleasant woman. Frankly, I was delighted when she died."

" Yes," said Poirot. " You are certainly frank ! "

She gave the same scornful smile.

Poirot said :

" I have a suggestion to make."

" Yes ? "

" Drastic means are required here. I suggest that somebody —possibly yourself—might write to the Home Office."

" What on earth do you mean ? "

" I mean that the best way of disposing of this story once

and for all is to get the body exhumed and an autopsy performed."

She took a step back from him. Her lips opened, then shut again. Poirot watched her.

" Well, Mademoiselle ? " he said at last.

Jean Moncrieffe said quietly :

" I don't agree with you."

" But why not ? Surely a verdict of death from natural causes would silence all tongues ? "

" *If* you got that verdict, yes."

" Do you know what you are suggesting, Mademoiselle ? "

Jean Moncrieffe said impatiently :

" I know what I'm talking about. You're thinking of arsenic poisoning—you could prove that she was not poisoned by arsenic. But there are other poisons—the vegetable alkaloids. After a year, I doubt if you'd find any traces of them even if they had been used. And I know what these official analyst people are like. They might return a non-committal verdict saying that there was nothing to show what caused death—and then the tongues would wag faster than ever ! "

Hercule Poirot was silent for a minute or two, then he said :

" Who in your opinion is the most inveterate talker in the village ? "

The girl considered. She said at last :

" I really think old Miss Leatheran is the worst cat of the lot."

" Ah ! Would it be possible for you to introduce me to Miss Leatheran—in a casual manner if possible ? "

" Nothing could be easier. All the old tabbies are prowling about doing their shopping at this time of the morning. We've only got to walk down the main street."

As Jean had said, there was no difficulty about the procedure. Outside the post office, Jean stopped and spoke to a tall, thin middle-aged woman with a long nose and sharp inquisitive eyes.

" Good-morning, Miss Leatheran."

" Good-morning, Jean. Such a lovely day, is it not ? "

The sharp eyes ranged inquisitively over Jean Moncrieffe's companion. Jean said :

" Let me introduce M. Poirot, who is staying down here for a few days."


### III


Nibbling delicately at a scone and balancing a cup of tea on his knee, Hercule Poirot allowed himself to become confidential with his hostess. Miss Leatheran had been kind enough to ask him to tea and had thereupon made it her business to find out exactly what this exotic little foreigner was doing in their midst.

For some time he parried her thrusts with dexterity—thereby whetting her appetite. Then, when he judged the moment ripe, he leant forward :

" Ah, Miss Leatheran," he said. " I can see that you are too clever for me ! You have guessed my secret. I am down here at the request of the Home Office. But please," he lowered his voice, " *keep this information to yourself*."

" Of course—of course——" Miss Leatheran was fluttered —thrilled to the core. " The Home Office—you don't mean— *not* poor Mrs. Oldfield ? "

Poirot nodded his head slowly several times.

" We-ell ! " Miss Leatheran breathed into that one word a whole gamut of pleasurable emotion.

Poirot said :

" It is a delicate matter, you understand. I have been ordered to report whether there is or is not a sufficient case for exhumation."

Mis Leatheran exclaimed :

" You are going to dig the poor thing up. How terrible ! "

If she had said " how splendid " instead of " how terrible " the words would have suited her tone of voice better.

" What is your own opinion, Miss Leatheran ? "

" Well, of course, M. Poirot, there has been a lot of *talk*. But I never listen to *talk*. There is always so *much* unreliable gossip going about. There is no doubt that Doctor Oldfield has been very odd in his manner ever since it happened, but as I have said repeatedly we surely need not put that down to a *guilty conscience*. It might be just grief. Not, of course, that he and his wife were on really affectionate terms. That I *do* know—on *first hand authority*. Nurse Harrison, who was with Mrs. Oldfield for three or four years up to the time of her death, has admitted *that* much. And I have always felt, you know, that Nurse Harrison *had her suspicions*—not that she ever *said* anything, but one can *tell*, can't one, from a person's manner ? "

Poirot said sadly :

" One has so little to go upon."

" Yes, I know, but of course, M. Poirot, if the body is exhumed then you will *know*."

" Yes," said Poirot, " then we will know."

" There have been cases like it before, of course," said Miss Leatheran, her nose twitching with pleasurable excitement. " Armstrong, for instance, and that other man—I can't remember his name—and then Crippen, of course. I've always wondered if Ethel Le Neve was in it with him or not. Of course, Jean Moncrieffe is a very nice girl, I'm sure . . . I wouldn't like to say she led him on exactly—but men do get rather *silly* about girls, don't they ? And, of course, they *were* thrown very much together ! "

Poirot did not speak. He looked at her with an innocent expression of inquiry calculated to produce a further spate of conversation. Inwardly he amused himself by counting the number of times the words " of course " occurred.

" And, of course, with a post-mortem and all that, so much would be bound to come out, wouldn't it ? Servants and all that. Servants always know so much, don't they ? And, of course, it's quite impossible to keep them from gossiping, isn't it ? The Oldfields' Beatrice was dismissed almost immediately after the funeral—and I've always thought that was *odd*—especially with the difficulty of getting maids nowadays. It looks as though Doctor Oldfield was afraid she might *know* something."

" It certainly seems as though there were grounds for an inquiry," said Poirot solemnly.

Miss Leatheran gave a little shiver of reluctance.

" One does so shrink from the idea," she said. " Our dear quiet little village—dragged into the newspapers—all the *publicity* ! "

" It appals you ? " asked Poirot.

" It does a little. I'm old-fashioned, you know."

" And, as you say, it is probably nothing but gossip ! "

" Well—I wouldn't like conscientiously to say *that*. You know, I do think it's so true—the saying that there's no smoke without fire."

" I myself was thinking exactly the same thing," said Poirot.

He rose.

" I can trust your discretion, Mademoiselle ? "

" Oh, *of course* ! I shall not say a *word* to *anybody*."

Poirot smiled and took his leave.

On the doorstep he said to the little maid who handed him his hat and coat :

" I am down here to inquire into the circumstances of Mrs. Oldfield's death, but I shall be obliged if you will keep that strictly to yourself."

Miss Leatheran's Gladys nearly fell backward into the umbrella stand. She breathed excitedly :

" Oh sir, then the doctor *did* do her in ? "

" You've thought so for some time, haven't you ? "

" Well, sir, it wasn't *me*. It was Beatrice. She was up there when Mrs. Oldfield died."

" And she thought there had been "—Poirot selected the melodramatic words deliberately—" ' foul play ' ? "

Gladys nodded excitedly.

" Yes, she did. And she said so did Nurse that was up there, Nurse Harrison. Ever so fond of Mrs. Oldfield Nurse was, and ever so distressed when she died, and Beatrice always said as how Nurse Harrison knew something about it because she turned right round against the doctor afterwards and she wouldn't of done that unless there was something wrong, would she ? "

" Where is Nurse Harrison now ? "

" She looks after old Miss Bristow—down at the end of the village. You can't miss it. It's got pillars and a porch."

IV

It was a very short time afterwards that Hercule Poirot found himself sitting opposite to the woman who certainly must know more about the circumstances that had given rise to the rumours than any one else.

Nurse Harrison was a still handsome woman nearing forty. She had the calm serene features of a Madonna with big sympathetic dark eyes. She listened to him patiently and attentively. Then she said slowly :

" Yes, I know that there are these unpleasant stories going about. I have done what I could to stop them, but it's hopeless. People like the excitement, you know."

Poirot said :

" But there must have been *something* to give rise to these rumours ? "

He noted that her expression of distress deepened. But she merely shook her head perplexedly.

" Perhaps," Poirot suggested, " Doctor Oldfield and his wife did not get on well together and it was that that started the rumour ? "

Nurse Harrison shook her head decidedly.

" Oh no, Doctor Oldfield was always extremely kind and patient with his wife."

" He was really very fond of her ? "

She hesitated.

" No—I would not quite say that. Mrs. Oldfield was a very difficult woman, not easy to please and making constant demands for sympathy and attention which were not always justified."

" You mean," said Poirot, " that she exaggerated her condition ? "

The nurse nodded.

" Yes—her bad health was largely a matter of her own imagination."

" And yet," said Poirot gravely, " she died. . . ."

" Oh, I know—I know. . . ."

He watched her for a minute or two ; her troubled perplexity—her palpable uncertainty,

He said: "I think—I am sure—that you *do* know what first gave rise to all these stories."

Nurse Harrison flushed.

She said:

"Well—I could, perhaps, make a guess. I believe it was the maid, Beatrice, who started all these rumours and I think I know what put it into her head."

"Yes?"

Nurse Harrison said rather incoherently:

"You see, it was something I happened to overhear—a scrap of conversation between Doctor Oldfield and Miss Moncrieffe—and I'm pretty certain Beatrice overheard it too, only I don't suppose she'd ever admit it."

"What was this conversation?"

Nurse Harrison paused for a minute as though to test the accuracy of her own memory, then she said:

"It was about three weeks before the last attack that killed Mrs. Oldfield. They were in the dining-room. I was coming down the stairs when I heard Jean Moncrieffe say:

"'How much longer will it be? I can't bear to wait much longer.'

And the doctor answered her:

"'Not much longer now, darling, I swear it.' And she said again:

"'I can't bear this waiting. You do think it will be all right, don't you?' And he said: 'Of course. Nothing can go wrong. This time next year we'll be married.'"

She paused.

"That was the very first inkling I'd had, M. Poirot, that there was anything between the doctor and Miss Moncrieffe. Of course I knew he admired her and that they were very good friends, but nothing more. I went back up the stairs again—it had given me quite a shock—but I did notice that the kitchen door was open and I've thought since that Beatrice must have been listening. And you can see, can't you, that the way they were talking could be taken two ways? It might just mean that the doctor knew his wife was very ill and couldn't live much longer—and I've no doubt that that was the way he meant it—but to any one like Beatrice it might sound differently—it might look as though the doctor and

Jean Moncrieffe were—well—were definitely planning to do away with Mrs. Oldfield."

" But *you* don't think so, yourself ? "

" No—no, of course not. . . ."

Poirot looked at her searchingly. He said :

" Nurse Harrison, is there something more that you know ? Something that you haven't told me ? "

She flushed and said violently :

" No. No. Certainly not. What could there be ? "

" I do not know. But I thought that there might be—something ? "

She shook her head. The old troubled look had come back.

Hercule Poirot said : " It is possible that the Home Office may order an exhumation of Mrs. Oldfield's body ! "

" Oh no ! " Nurse Harrison was horrified. " What a horrible thing ! "

" You think it would be a pity ? "

" I think it would be *dreadful* ! Think of the talk it would create ! It would be terrible—quite terrible for poor Doctor Oldfield."

" You don't think that it might really be a good thing for him ? "

" How do you mean ? "

Poirot said : " If he is innocent—his innocence will be proved."

He broke off. He watched the thought take root in Nurse Harrison's mind, saw her frown perplexedly, and then saw her brow clear.

She took a deep breath and looked at him.

" I hadn't thought of that," she said simply. " Of course, it is the only thing to be done."

There were a series of thumps on the floor overhead. Nurse Harrison jumped up.

" It's my old lady, Miss Bristow. She's woken up from her rest. I must go and get her comfortable before her tea is brought to her and I go out for my walk. Yes, M. Poirot, I think you are quite right. An autopsy will settle the business once for all. It will scotch the whole thing and all these dreadful rumours against poor Doctor Oldfield will die down."

She shook hands and hurried out of the room.

V

Hercule Poirot walked along to the post office and put through a call to London.

The voice at the other end was petulant.

" *Must* you go nosing out these things, my dear Poirot ? Are you *sure* it's a case for us ? You know what these country town rumours usually amount to—just nothing at all."

" This," said Hercule Poirot, " is a special case."

" Oh well—if you say so. You have such a tiresome habit of being right. But if it's all a mare's nest we shan't be pleased with you, you know."

Hercule Poirot smiled to himself. He murmured :

" No, *I* shall be the one who is pleased."

" What's that you say ? Can't hear."

" Nothing. Nothing at all."

He rang off.

Emerging into the post office he leaned across the counter. He said in his most engaging tones :

" Can you by any chance tell me, Madame, where the maid who was formerly with Doctor Oldfield—Beatrice her Christian name was—now resides ? "

" Beatrice King ? She's had two places since then. She's with Mrs. Marley over the Bank now."

Poirot thanked her, bought two postcards, a book of stamps and a piece of local pottery. During the purchase, he contrived to bring the death of the late Mrs. Oldfield into the conversation. He was quick to note the peculiar furtive expression that stole across the post-mistress's face. She said :

" Very sudden, wasn't it ? It's made a lot of talk as you may have heard."

A gleam of interest came into her eyes as she asked :

" Maybe that's what you'd be wanting to see Beatrice King for ? We all thought it odd the way she was got out of there all of a sudden. Somebody thought she knew something—and *maybe she did*. She's dropped some pretty broad hints."

Beatrice King was a short rather sly-looking girl with adenoids. She presented an appearance of stolid stupidity but her eyes were more intelligent than her manner would have

led one to expect. It seemed, however, that there was nothing
to be got out of Beatrice King. She repeated :

"I don't know nothing about anything ... It's not for me to
say what went on up there ... I don't know what you mean
by overhearing a conversation between the doctor and Miss
Moncrieffe. I'm not one to go listening to doors, and you've
no right to say I did. I don't know nothing."

Poirot said :

"Have you ever heard of poisoning by arsenic ? "

A flicker of quick furtive interest came into the girl's sullen
face.

She said :

"So *that's* what it was in the medicine bottle ? "

"What medicine bottle ? "

Beatrice said :

"One of the bottles of medicine what that Miss Moncrieffe
made up for the Missus. Nurse was all upset—I could see that.
Tasted it, she did, and smelt it, and then poured it away down
the sink and filled up the bottle with plain water from the tap.
It was white medicine like water, anyway. And once, when
Miss Moncrieffe took up a pot of tea to the Missus, Nurse
brought it down again and made it fresh—said it hadn't been
made with boiling water but that was just my eye, that was !
I thought it was just the sort of fussing way nurses have at
the time—but I dunno—it may have been more than that."

Poirot nodded. He said :

"Did you like Miss Moncrieffe, Beatrice ? "

"I didn't mind her . . . . A bit standoffish. Of course, I
always knew as she was sweet on the doctor. You'd only to
see the way she looked at him."

Again Poirot nodded his head. He went back to the inn.
There he gave certain instructions to George.


VI


Dr. Alan Garcia, the Home Office Analyst, rubbed his hands
and twinkled at Hercule Poirot. He said :

"Well, this suits you, M. Poirot, I suppose ? The man who's
always right."

Poirot said:

" You are too kind."

" What put you on to it ?  Gossip ? "

" As you say—Enter Rumour, painted full of tongues."

The following day Poirot once more took a train to Market Loughborough.

Market Loughborough was buzzing like a beehive.  It had buzzed mildly ever since the exhumation proceedings.

Now that the findings of the autopsy had leaked out, excitement had reached fever heat.

Poirot had been at the inn for about an hour and had just finished a hearty lunch of steak and kidney pudding washed down by beer when word was brought to him that a lady was waiting to see him.

It was Nurse Harrison.  Her face was white and haggard.

She came straight to Poirot.

" Is this true ?  Is this really true, M. Poirot ? "

He put her gently into a chair.

" Yes.  More than sufficient arsenic to cause death has been found."

Nurse Harrison cried:

" I never thought—I never for one moment thought——"
and burst into tears.

Poirot said gently:

" The truth had to come out, you know."

She sobbed.

" Will they hang him ? "

Poirot said:

" A lot has to be proved still.  Opportunity—access to poison—the vehicle in which it was administered."

" But supposing, M. Poirot, that he had nothing to do with it—nothing at all."

" In that case," Poirot shrugged his shoulders, " he will be acquitted."

Nurse Harrison said slowly:

" There is something—something that, I suppose, I ought to have told you before—but I didn't think that there was really anything in it.  It was just *queer*."

" I knew there was something," said Poirot.  " You had better tell it to me now."

" It isn't much. It's just that one day when I went down to the dispensary for something, Jean Moncrieffe was doing something rather—odd."

" Yes ? "

" It sounds so silly. It's only that she was filling up her powder compact—a pink enamel one——"

" Yes ? "

" But she wasn't filling it up with powder—with face powder, I mean. She was tipping something into it from one of the bottles out of the poison cupboard. When she saw me she started and shut up the compact and whipped it into her bag—and put back the bottle quickly into the cupboard so that I couldn't see what it was. I daresay it doesn't mean anything—but now that I know that Mrs. Oldfield really was poisoned——" She broke off.

Poirot said : " You will excuse me ? "

He went out and telephoned to Detective Sergeant Grey of the Berkshire Police.

Hercule Poirot came back and he and Nurse Harrison sat in silence.

Poirot was seeing the face of a girl with red hair and hearing a clear hard voice say : " I don't agree." *Jean Moncrieffe had not wanted an autopsy*. She had given a plausible enough excuse, but the fact remained. A competent girl—efficient—resolute. In love with a man who was tied to a complaining invalid wife, who might easily live for years since, according to Nurse Harrison, she had very little the matter with her.

Hercule Poirot sighed.

Nurse Harrison said :

" What are you thinking of ? "

Poirot answered :

" The pity of things. . . ."

Nurse Harrison said :

" I don't believe for a minute *he* knew anything about it."

Poirot said :

" No. I am sure he did not."

The door opened and Detective Sergeant Grey came in. He had something in his hand, wrapped in a silk handkerchief. He unwrapped it and set it carefully down. It was a bright rose pink enamel compact.

Nurse Harrison said :

" That's the one I saw."

Grey said :

" Found it pushed right to the back of Miss Moncrieffe's bureau drawer. Inside a handkerchief sachet. As far as I can see there are no fingerprints on it, but I'll be careful."

With the handkerchief over his hand he pressed the spring. The case flew open. Grey said :

" This stuff isn't face powder."

He dipped a finger and tasted it gingerly on the tip of his tongue.

" No particular taste."

Poirot said :

" White arsenic does not taste."

Grey said :

" It will be analysed at once." He looked at Nurse Harrison. " You can swear to this being the same case ? "

" Yes. I'm positive. That's the case I saw Miss Moncrieffe with in the dispensary about a week before Mrs. Oldfield's death."

Sergeant Grey sighed. He looked at Poirot and nodded. The latter rang the bell.

" Send my servant here, please."

George, the perfect valet, discreet, unobtrusive, entered and looked inquiringly at his master.

Hercule Poirot said :

" You have identified this powder compact, Miss Harrison, as one you saw in the possession of Miss Moncrieffe over a year ago. *Would you be surprised to learn that this particular case was sold by Messrs. Woolworth only a few weeks ago and that, more-over, it is of a pattern and colour that has only been manufactured for the last three months ? *"

Nurse Harrison gasped. She stared at Poirot, her eyes round and dark. Poirot said :

" Have you seen this compact before, Georges ? "

George stepped forward :

" Yes, sir. I observed this person, Nurse Harrison, purchase it at Woolworth's on Friday the 18th. Pursuant to your instructions I followed this lady whenever she went out. She took a bus over to Darnington on the day I have mentioned and purchased this compact. She took it home with her. Later, the same day, she came to the house in which Miss Moncrieffe lodges. Acting as by your instructions, I was already in the house. I observed her go into Miss Moncrieffe's bedroom and hide this in the back of the bureau drawer. I had a good view through the crack of the door. She then left the house believing herself unobserved. I may say that no one locks their front doors down here and it was dusk."

Poirot said to Nurse Harrison, and his voice was hard and venomous:

"Can you explain these facts, Nurse Harrison ? *I think not.* There was no arsenic in that box when it left Messrs. Woolworth, but there was when it left Miss Bristow's house." He added softly, "*It was unwise of you to keep a supply of arsenic in your possession.*"

Nurse Harrison buried her face in her hands. She said in a low dull voice:

"*It's true—it's all true ... I killed her. And all for nothing —nothing ... I was mad.*"

## VII

Jean Moncrieffe said :

"I must ask you to forgive me, M. Poirot. I have been so angry with you—so terribly angry with you. It seemed to me that you were making everything so much worse."

Poirot said with a smile :

"So I was to begin with. It is like in the old legend of the Lernean Hydra. Every time a head was cut off, two heads grew in its place. So, to begin with, the rumours grew and multiplied. But you see my task, like that of my namesake Hercules, was to reach the first—the original head. Who had started this rumour ? It did not take me long to discover that the originator of the story was Nurse Harrison. I went to see her. She appeared to be a very nice woman—intelligent and sympathetic. But almost at once she made a bad mistake— she repeated to me a conversation which she had overheard taking place between you and the doctor, and that conversation, you see, *was all wrong*. It was psychologically most unlikely. *If* you and the doctor had planned together to kill Mrs. Oldfield, you are both of you far too intelligent and level-headed to hold such a conversation in a room with an open door, easily overheard by someone on the stairs or someone in the kitchen. Moreover, the words attributed to you did not fit in at all with your mental make-up. They were the words of a much *older* woman and of one of a quite different type. They were words such as would be imagined by Nurse Harrison as being used *by herself in like circumstances*.

" I had, up to then, regarded the whole matter as fairly simple. Nurse Harrison, I realised, was a fairly young and still handsome woman—she had been thrown closely with Doctor Oldfield for nearly three years—the doctor had been very fond of her and grateful to her for her tact and sympathy. She had formed the impression that *if Mrs. Oldfield died*, the doctor would probably ask her to marry him. Instead of that, after Mrs. Oldfield's death, she learns that *Doctor Oldfield is in love with you*. Straightaway, driven by anger and jealousy, she starts spreading the rumour that Doctor Oldfield has poisoned his wife.

" That, as I say, was how I had visualised the position at first. It was a case of a jealous woman and a lying rumour. But the old trite phrase ' no smoke without fire ' recurred to me significantly. I wondered if Nurse Harrison had done *more* than spread a rumour. Certain things she said rang strangely. She told me that Mrs. Oldfield's illness was largely imaginary— that she did not really suffer much pain. But the *doctor himself* had been in no doubt about the reality of his wife's suffering. *He* had not been surprised by her death. He had called in another doctor shortly before her death and the other doctor had realised the gravity of her condition. Tentatively I brought forward the suggestion of exhumation . . . Nurse Harrison was at first frightened out of her wits by the idea. Then, almost at once, her jealousy and hatred took command of her. Let them find arsenic—no suspicion would attach to *her*. It would be the doctor and Jean Moncrieffe who would suffer.

" There was only one hope. *To make Nurse Harrison over-reach herself*. If there were a chance that Jean Moncrieffe would escape, I fancied that Nurse Harrison would strain every nerve to involve her in the crime. I gave instructions to my faithful Georges—the most unobtrusive of men whom she did not know by sight. He was to follow her closely. And so—all ended well."

Jean Moncrieffe said :

" You've been *wonderful*."

Dr. Oldfield chimed in. He said :

" Yes, indeed. I can never thank you enough. What a blind fool I was ! "

Poirot asked curiously :

" Were you as blind, Mademoiselle ? "

Jean Moncrieffe said slowly :

" I have been terribly worried. You see, the arsenic in the poison cupboard didn't tally. . . ."

Oldfield cried :

" Jean—you didn't think—— ? "

" No, no—not *you*. What I *did* think was that Mrs. Oldfield had somehow or other got hold of it—and that she was taking it so as to make herself ill and get sympathy and that she had inadvertently taken too much. But I was afraid that if there *was* an autopsy and arsenic was found, they would never consider that theory and would leap to the conclusion that *you'd* done it. That's why I never said anything about the missing arsenic. I even cooked the poison book ! But the last person I would ever have suspected was Nurse Harrison."

Oldfield said :

" I too. She was such a gentle womanly creature. Like a Madonna."

Poirot said sadly :

" Yes, she would have made, probably, a good wife and mother . . . Her emotions were just a little too strong for her."

He sighed and murmured once more under his breath :

" *The pity of it*."

Then he smiled at the happy-looking middle-aged man and the eager-faced girl opposite him. He said to himself :

" These two have come out of its shadow into the sun . . . and I—I have performed the second Labour of Hercules."

# III

# THE ARCADIAN DEER

## I

HERCULE POIROT stamped his feet, seeking to warm them. He blew upon his fingers. Flakes of snow melted and dripped from the corners of his moustache.

There was a knock at the door and a chambermaid appeared. She was a slow-breathing thickset country girl and she stared with a good deal of curiosity at Hercule Poirot. It was possible that she had never seen anything quite like him before.

She asked : " Did you ring ? "

" I did. Will you be so good as to light the fire ? "

She went out and came back again immediately with paper and sticks. She knelt down in front of the big Victorian grate and began to lay a fire.

Hercule Poirot continued to stamp his feet, swing his arms and blow on his fingers.

He was annoyed. His car—an expensive Messarro Gratz—had not behaved with that mechanical perfection which he expected of a car. His chauffeur, a young man who enjoyed a handsome salary, had not succeeded in putting things right. The car had staged a final refusal in a secondary road a mile and a half from anywhere with a fall of snow beginning. Hercule Poirot, wearing his usual smart patent leather shoes, had been forced to walk that mile and a half to reach the riverside village of Hartly Dene—a village which, though showing every sign of animation in summer-time, was completely moribund in winter. The Black Swan had registered something like dismay at the arrival of a guest. The landlord had been almost eloquent as he pointed out that the local garage could supply a car in which the gentleman could continue his journey.

Hercule Poirot repudiated the suggestion. His Latin thrift was offended. Hire a car ? He already *had* a car—a large car —an expensive car. In that car and no other he proposed to

63

continue his journey back to town. And in any case, even if repairs to it could be quickly effected, he was not going on in this snow until next morning. He demanded a room, a fire and a meal. Sighing, the landlord showed him to the room, sent the maid to supply the fire and then retired to discuss with his wife the problem of the meal.

An hour later, his feet stretched out towards the comforting blaze, Hercule Poirot reflected leniently on the dinner he had just eaten. True, the steak had been both tough and full of gristle, the brussels-sprouts had been large, pale, and definitely watery, the potatoes had had hearts of stone. Nor was there much to be said for the portion of stewed apple and custard which had followed. The cheese had been hard, and the biscuits soft. Nevertheless, thought Hercule Poirot, looking graciously at the leaping flames, and sipping delicately at a cup of liquid mud euphemistically called coffee, it was better to be full than empty, and after tramping snowbound lanes in patent leather shoes, to sit in front of a fire was Paradise !

There was a knock on the door and the chambermaid appeared.

" Please, sir, the man from the garage is here and would like to see you."

Hercule Poirot replied amiably :

" Let him mount."

The girl giggled and retired. Poirot reflected kindly that her account of him to her friends would provide entertainment for many winter days to come.

There was another knock—a different knock—and Poirot called :

" Come in."

He looked up with approval at the young man who entered and stood there looking ill at ease, twisting his cap in his hands.

Here, he thought, was one of the handsomest specimens of humanity he had ever seen, a simple young man with the outward semblance of a Greek god.

The young man said in a low husky voice :

" About the car, sir, we've brought it in. And we've got at the trouble. It's a matter of an hour's work or so."

Poirot said :

" What is wrong with it ? "

The young man plunged eagerly into technical details. Poirot nodded his head gently, but he was not listening. Perfect physique was a thing he admired greatly. There were, he considered, too many rats in spectacles about. He said to himself approvingly : " Yes, a Greek god—a young shepherd in Arcady."

The young man stopped abruptly. It was then that Hercule Poirot's brows knitted themselves for a second. His first reaction had been æsthetic, his second mental. His eyes narrowed themselves curiously, as he looked up.

He said :

" I comprehend. Yes, I comprehend." He paused and then added : " My chauffeur, he has already told me that which you have just said."

He saw the flush that came to the other's cheek, saw the fingers grip the cap nervously.

The young man stammered :

" Yes—er—yes, sir. I know."

Hercule Poirot went on smoothly :

" But you thought that you would also come and tell me yourself ? "

" Er—yes, sir, I thought I'd better."

" That," said Hercule Poirot, " was very conscientious of you. Thank you."

There was a faint but unmistakable note of dismissal in the last words but he did not expect the other to go and he was right. The young man did not move.

His fingers moved convulsively, crushing the tweed cap, and he said in a still lower embarrassed voice :

" Er—excuse me, sir—but it's true, isn't it, that you're the detective gentleman—you're Mr. Hercules Pwarrit ? " He said the name carefully.

Poirot said : " That is so."

Red crept up the young man's face. He said :

" I read a piece about you in the paper."

" Yes ? "

The boy was now scarlet. There was distress in his eyes—distress and appeal. Hercule Poirot came to his aid. He said gently :

" Yes ?  What is it you want to ask me ? "

The words came with a rush now.

" I'm afraid you may think it's awful cheek of me, sir.  But your coming here by chance like this—well, it's too good to be missed.  Having read about you and the clever things you've done.  Anyway, I said as after all I might as well ask you.  There's no harm in asking, is there ? "

Hercule Poirot shook his head.  He said :

" You want my help in some way ? "

The other nodded.  He said, his voice husky and embarrassed :

" It's—it's about a young lady.  If—if you could find her for me."

" Find her ?  Has she disappeared, then ? "

" That's right, sir."

Hercule Poirot sat up in his chair.  He said sharply :

" I could help you, perhaps, yes.  But the proper people for you to go to are the police.  It is their job and they have far more resources at their disposal than I have."

The boy shuffled his feet.  He said awkwardly :

" I couldn't do that, sir.  It's not like that at all.  It's all rather peculiar, so to speak."

Hercule Poirot stared at him.  Then he indicated a chair.

" *Eh bien*, then, sit down—what is your name ? "

" Williamson, sir, Ted Williamson."

" Sit down, Ted.  And tell me all about it."

" Thank you, sir."  He drew forward the chair and sat down carefully on the edge of it.  His eyes had still that appealing doglike look.

Hercule Poirot said gently :

" Tell me."

Ted Williamson drew a deep breath.

" Well, you see, sir, it was like this.  I never saw her but the once.  And I don't know her right name nor anything.  But it's queer like, the whole thing, and my letter coming back and everything."

" Start," said Hercule Poirot, " at the beginning.  Do not hurry yourself.  Just tell me everything that occurred."

" Yes, sir.  Well, perhaps you know Grasslawn, sir, that big house down by the river past the bridge ? "

" I know nothing at all."

"Belongs to Sir George Sanderfield, it does. He uses it in the summer-time for week-ends and parties—rather a gay lot he has down as a rule. Actresses and that. Well, it was last June—and the wireless was out of order and they sent me up to see to it."

Poirot nodded.

"So I went along. The gentleman was out on the river with his guests and the cook was out and his manservant had gone along to serve the drinks and all that on the launch. There was only this girl in the house—she was the lady's-maid to one of the guests. She let me in and showed me where the set was, and stayed there while I was working on it. And so we got to talking and all that ... Nita her name was, so she told me, and she was lady's-maid to a Russian dancer who was staying there."

"What nationality was she, English?"

"No, sir, she'd be French, I think. She'd a funny sort of accent. But she spoke English all right. She—she was friendly and after a bit I asked her if she could come out that night and go to the pictures, but she said her lady would be needing her. But then she said as how she could get off early in the afternoon because as how they wasn't going to be back off the river till late. So the long and the short of it was that I took the afternoon off without asking (and nearly got the sack for it too) and we went for a walk along by the river."

He paused. A little smile hovered on his lips. His eyes were dreamy. Poirot said gently:

"And she was pretty, yes?"

"She was just the loveliest thing you ever saw. Her hair was like gold—it went up each side like wings—and she had a gay kind of way of tripping along. I—I—well, I fell for her right away, sir. I'm not pretending anything else."

Poirot nodded. The young man went on:

"She said as how her lady would be coming down again in a fortnight and we fixed up to meet again then." He paused. "But she never came. I waited for her at the spot she'd said, but not a sign of her, and at last I made bold to go up to the house and ask for her. The Russian lady was staying there all right and her maid too, they said. Sent for her, they did, but when she came, why, it wasn't Nita at all! Just a dark catty-looking girl—a bold lot if there ever was one. Marie, they called her. ' You want to see me ? ' she says, simpering all over. She must have seen I was took aback. I said was she the Russian lady's maid and something about her not being the one I'd seen before, and then she laughed and said that the last maid had been sent away sudden. ' Sent away ? ' I said. ' What for ? ' She sort of shrugged her shoulders and stretched out her hands. ' How should I know ? ' she said. ' I was not there.'

" Well, sir, it took me aback. At the moment I couldn't think of anything to say. But afterwards I plucked up courage and I got to see this Marie again and asked her to get me Nita's address. I didn't let on to her that I didn't even know Nita's last name. I promised her a present if she did what I asked—she was the kind as wouldn't do anything for you for nothing. Well, she got it all right for me—an address in North London, it was, and I wrote to Nita there—but the letter came back after a bit—sent back through the post office with *no longer at this address* scrawled on it."

Ted Williamson stopped. His eyes, those deep blue steady eyes, looked across at Poirot. He said :

" You see how it is, sir ? It's not a case for the police. But I want to find her. And I don't know how to set about it. If—if you could find her for me." His colour deepened. " I've —I've a bit put by. I could manage five pounds—or even ten."

Poirot said gently :

" We need not discuss the financial side for the moment. First reflect on this point—this girl, this Nita—she knew your name and where you worked ? "

" Oh yes, sir."

" She could have communicated with you if she had wanted to ? "

Ted said more slowly :

" Yes, sir."

" Then do you not think—perhaps——"

Ted Williamson interrupted him.

" What you're meaning, sir, is that I fell for her but she didn't fall for me ? Maybe that's true in a way . . . But she liked me—she *did* like me—it wasn't just a bit of fun to her.

... And I've been thinking, sir, as there might be a *reason* for all this. You see, sir, it was a funny crowd she was mixed up in. She might be in a bit of trouble, if you know what I mean."

"You mean she might have been going to have a child? Your child?"

"Not mine, sir." Ted flushed. "There wasn't nothing wrong between us."

Poirot looked at him thoughtfully. He murmured:

"And if what you suggest is true—you still want to find her?"

The colour surged up in Ted Williamson's face. He said:

"Yes, I do, and that's flat! I want to marry her if she'll have me. And that's no matter what kind of a jam she's in! If you'll only try and find her for me, sir?"

Hercule Poirot smiled. He said, murmuring to himself:

"'Hair like wings of gold.' Yes, I think this is the third Labour of Hercules ... If I remember rightly, that happened in Arcady. ..."

## II

Hercule Poirot looked thoughtfully at the sheet of paper on which Ted Williamson had laboriously inscribed a name and address.

Miss Valetta, 17 Upper Renfrew Lane, N.15.

He wondered if he would learn anything at that address. Somehow he fancied not. But it was the only help Ted could give him.

No. 17 Upper Renfrew Lane was a dingy but respectable street. A stout woman with bleary eyes opened the door to Poirot's knock.

"Miss Valetta?"

"Gone away a long time ago, she has."

Poirot advanced a step into the doorway just as the door was about to close.

"You can give me, perhaps, her address?"

"Couldn't say, I'm sure. She didn't leave one."

"When did she go away?"

"Last summer it was."

" Can you tell me exactly *when* ? "

A gentle clinking noise came from Poirot's right hand where two half-crowns jostled each other in friendly fashion.

The bleary-eyed woman softened in an almost magical manner. She became graciousness itself.

" Well, I'm sure I'd like to help you, sir. Let me see now. August, no, before that—July—yes, July it must have been. About the first week in July. Went off in a hurry, she did. Back to Italy, I believe."

" She was an Italian, then ? "

" That's right, sir."

" And she was at one time lady's-maid to a Russian dancer, was she not ? "

" That's right. Madame Semoulina or some such name. Danced at the Thespian in this Bally everyone's so wild about. One of the stars, she was."

Poirot said :

" Do you know why Miss Valetta left her post ? "

The woman hesitated a moment before saying :

" I couldn't say, I'm sure."

" She was dismissed, was she not ? "

" Well—I believe there was a bit of a dust up ! But mind you, Miss Valetta didn't let on much about it. *She* wasn't one to give things away. But she looked wild about it. Wicked temper she had—real Eyetalian—her black eyes all snapping and looking as if she'd like to put a knife into you. I wouldn't have crossed her when she was in one of her moods ! "

" And you are quite sure you do not know Miss Valetta's present address ? "

The half-crowns clinked again encouragingly.

The answer rang true enough.

" I wish I did, sir. I'd be only too glad to tell you. But there—she went off in a hurry and there it is ! "

Poirot said to himself thoughtfully :

" Yes, there it is . . ."

III

Ambrose Vandel, diverted from his enthusiastic account of the *décor* he was designing for a forthcoming ballet, supplied information easily enough.

" Sanderfield ? George Sanderfield ? Nasty fellow. Rolling in money but they say he's a crook. Dark horse ! Affair with a dancer ? But of course, my dear—he had an affair with *Katrina*. Katrina Samoushenka. You *must* have seen her ? Oh, my dear—too delicious. Lovely technique. *The Swan of Tuolela*—you must have seen *that* ? *My décor !* And that other thing of Debussy or is it Mannine ' *La Biche au Bois* ' ? She danced it with Michael Novgin. He's *so* marvellous, isn't he ? "

" And she was a friend of Sir George Sanderfield ? "

" Yes, she used to week-end with him at his house on the river. Marvellous parties I believe he gives."

" Would it be possible, *mon cher*, for you to introduce me to Mademoiselle Samoushenka ? "

" But, my dear, she isn't *here* any longer. She went to Paris or somewhere quite suddenly. You know, they do say that *she* was a Bolshevik spy or something—not that I believed it *myself*—you know people love saying things like that. Katrina always pretended that she was a White Russian—her father was a Prince or a Grand Duke—the usual thing ! It goes *down* so much better." Vandel paused and returned to the absorbing subject of himself. " Now as I was saying, if you want to get the *spirit* of Bathsheba you've got to steep yourself in the Semitic tradition. I express it by——"

He continued happily.

IV

The interview that Hercule Poirot managed to arrange with Sir George Sanderfield did not start too auspiciously.

The " dark horse," as Ambrose Vandel had called him, was slightly ill at ease. Sir George was a short square man with dark coarse hair and a roll of fat in his neck.

He said :

" Well, M. Poirot, what can I do for you ? Er—we haven't
met before, I think ? "

" No, we have not met."

" Well, what is it ?  I confess, I'm quite curious."

" Oh, it is very simple—a mere matter of information."
The other gave an uneasy laugh.

" Want me to give you some inside dope, eh ?  Didn't know
you were interested in finance."

" It is not a matter of *les affaires*.  It is a question of a certain
lady."

" Oh, a woman."  Sir George Sanderfield leant back in his
arm-chair.  He seemed to relax.  His voice held an easier note.
Poirot said :

" You were acquainted, I think, with Mademoiselle Katrina
Samoushenka ? "

Sanderfield laughed.

" Yes.  An enchanting creature.  Pity she's left London."

" Why did she leave London ? "

" My dear fellow, *I* don't know.  Row with the management,
I believe.  She was temperamental, you know—very Russian
in her moods.  I'm sorry that I can't help you but I haven't the
least idea where she is now.  I haven't kept up with her at all."

There was a note of dismissal in his voice as he rose to his
feet.

Poirot said :

" But it is not Mademoiselle Samoushenka that I am anxious
to trace."

" It isn't ? "

" No, it is a question of her maid."

" Her *maid* ? "  Sanderfield stared at him.

Poirot said :

" Do you—perhaps—remember her maid ? "

All Sanderfield's uneasiness had returned.  He said
awkwardly :

" Good Lord, no, how should I ?  I remember she *had* one,
of course . . .  Bit of a bad lot, too, I should say.  Sneaking,
prying sort of girl.  If I were you I shouldn't put any faith in
a word that girl says.  She's the kind of girl who's a born liar."

Poirot murmured :

" So actually, you remember quite a lot about her ? "

Sanderfield said hastily :

" Just an impression, that's all . . . Don't even remember her name. Let me see, Marie something or other—no, I'm afraid I can't help you to get hold of her. Sorry."

Poirot said gently :

" I have already got the name of Marie Hellin from the Thespian Theatre—and her address. But I am speaking, Sir George, of the maid who was with Mademoiselle Samoushenka *before* Marie Hellin. I am speaking of Nita Valetta."

Sanderfield stared. He said :

" Don't remember her at all. Marie's the only one *I* remember. Little dark girl with a nasty look in her eye."

Poirot said :

" The girl I mean was at your house Grasslawn last June."

Sanderfield said sulkily :

" Well, all I can say is I don't remember her. Don't believe she had a maid with her. I think you're making a mistake."

Hercule Poirot shook his head. He did not think he was making a mistake.

### V

Marie Hellin looked swiftly at Poirot out of small intelligent eyes and as swiftly looked away again. She said in smooth, even tones :

" But I remember *perfectly*, Monsieur. I was engaged by Madame Samoushenka the last week in June. Her former maid had departed in a hurry."

" Did you ever hear why that maid left ? "

" She went—suddenly—that is all I know ! It may have been illness—something of that kind. Madame did not say."

Poirot said :

" Did you find your mistress easy to get on with ? "

The girl shrugged her shoulders.

" She had great moods. She wept and laughed in turns. Sometimes she was so despondent she would not speak or eat. Sometimes she was wildly gay. They are like that, these dancers. It is temperament."

" And Sir George ? "

The girl looked up alertly. An unpleasant gleam came into her eyes.

"Ah, Sir George Sanderfield? You would like to know about *him*? Perhaps it is that that you really want to know? The other was only an excuse, eh? Ah, Sir George, I could tell you some curious things about him, I could tell you——"

Poirot interrupted:

"It is not necessary."

She stared at him, her mouth open. Angry disappointment showed in her eyes.


## VI


"I always say you know everything, Alexis Pavlovitch."

Hercule Poirot murmured the words with his most flattering intonation.

He was reflecting to himself that this third Labour of Hercules had necessitated more travelling and more interviews than could have been imagined possible. This little matter of a missing lady's-maid was proving one of the longest and most difficult problems he had ever tackled. Every clue, when examined, led exactly nowhere.

It had brought him this evening to the Samovar Restaurant in Paris whose proprietor, Count Alexis Pavlovitch, prided himself on knowing everything that went on in the artistic world.

He nodded now complacently:

"Yes, yes, my friend, *I* know—I always know. You ask me where she is gone—the little Samoushenka, the exquisite dancer? Ah! she was the real thing, that little one." He kissed his fingertips. "What fire—what abandon! She would have gone far—she would have been the Première Ballerina of her day—and then suddenly it all ends—she creeps away—to the end of the world—and soon, ah! so soon, they forget her."

"Where is she then?" demanded Poirot.

"In Switzerland. At Vagray les Alpes. It is there that they go, those who have the little dry cough and who grow thinner and thinner. She will die, yes, she will die! She has a fatalistic nature. She will surely die."

Poirot coughed to break the tragic spell. He wanted information.

"You do not, by chance, remember a maid she had? A maid called Nita Valetta?"

"Valetta? Valetta? I remember seeing a maid once— at the station when I was seeing Katrina off to London. She was an Italian from Pisa, was she not? Yes, I am sure she was an Italian who came from Pisa."

Hercule Poirot groaned.

"In that case," he said, "I must now journey to Pisa."


## VII


Hercule Poirot stood in the Campo Santo at Pisa and looked down on a grave.

So it was here that his quest had come to an end—here by this humble mound of earth. Underneath it lay the joyous creature who had stirred the heart and imagination of a simple English mechanic.

Was this perhaps the best end to that sudden strange romance? Now the girl would live always in the young man's memory as he had seen her for those few enchanted hours of a June afternoon. The clash of opposing nationalities, of different standards, the pain of disillusionment, all that was ruled out for ever.

Hercule Poirot shook his head sadly. His mind went back to his conversation with the Valetta family. The mother, with her broad peasant face, the upright grief-stricken father, the dark hard-lipped sister.

"It was sudden, Signor, it was very sudden. Though for many years she had had pains on and off . . . The doctor gave us no choice—he said there must be an operation immediately for the appendicitis. He took her off to the hospital then and there . . . *Si, si*, it was under the anæsthetic she died. She never recovered consciousness."

The mother sniffed, murmuring:

"Bianca was always such a clever girl. It is terrible that she should have died so young. . . ."

Hercule Poirot repeated to himself:

" She died young. . . ."

That was the message he must take back to the young man who had asked his help so confidingly.

" *She is not for you, my friend. She died young.*"

His quest had ended—here where the leaning Tower was silhouetted against the sky and the first spring flowers were showing pale and creamy with their promise of life and joy to come.

Was it the stirring of spring that made him feel so rebelliously disinclined to accept this final verdict ? Or was it something else ? Something stirring at the back of his brain —words—a phrase—a name ? Did not the whole thing finish too neatly—dovetail too obviously ?

Hercule Poirot sighed. He must take one more journey to put things beyond any possible doubt. He must go to Vagray les Alpes.

## VIII

Here, he thought, really was the world's end. This shelf of snow—these scattered huts and shelters in each of which lay a motionless human being fighting an insidious death.

So he came at last to Katrina Samoushenka. When he saw her, lying there with hollow cheeks in each of which was a vivid red stain, and long thin emaciated hands stretched out on the coverlet, a memory stirred in him. He had not remembered her name, but he *had* seen her dance—had been carried away and fascinated by the supreme art that can make you forget art.

He remembered Michael Novgin, the Hunter, leaping and twirling in that outrageous and fantastic forest that the brain of Ambrose Vandel had conceived. And he remembered the lovely flying Hind, eternally pursued, eternally desirable—a golden beautiful creature with horns on her head and twinkling bronze feet. He remembered her final collapse, shot and wounded, and Michael Novgin standing bewildered, with the body of the slain Deer in his arms.

Katrina Samoushenka was looking at him with faint curiosity. She said :

" I have never seen you before, have I ? What is it you want of me ? "

Hercule Poirot made her a little bow.

" First, Madame, I wish to thank you—for your art which made for me once an evening of beauty."

She smiled faintly.

" But also I am here on a matter of business. I have been looking, Madame, for a long time for a certain maid of yours— her name was Nita."

" Nita ? "

She stared at him. Her eyes were large and startled. She said :

" What do you know about—Nita ? "

" I will tell you."

He told her of the evening when his car had broken down and of Ted Williamson standing there twisting his cap between his fingers and stammering out his love and his pain. She listened with close attention.

She said when he had finished :

" It is touching, that—yes, it is touching. . . ."

Hercule Poirot nodded.

" Yes," he said. " It is a tale of Arcady, is it not ? What can you tell me, Madame, of this girl ? "

Katrina Samoushenka sighed.

" I had a maid—Juanita. She was lovely, yes—gay, light of heart. It happened to her what happens so often to those the gods favour. She died young."

They had been Poirot's own words—final words—irrevocable words—Now he heard them again—and yet he persisted. He asked :

" She is dead ? "

" Yes, she is dead."

Hercule Poirot was silent a minute, then he said :

" Yet there is one thing I do not quite understand. I asked Sir George Sanderfield about this maid of yours and he seemed afraid. Why was that ? "

There was a faint expression of disgust on the dancer's face.

" You just said a maid of mine. He thought you meant Marie—the girl who came to me after Juanita left. She tried to blackmail him, I believe, over something that she found out about him. She was an odious girl—inquisitive, always prying into letters and locked drawers."

Poirot murmured :

" Then that explains that."

He paused a minute, then he went on, still persistent :

" Juanita's other name was Valetta and she died of an operation for appendicitis in Pisa. Is that correct ? "

He noted the hesitation, hardly perceptible but nevertheless there, before the dancer bowed her head.

" Yes, that is right. . . ."

Poirot said meditatively :

" And yet—there is still a little point—her people spoke of her, not as Juanita but as *Bianca*."

Katrina shrugged her thin shoulders. She said : " Bianca—Juanita, does it matter ? I suppose her real name was Bianca but she thought the name of Juanita was more romantic and so chose to call herself by it."

" Ah, you think that ? " He paused and then, his voice changing, he said : " For me, there is another explanation."

" What is it ? "

Poirot leaned forward. He said :

" The girl that Ted Williamson saw had hair that he described as being like wings of gold."

He leaned still a little further forward. His finger just touched the two springing waves of Katrina's hair.

" Wings of gold, horns of gold ? It is as you look at it, it is whether one sees you as devil or as angel ! You might be either. Or are they perhaps only the golden horns of the stricken deer ? "

Katrina murmured :

" *The stricken deer.* . . ." and her voice was the voice of one without hope.

Poirot said :

" All along Ted Williamson's description has worried me—it brought something to my mind—that something was *you*, dancing on your twinkling bronze feet through the forest. Shall I tell you what *I* think, Mademoiselle ? I think there was a week when you had *no* maid, when you went down alone to Grasslawn, for Bianca Valetta had returned to Italy and you had not yet engaged a new maid. Already you were feeling the illness which has since overtaken you, and you stayed in the house one day when the others went on an all day excursion on the river. There was a ring at the door and you went to it and you saw—*shall I tell you what you saw?* You saw a young man who was as simple as a child and as handsome as a god! And you invented for him a girl—not *Juanita*—but *Incognita* —and for a few hours you walked with him in Arcady. . . ."

There was a long pause. Then Katrina said in a low hoarse voice :

" In one thing at least I have told you the truth. I have given you the right end to the story. Nita will die young."

" *Ah non !* " Hercule Poirot was transformed. He struck his hand on the table. He was suddenly prosaic, mundane, practical.

He said :

" It is quite unnecessary ! *You need not die.* You can fight for your life, can you not, as well as another ? "

She shook her head—sadly, hopelessly——

" What life is there for me ? "

" Not the life of the stage, *bien entendu !* But think, there is another life. Come now, Mademoiselle, be honest, was your father really a Prince or a Grand Duke, or even a General ? "

She laughed suddenly. She said :

" He drove a lorry in Leningrad ! "

" Very good ! And why should you not be the wife of a garage hand in a country village ? And have children as beautiful as gods, and with feet, perhaps, that will dance as you once danced."

Katrina caught her breath.

" But the whole idea is fantastic ! "

" Nevertheless," said Hercule Poirot with great self-satisfaction, " I believe it is going to come true ! "

# IV

## THE ERYMANTHIAN BOAR

### I

THE ACCOMPLISHMENT of the third Labour of Hercules having brought him to Switzerland, Hercule Poirot decided that being there, he might take advantage of the fact and visit certain places which were up to now unknown to him.

He passed an agreeable couple of days at Chamonix, lingered a day or two at Montreux and then went on to Aldermatt, a spot which he had heard various friends praise highly.

Aldermatt, however, affected him unpleasantly. It was at the end of a valley with towering snow-peaked mountains shutting it in. He felt, unreasonably, that it was difficult to breathe.

"Impossible to remain here," said Hercule Poirot to himself. It was at that moment that he caught sight of a funicular railway. "Decidedly, I must mount."

The funicular, he discovered, ascended first to Les Avines, then to Caurouchet and finally to Rochers Neiges, ten thousand feet above sea level.

Poirot did not propose mounting as high as all that. Les Avines, he thought, would be quite sufficiently his affair.

But here he reckoned without that element of chance which plays so large a part in life. The funicular had started when the conductor approached Poirot and demanded his ticket. After he had inspected it and punched it with a fearsome pair of clippers, he returned it with a bow. At the same time Poirot felt a small wad of paper pressed into his hand with the ticket.

The eyebrows of Hercule Poirot rose a little on his forehead. Presently, unostentatiously, without hurrying himself, he smoothed out the wad of paper. It proved to be a hurriedly scribbled note written in pencil.

*Impossible* (it ran) *to mistake those moustaches! I salute*

*you, my dear colleague. If you are willing, you can be of great
assistance to me. You have doubtless read of the affaire Salley?
The killer—Marrascaud—is believed to have a rendezvous with
some members of his gang at Rochers Neiges—of all places in
the world! Of course the whole thing may be a blague—but our
information is reliable—there is always someone who squeals,
is there not? So keep your eyes open, my friend. Get in touch
with Inspector Drouet who is on the spot. He is a sound man—
but he cannot pretend to the brilliance of Hercule Poirot. It is
important, my friend, that Marrascaud should be taken—and
taken alive. He is not a man—he is a wild boar—one of the
most dangerous killers alive to-day. I did not risk speaking to
you at Aldermatt as I might have been observed and you will
have a freer hand if you are thought to be a mere tourist. Good
hunting! Your old friend—Lementeuil.*

Thoughtfully, Hercule Poirot caressed his moustaches.
Yes, indeed, impossible to mistake the moustaches of Hercule
Poirot. Now what was all this? He had read in the papers
the details of *l'affaire Salley*—the cold blooded murder of a
well-known Parisian bookmaker. The identity of the murderer
was known. Marrascaud was a member of a well-known racecourse gang. He had been suspected of many other killings—
but this time his guilt was proved up to the hilt. He had got
away, out of France it was thought, and the police in every
country in Europe were on the look out for him.

So Marrascaud was said to have a rendezvous at Rochers
Neiges. . . .

Hercule Poirot shook his head slowly. He was puzzled.
For Rochers Neiges was above the snow line. There was a
hotel there, but it communicated with the world only by the
funicular, standing as it did on a long narrow ledge overhanging the valley. The hotel opened in June, but there was
seldom any one there until July and August. It was a place
ill-supplied with entrances and exits—if a man were tracked
there, he was caught in a trap. It seemed a fantastic place to
choose as the rendezvous of a gang of criminals.

And yet, if Lementeuil said his information was reliable,
then Lementeuil was probably right. Hercule Poirot respected
the Swiss Commissaire of Police. He knew him as a sound and
dependable man.

Some reason unknown was bringing Marrascaud to this meeting-place far above civilisation.

Hercule Poirot sighed. To hunt down a ruthless killer was not his idea of a pleasant holiday. Brain work from an arm-chair, he reflected, was more in his line. Not to ensnare a wild boar upon a mountainside.

*A wild boar*—that was the term Lementeuil had used. It was certainly an odd coincidence. . . .

He murmured to himself : " The fourth Labour of Hercules. The Erymanthian Boar ? "

Quietly, without ostentation, he took careful stock of his fellow passengers.

On the seat opposite him was an American tourist. The pattern of his clothes, of his overcoat, the grip he carried, down to his hopeful friendliness and his naïve absorption in the scenery, even the guide book in his hand, all gave him away and proclaimed him a small town American seeing Europe for the first time. In another minute or two, Poirot judged, he would break into speech. His wistful dog-like expression could not be mistaken.

On the other side of the carriage a tall, rather distinguished looking man with greyish hair and a big curved nose was reading a German book. He had the strong mobile fingers of a musician or a surgeon.

Farther away still were three men all of the same type. Men with bowed legs and an indescribable suggestion of horsi-ness about them. They were playing cards. Presently, perhaps, they would suggest a stranger cutting in on the game. At first the stranger would win. Afterwards, the luck would run the other way.

Nothing very unusual about the three men. The only thing that was unusual was the place where they were.

One might have seen them in any train on the way to a race meeting—or on an unimportant liner. But in an almost empty funicular—no !

There was one other occupant of the carriage—a woman. She was tall and dark. It was a beautiful face—a face that might have expressed a whole gamut of emotion—but which instead was frozen into a strange inexpressiveness. She looked at no one, staring out at the valley below.

Presently, as Poirot had expected, the American began to talk. His name, he said, was Schwartz. It was his first visit to Europe. The scenery, he said, was just grand. He'd been very deeply impressed by the Castle of Chillon. He didn't think much of Paris as a city—overrated—he'd been to the Folies Bergères and the Louvre and Nôtre Dame—and he'd noticed that none of these restaurants and cafés could play hot jazz properly. The Champs Elysées, he thought, was pretty good, and he liked the fountains especially when they were floodlit.

Nobody got out at Les Avines or at Caurouchet. It was clear that everyone in the funicular was going up to Rochers Neiges.

Mr. Schwartz explained his own reasons. He had always wished, he said, to be high up among snow mountains. Ten thousand feet was pretty good—he'd heard that you couldn't boil an egg properly when you were as high up as that.

In the innocent friendliness of his heart, Mr. Schwartz endeavoured to draw the tall, grey-haired man on the other side of the carriage into the conversation, but the latter merely stared at him coldly over his pince-nez and returned to the perusal of his book.

Mr. Schwartz then offered to exchange places with the dark lady—she would get a better view, he explained.

It was doubtful whether she understood English. Anyway, she merely shook her head and shrank closer into the fur collar of her coat.

Mr. Schwartz murmured to Poirot :

" Seems kind of wrong to see a woman travelling about alone with no one to see to things for her. A woman needs a lot of looking after when she's travelling."

Remembering certain American women he had met on the Continent, Hercule Poirot agreed.

Mr. Schwartz sighed. He found the world unfriendly. And surely, his brown eyes said expressively, there's no harm in a little friendliness all round ?

## II

To be received by a hotel manager correctly garbed in frock coat and patent leather shoes seemed somehow ludicrous in this out of the world, or rather above-the-world, spot.

The manager was a big handsome man, with an important manner. He was very apologetic.

So early in the season . . . The hot-water system was out of order . . . things were hardly in running order . . . Naturally, he would do everything he could . . . Not a full staff yet . . . He was quite confused by the unexpected number of visitors.

It all came rolling out with professional urbanity and yet it seemed to Poirot that behind the urbane *façade* he caught a glimpse of some poignant anxiety. This man, for all his easy manner, was *not* at ease. He was worried about something:

Lunch was served in a long room overlooking the valley far below. The solitary waiter, addressed as Gustave, was skilful and adroit. He darted here and there, advising on the menu, whipping out his wine list. The three horsy men sat at a table together. They laughed and talked in French, their voices rising.

Good old Joseph!—What about the little Denise, mon vieux ?—Do you remember that sacré pig of a horse that let us all down at Auteuil ?

It was all very hearty, very much in character—and incongruously out of place !

The woman with the beautiful face sat alone at a table in the corner. She looked at no one.

Afterwards, as Poirot was sitting in the lounge, the manager came to him and was confidential.

Monsieur must not judge the hotel too hardly. It was out of the season. No one came here till the end of July. That lady, Monsieur had noticed her, perhaps ? She came at this time every year. Her husband had been killed climbing three years ago. It was very sad. They had been very devoted. She came here always before the season commenced—so as to be quiet. It was a sacred pilgrimage. The elderly gentleman was a famous doctor, Dr. Karl Lutz, from Vienna. He had come here, so he said, for quiet and repose.

"It is peaceful, yes," agreed Hercule Poirot. "And *ces Messieurs* there?" He indicated the three horsy men. "Do they also seek repose, do you think?"

The manager shrugged his shoulders. Again there appeared in his eyes that worried look. He said vaguely:

"Ah, the tourists, they wish always a new experience . . . The altitude—that alone is a new sensation."

It was not, Poirot thought, a very pleasant sensation. He was conscious of his own rapidly beating heart. The lines of a nursery rhyme ran idiotically through his mind. "*Up above the world so high, Like a tea tray in the sky.*"

Schwartz came into the lounge. His eyes brightened when he saw Poirot. He came over to him at once.

"I've been talking to that doctor. He speaks English after a fashion. He's a Jew—been turned out of Austria by the Nazis. Say, I guess those people are just crazy! This Doctor Lutz was quite a big man, I gather—nerve specialist—psycho-analysis—that kind of stuff."

His eyes went to where the tall woman was looking out of a window at remorseless mountains. He lowered his voice.

"I got her name from the waiter. She's a Madame Grandier. Her husband was killed climbing. That's why she comes here. I sort of feel, don't you, that we ought to do something about it—try to take her out of herself?"

Hercule Poirot said:

"If I were you I should not attempt it."

But the friendliness of Mr. Schwartz was indefatigable.

Poirot saw him make his overtures, saw the remorseless way in which they were rebuffed. The two stood together for a minute silhouetted against the light. The woman was taller than Schwartz. Her head was thrown back and her expression was cold and forbidding.

He did not hear what she said, but Schwartz came back looking crestfallen.

"Nothing doing," he said. He added wistfully: "Seems to me that as we're all human beings together there's no reason we shouldn't be friendly to one another. Don't you agree, Mr.—— You know, I don't know *your* name?"

"My name," said Poirot, "is Poirier." He added: "I am a silk merchant from Lyons."

" I'd like to give you my card, M. Poirier, and if ever you come to Fountain Springs you'll be sure of a welcome."

Poirot accepted the card, clapped his hand to his own pocket, murmured:

" Alas, I have not a card on me at the moment. . . ."

That night, when he went to bed, Poirot read through Lementeuil's letter carefully before replacing it, neatly folded, in his wallet. As he got into bed he said to himself:

" It is curious—I wonder if . . ."

## III

Gustave the waiter brought Hercule Poirot his breakfast of coffee and rolls. He was apologetic over the coffee.

" Monsieur comprehends, does he not, that at this altitude it is impossible to have the coffee really hot? Lamentably, it boils too soon."

Poirot murmured:

" One must accept these vagaries of Nature's with fortitude."

Gustave murmured:

" Monsieur is a philosopher."

He went to the door, but instead of leaving the room, he took one quick look outside, then shut the door again and returned to the bedside. He said:

" M. Hercule Poirot? I am Drouet, Inspector of Police."

" Ah," said Poirot, " I had already suspected as much."

Drouet lowered his voice.

" M. Poirot, something very grave has occurred  There has been an accident to the funicular ! "

" An accident ? " Poirot sat up. " What kind of an accident ? "

" Nobody has been injured. It happened in the night. It was occasioned, perhaps, by natural causes—a small avalanche that swept down boulders and rocks. But it is possible that there was human agency at work. One does not know. In any case the result is that it will take many days to repair and that in the meantime *we are cut off up here.* So early in the season, when the snow is still heavy, it is impossible to communicate with the valley below."

Hercule Poirot sat up in bed. He said softly :
" That is very interesting."

The Inspector nodded.

" Yes," he said. " It shows that our commissaire's information was correct. Marrascaud *has* a *rendezvous* here, and
he has made sure that that *rendezvous* shall not be interrupted."

Hercule Poirot cried impatiently :
" But it is fantastic ! "

" I agree." Inspector Drouet threw up his hands. " It does
not make the commonsense—*but there it is*. This Marrascaud,
you know, is a fantastic creature ! Myself," he nodded, " I
think he is *mad*."

Poirot said :
" A madman *and* a murderer ! "

Drouet said dryly :
" It is not amusing. I agree."

Poirot said slowly :
" But if he has a *rendezvous* here, on this ledge of snow
high above the world, then it also follows that *Marrascaud
himself is here already*, since communications are now cut."

Drouet said quietly :
" I know."

Both men were silent for a minute or two. Then Poirot
asked :
" Dr. Lutz ? Can he be Marrascaud ? "

Drouet shook his head.

" I do not think so. There is a real Dr. Lutz—I have seen
his pictures in the papers—a distinguished and well-known
man. This man resembles these photographs closely."

Poirot murmured :
" If Marrascaud is an artist in disguise, he might play the
part successfully."

" Yes, but is he ? I never heard of him as an expert in
disguise. He has not the guile and cunning of the serpent.
He is a wild boar, ferocious, terrible, who charges in blind
fury."

Poirot said :
" All the same. . . ."

Drouet agreed quickly.

" Ah yes, he is a fugitive from justice. Therefore he is forced to dissemble. So he may—in fact he must be—more or less disguised."

" You have his description ? "

The other shrugged his shoulders.

" Roughly only. The official Bertillon photograph and measurements were to have been sent up to me to-day. I know only that he is a man of thirty odd, of a little over medium height and of dark complexion. No distinguishing marks."

Poirot shrugged his shoulders.

" That could apply to anybody. What about the American, Schwartz ? "

" I was going to ask you that. You have spoken with him, and you have lived, I think, much with the English and the Americans. To a casual glance he appears to be the normal travelling American. His passport is in order. It is perhaps strange that he should elect to come here—but Americans when travelling are quite incalculable. What do you think yourself ? "

Hercule Poirot shook his head in perplexity.

He said :

" On the surface, at any rate, he appears to be a harmless slightly over-friendly, man. He might be a bore, but it seems difficult to regard him as a danger." He went on : " But there are three more visitors here."

The Inspector nodded, his face suddenly eager.

" Yes, and they *are* the type we are looking for. I'll take my oath, M. Poirot, that those three men are at any rate members of Marrascaud's gang. They're racecourse toughs if I ever saw them ! and one of the three may be Marrascaud himself."

Hercule Poirot reflected. He recalled the three faces.

One was a broad face with overhanging brows and a fat jowl—a hoggish, bestial face. One was lean and thin with a sharp narrow face and cold eyes. The third man was a pasty-faced fellow with a slight dandiacal air.

Yes, one of the three might well be Marrascaud, but if so, the question came insistently, *why* ? Why should Marrascaud, and two members of his gang journey together and ascend into a rat-trap on a mountain side? A meeting surely could be arranged in safer and less fantastic surroundings—in a café—in a railway station—in a crowded cinema—in a public park—somewhere where there were exits in plenty—not here far above the world in a wilderness of snow.

Something of this he tried to convey to Inspector Drouet and the latter agreed readily enough.

" But yes, it is fantastic, it does not make sense."

" If it is a *rendezvous*, why do they travel *together*? No, indeed, it does not make sense."

Drouet said, his face worried :

" In that case, we have to examine a second supposition. These three men are members of Marrascaud's gang and they have come here to meet Marrascaud himself. Who then *is* Marrascaud? "

Poirot asked :

" What about the staff of the hotel? "

Drouet shrugged his shoulders.

" There is no staff to speak of. There is an old woman who cooks, there is her old husband Jacques—they have been here for fifty years I should think. There is the waiter whose place I have taken, that is all."

Poirot said :

" The manager, he knows of course who you are? "

" Naturally. It needed his co-operation."

" Has it struck you," said Hercule Poirot, " that he looks worried? "

The remark seemed to strike Drouet. He said thoughtfully :

" Yes, that is true."

" It may be that it is merely the anxiety of being involved in police proceedings."

" But you think it may be more than that? You think that he may—know something? "

" It occurred to me, that is all."

Drouet said sombrely : " I wonder."

He paused and then went on :

" Could one get it out of him, do you think? "

Poirot shook his head doubtfully. He said :

" It would be better, I think, not to let him know of our suspicions. Keep your eye on him, that is all."

Drouet nodded. He turned towards the door.

" You've no suggestions, M. Poirot ? I—I know your reputation. We have heard of you in this country of ours."

Poirot said perplexedly :

" For the moment I can suggest nothing. It is the *reason*
which escapes me—the reason for a *rendezvous* in this place.
In fact, the reason for a *rendezvous* at all ? "

" Money," said Drouet succinctly.

" He was robbed, then, as well as murdered, this poor
fellow Salley ? "

" Yes, he had a very large sum of money on him which has
disappeared."

" And the *rendezvous* is for the purpose of sharing out, you
think ? "

" It is the most obvious idea."

Poirot shook his head in a dissatisfied manner.

" Yes, but why *here* ? " He went on slowly : " The worst
place possible for a *rendezvous* of criminals. But it is a place,
this, where one might come to meet a woman. . . ."

Drouet took a step forward eagerly.

He said excitedly :

" You think—— ? "

" I think," said Poirot, " that Madame Grandier is a very
beautiful woman. I think that anyone might well mount ten
thousand feet for her sake—that is, if she had suggested such
a thing."

" You know," said Drouet, " that's interesting. I never
thought of her in connection with the case. After all, she's
been to this place several years running."

Poirot said gently :

" Yes—*and therefore her presence would not cause comment.*
It would be a reason, would it not, why Rochers Neiges should
have been the spot selected ? "

Drouet said excitedly :

" You've had an idea, M. Poirot. I'll look into that angle."

## IV

The day passed without incident. Fortunately the hotel was well provisioned. The manager explained that there need be no anxiety. Supplies were assured.

Hercule Poirot endeavoured to get into conversation with Dr. Karl Lutz and was rebuffed. The doctor intimated plainly that psychology was his professional preoccupation and that he was not going to discuss it with amateurs. He sat in a corner reading a large German tome on the subconscious and making copious notes and annotations.

Hercule Poirot went outside and wandered aimlessly round to the kitchen premises. There he entered into conversation with the old man Jacques, who was surly and suspicious. His wife, the cook, was more forthcoming. Fortunately, she explained to Poirot, there was a large reserve of tinned food— but she herself thought little of food in tins. It was wickedly expensive and what nourishment could there be in it ? The good God had never intended people to live out of tins.

The conversation came round to the subject of the hotel staff. Early in July the chambermaids and the extra waiters arrived. But for the next three weeks, there would be nobody or next to nobody. Mostly people who came up and had lunch and then went back again. She and Jacques and one waiter could manage that easily.

Poirot asked :

" There was already a waiter here before Gustave came, was there not ? "

" But yes, indeed, a poor kind of a waiter. No skill, no experience. No class at all."

" How long was he here before Gustave replaced him ? "

" A few days only—the inside of a week. Naturally he was dismissed. We were not surprised. It was bound to come."

Poirot murmured :

" He did not complain unduly ? "

" Ah no, he went quietly enough. After all, what could he expect ? This is a hotel of good class. One must have proper service here."

Poirot nodded. He asked :

" Where did he go ? "

" That Robert, you mean ? " She shrugged her shoulders.
" Doubtless back to the obscure café he came from."

" He went down in the funicular ? "

She looked at him curiously.

" Naturally, Monsieur. What other way is there to go ? "

Poirot asked :

" Did anyone *see* him go ? "

They both stared at him.

" Ah ! do you think it likely that one goes to see off an
animal like that—that one gives him the grand farewell ?
One has one's own affairs to occupy one."

" Precisely," said Hercule Poirot.

He walked slowly away, staring up as he did so at the
building above him. A large hotel—with only one wing open
at present. In the other wings were many rooms, closed and
shuttered where no one was likely to enter. . . .

He came round the corner of the hotel and nearly ran into
one of the three card-playing men. It was the one with the
pasty face and pale eyes. The eyes looked at Poirot without
expression. Only the lips curled back a little showing the
teeth like a vicious horse.

Poirot passed him and went on. There was a figure ahead
of him—the tall graceful figure of Madame Grandier.

He hastened his pace a little and caught her up. He said :

" This accident to the funicular, it is distressing. I hope,
Madame, that it has not inconvenienced you ? "

She said :

" It is a matter of indifference to me."

Her voice was very deep—a full contralto. She did not
look at Poirot. She swerved aside and went into the hotel
by a small side door.

v

Hercule Poirot went to bed early. He was awakened some
time after midnight.

Someone was fumbling with the lock of the door.

He sat up, putting on the light. At the same moment the

lock yielded to manipulation and the door swung open. Three men stood there, the three card-playing men. They were, Poirot thought, slightly drunk. Their faces were foolish and yet malevolent. He saw the gleam of a razor blade.

The big thickset man advanced. He spoke in a growling voice.

" Sacred pig of a detective ! Bah ! "

He burst into a torrent of profanity. The three of them advanced purposefully on the defenceless man in the bed.

" We'll carve him up, boys. Eh, little horses ? We'll slash Monsieur Detective's face open for him. He won't be the first one to-night."

They came on, steady, purposeful—the razor blades flashed. . . .

And then, startling in its crisp transatlantic tones, a voice said :

" Stick 'em up."

They swerved round. Schwartz, dressed in a peculiarly vivid set of striped pyjamas stood in the doorway. In his hand he held an automatic.

" Stick 'em up, guys. I'm pretty good at shooting."

He pressed the trigger—and a bullet sang past the big man's ear and buried itself in the woodwork of the window.

Three pairs of hands were raised rapidly.

Schwartz said : " Can I trouble you, M. Poirier ? "

Hercule Poirot was out of bed in a flash. He collected the gleaming weapons and passed his hands over the three men's bodies to make sure that they were not armed.

Schwartz said :

" Now then, march ! There's a big cupboard just along the corridor. No window in it. Just the thing."

He marched them into it and turned the key on them. He swung round to Poirot, his voice breaking with pleasurable emotion.

" If that doesn't just show ? Do you know, M. Poirier, there were folks in Fountain Springs who laughed at me because I said I was going to take a gun abroad with me. ' Where do you think you're going ? ' they asked. ' Into the jungle ? ' Well, sir, I'd say the laugh is with me. Did you ever see such an ugly bunch of toughs ? "

Poirot said :

" My dear Mr. Schwartz, you appeared in the nick of time. It might have been a drama on the stage ! I am very much in your debt."

" That's nothing. Where do we go from here ? We ought to turn these boys over to the police and that's just what we can't do ! It's a knotty problem. Maybe we'd better consult the manager."

Hercule Poirot said :

" Ah, the manager. I think first we will consult the waiter—Gustave—alias Inspector Drouet. But yes—the waiter Gustave is really a detective."

Schwartz stared at him.

" So that's why they did it ! "

" That is why who did what ? "

" This bunch of crooks got to you second on the list. They'd already carved up Gustave."

" *What ?* "

" Come with me. The doc's busy on him now."

Drouet's room was a small one on the top floor. Dr. Lutz, in a dressing-gown, was busy bandaging the injured man's face.

He turned his head as they entered.

" Ah ! It is you, Mr. Schwartz ? A nasty business, this. What butchers ! What inhuman monsters ! "

Drouet lay still, moaning faintly.

Schwartz asked :  " Is he in danger ? "

" He will not die if that is what you mean. But he must not speak—there must be no excitement. I have dressed the wounds—there will be no risk of septicæmia."

The three men left the room together. Schwartz said to Poirot :

" Did you say Gustave was a police officer ? "

Hercule Poirot nodded.

" But what was he doing up at Rochers Neiges ? "

" He was engaged in tracking down a very dangerous criminal."

In a few words Poirot explained the situation.

Dr. Lutz said :

" Marrascaud ? I read about the case in the paper. I

should much like to meet that man. There is some deep abnormality there! I should like to know the particulars of his childhood."

" For myself," said Hercule Poirot, " I should like to know exactly where he is at this minute."

Schwartz said :

" Isn't he one of the three we locked in the cupboard ? "

Poirot said in a dissatisfied voice :

" It is possible—yes, but me, I am not sure. . . . I have an idea—"

He broke off, staring down at the carpet. It was of a light buff colour and there were marks on it of a deep rusty brown.

Hercule Poirot said :

" Footsteps—footsteps that have trodden, I think, in blood and they lead from the unused wing of the hotel. Come— we must be quick ! "

They followed him, through a swing door and along a dim, dusty corridor. They turned the corner of it, still following the marks on the carpet until the tracks led them to a half-open doorway.

Poirot pushed the door open and entered.

He uttered a sharp, horrified exclamation.

The room was a bedroom. The bed had been slept in and there was a tray of food on the table.

In the middle of the floor lay the body of a man. He was of just over middle height and he had been attacked with savage and unbelievable ferocity. There were a dozen wounds on his arms and chest and his head and face had been battered almost to a pulp.

Schwartz gave a half-stifled exclamation and turned away looking as though he might be sick.

Dr. Lutz uttered a horrified exclamation in German.

Schwartz said faintly :

" Who is this guy ? Does anyone know ? "

" I fancy," said Poirot, " that he was known here as Robert, a rather unskilful waiter. . . ."

Lutz had gone nearer, bending over the body. He pointed with a finger.

There was a paper pinned to the dead man's breast. It had some words scrawled on it in ink.

*Marrascaud will kill no more—nor will he rob his friends !*
Schwartz ejaculated :

" *Marrascaud ?* So this is *Marrascaud !* But what brought
him up here to this out of the way spot ? And why do you say
his name is Robert ? "

Poirot said :

" He was here masquerading as a waiter—and by all accounts
he was a very bad waiter. So bad that no one was surprised
when he was given the sack. He left—presumably to return
to Andermatt. *But nobody saw him go.*"

Lutz said in his slow rumbling voice :

" So—and what do you think happened ? "

Poirot replied :

" I think we have here the explanation of a certain worried
expression on the hotel manager's face. Marrascaud must
have offered him a big bribe to allow him to remain hidden in
the unused part of the hotel . . ."

He added thoughtfully : " But the manager was not happy
about it. Oh no, he was not happy at all."

" And Marrascaud continued to live in this unused wing
with no one but the manager knowing about it ? "

" So it seems. It would be quite possible, you know."

Dr. Lutz said :

" And why was he killed ? And who killed him ? "

Schwartz cried :

" That's easy. He was to share out the money with his
gang. He didn't. He double-crossed them. He came here,
to this out of the way place, to lie low for a while. He thought
it was the last place in the world they'd ever think of. He was
wrong. Somehow or other they got wise to it and followed
him." He touched the dead body with the tip of his shoe.
" And they settled his account—like this."

Hercule Poirot murmured :

" Yes, it was not quite the kind of *rendezvous* we thought."

Dr. Lutz said irritably :

" These hows and whys may be very interesting, but I am
concerned with our present position. Here we have a dead
man. I have a sick man on my hands and a limited amount of
medical supplies. And we are cut off from the world ! For
how long ? "

Schwartz added:

"*And* we've got three murderers locked in a cupboard! It's what I'd call kind of an interesting situation."

Dr. Lutz said:

"What do we do?"

Poirot said:

"First, we get hold of the manager. He is not a criminal, that one, only a man who was greedy for money. He is a coward, too. He will do everything we tell him. My good friend Jacques, or his wife, will perhaps provide some cord. Our three miscreants must be placed where we can guard them in safety until the day when help comes. I think that Mr. Schwartz's automatic will be effective in carrying out any plans we may make."

Dr. Lutz said:

"And I? What do I do?"

"You, doctor," said Poirot gravely, "will do all you can for your patient. The rest of us will employ ceaseless vigilance—and wait. There is nothing else we can do."


## VI


It was three days later that a little party of men appeared in front of the hotel in the early hours of the morning.

It was Hercule Poirot who opened the front door to them with a flourish.

"Welcome, *mon vieux*."

Monsieur Lementeuil, Commissaire of Police, seized Poirot by both hands.

"Ah, my friend, with what emotion I greet you! What stupendous events—what emotions you have passed through! And we below, our anxiety, our fears—knowing nothing—fearing everything. No wireless—no means of communication. To heliograph, that was indeed a stroke of genius on your part."

"No, no," Poirot endeavoured to look modest. "After all, when the inventions of man fail, one falls back upon nature. There is always the sun in the sky."

The little party filed into the hotel. Lementeuil said:

"We are not expected?" His smile was somewhat grim.

Poirot smiled also. He said :

" But no ! It is believed that the funicular is not nearly repaired yet."

Lementeuil said with emotion :

" Ah, this is a great day. There is no doubt, you think ? It is really Marrascaud ? "

" It is Marrascaud all right. Come with me."

They went up the stairs. A door opened and Schwartz came out in his dressing-gown. He stared when he saw the men.

" I heard voices," he explained. " Why, what's this ? "

Hercule Poirot said grandiloquently :

" Help has come ! Accompany us, monsieur. This is a great moment."

He started up the next flight of stairs.

Schwartz said :

" Are you going up to Drouet ? How is he, by the way ? "

" Dr. Lutz reported him going on well last night."

They came to the door of Drouet's room. Poirot flung it open. He announced :

" *Here is your wild boar, gentlemen.* Take him alive and see to it that he does not cheat the guillotine."

The man in the bed, his face still bandaged, started up. But the police officers had him by the arms before he could move.

Schwartz cried bewildered :

" But that's Gustave the waiter—that's Inspector Drouet."

" It is Gustave, yes—*but it is not Drouet.* Drouet was the *first* waiter, the waiter Robert who was imprisoned in the unused part of the hotel and whom Marrascaud killed the same night as the attack was made on me."

## VII

Over breakfast, Poirot explained gently to the bewildered American.

" You comprehend, there are certain things one *knows*—knows quite certainly in the course of one's profession. One knows, for instance, the difference between a detective and a murderer ! Gustave was no waiter—that I suspected at once—

but equally *he was not a policeman*. I have dealt with policemen all my life and I *know*. He could pass as a detective to an outsider—but not to a man who was *a policeman himself*.

"And so, at once, I was suspicious. That evening, I did not drink my coffee. I poured it away. And I was wise. Late that evening a man came into my room, came in with the easy confidence of one who knows that the man whose room he is searching is drugged. He looked through my affairs and he found the letter in my wallet—where I had left it for him to find! The next morning Gustave comes into my room with my coffee. He greets me by name and acts his part with complete assurance. But he is anxious—horribly anxious—for somehow or other the police have got on his track! They have learnt where he is and that is for him a terrible disaster. It upsets all his plans. He is caught up here like a rat in a trap."

Schwartz said :

"The damn fool thing was ever to come here! Why did he?"

Poirot said gravely :

"It is not so foolish as you think. He had need, urgent need, of a retired spot, away from the world, where he could meet a certain person, and where a certain happening could take place."

"What person?"

"Dr. Lutz."

"Dr. Lutz? Is he a crook too?"

"Dr. Lutz is really Dr. Lutz—but he is not a nerve specialist —not a psycho-analyst. He is a surgeon, my friend, *a surgeon who specialises in facial surgery*. That is why he was to meet Marrascaud here. He is poor now, turned out of his country. He was offered a huge fee to meet a man here and change that man's appearance by means of his surgical skill. He may have guessed that that man was a criminal, but if so, he shut his eyes to the fact. Realise this, they dared not risk a nursing home in some foreign country. No, up here, where no one ever comes so early in the season except for an odd visit, where the manager is a man in need of money who can be bribed, was an ideal spot.

"But, as I say, matters went wrong. Marrascaud was betrayed. The three men, his bodyguard, who were to meet him here and look after him had not yet arrived, but Marrascaud acts at once. The police officer who is pretending to be a waiter is kidnapped and Marrascaud *takes his place*. The gang arrange for the funicular to be wrecked. It is a matter of *time*. The following evening Drouet is killed and a paper is pinned on the dead body. It is hoped that by the time that communications are established with the world Drouet's body may have been buried as that of Marrascaud. Dr. Lutz performs his operation without delay. But one man must be silenced— Hercule Poirot. So the gang are sent to attack me. Thanks to you, my friend——"

Hercule Poirot bowed gracefully to Schwartz who said: " So you're really Hercule Poirot ? "

" Precisely."

" And you were never fooled by that body for a minute ? You knew all along that it *wasn't* Marrascaud ? "

" Certainly."

" Why didn't you say so ? "

Hercule Poirot's face was suddenly stern.

" Because I wanted to be quite sure of handing the real Marrascaud over to the police."

He murmured below his breath :

" *To capture alive the wild boar of Erymanthea. . . .*"

# V

## THE AUGEAN STABLES

### I

"The situation is an extremely delicate one, M. Poirot."

A faint smile flitted across Hercule Poirot's lips. He almost replied :

"It always is ! "

Instead, he composed his face and put on what might be described as a bedside manner of extreme discretion.

Sir George Conway proceeded weightily. Phrases fell easily from his lips—the extreme delicacy of the Government's position—the interests of the public—the solidarity of the Party—the necessity of presenting a united front—the power of the Press—the welfare of the Country. . . .

It all sounded well—and meant nothing. Hercule Poirot felt that familiar aching of the jaw when one longs to yawn and politeness forbids. He had felt the same sometimes when reading the parliamentary debates. But on those occasions there had been no need to restrain his yawns.

He steeled himself to endure patiently. He felt, at the same time, a sympathy for Sir George Conway. The man obviously wanted to tell him something—and as obviously had lost the art of simple narration. Words had become to him a means of obscuring facts—not of revealing them. He was an adept in the art of the useful phrase—that is to say the phrase that falls soothingly on the ear and is quite empty of meaning.

The words rolled on—poor Sir George became quite red in the face. He shot a desperate glance at the other man sitting at the head of the table, and that other man responded.

Edward Ferrier said :

"All right, George. I'll tell him."

Hercule Poirot shifted his gaze from the Home Secretary to the Prime Minister. He felt a keen interest in Edward Ferrier—an interest aroused by a chance phrase from an old

man of eighty-two. Professor Fergus MacLeod, after disposing
of a chemical difficulty in the conviction of a murderer, had
touched for a moment on politics. On the retirement of the
famous and beloved John Hammett (now Lord Cornworthy)
his son-in-law, Edward Ferrier, had been asked to form a
Cabinet. As politicians go he was a young man—under fifty.
Professor MacLeod had said : " Ferrier was once one of my
students. He's a sound man."

That was all, but to Hercule Poirot it represented a good
deal. If MacLeod called a man sound it was a testimonial to
character compared with which no popular or press enthusiasm
counted at all.

It coincided, it was true, with the popular estimate. Edward
Ferrier was considered sound—just that—not brilliant, not
great, not a particularly eloquent orator, not a man of deep
learning. He was a sound man—a man bred in the tradition—
a man who had married John Hammett's daughter—who had
been John Hammett's right hand man and who could be
trusted to carry on the government of the country in the John
Hammett tradition.

For John Hammett was particularly dear to the people and
Press of England. He represented every quality which was
dear to Englishmen. People said of him : " One does feel
that Hammett's honest." Anecdotes were told of his simple
home life, of his fondness for gardening. Corresponding to
Baldwin's pipe and Chamberlain's umbrella, there was John
Hammett's raincoat. He always carried it—a weather-worn
garment. It stood as a symbol—of the English climate, of the
prudent forethought of the English race, of their attachment
to old possessions. Moreover, in his bluff British way, John
Hammett was an orator. His speeches, quietly and earnestly
delivered, contained those simple sentimental clichés which
are so deeply rooted in the English heart. Foreigners sometimes criticise them as being both hypocritical and unbearably
noble. John Hammett did not in the least mind being noble—
in a sporting, public school, deprecating fashion.

Moreover, he was a man of fine presence, tall, upstanding,
with fair colouring and very bright blue eyes. His mother had
been a Dane and he himself had been for many years First
Lord of the Admiralty, which gave rise to his nickname of

'the Viking'. When at last ill-health forced him to give up the reins of office, deep uneasiness was felt. Who would succeed him? The brilliant Lord Charles Delafield? (Too brilliant—England didn't need brilliance.) Evan Whittler? (Clever—but perhaps a little unscrupulous.) John Potter? (The sort of man who might fancy himself as Dictator—and we didn't want any dictators in *this* country, thank you very much.) So a sigh of relief went up when the quiet Edward Ferrier assumed office. Ferrier was all right. He had been trained by the Old Man, he had married the Old Man's daughter. In the classic British phrase, Ferrier would "carry on."

Hercule Poirot studied the quiet dark-faced man with the low pleasant voice. Lean and dark and tired-looking.

Edward Ferrier was saying:

"Perhaps, M. Poirot, you are acquainted with a weekly periodical called the *X-ray News*?"

"I have glanced at it," admitted Poirot, blushing slightly.

The Prime Minister said:

"Then you know more or less of what it consists. Semi-libellous matter. Snappy paragraphs hinting at sensational secret history. Some of them true, some of them harmless—but all served up in a spicy manner. Occasionally—"

He paused and then said, his voice altering a little:

"Occasionally something more."

Hercule Poirot did not speak. Ferrier went on:

"For two weeks now there have been hints of impending disclosures of a first-class scandal in 'the highest political circles'. 'Astonishing revelations of corruption and jobbery.'"

Hercule Poirot said, shrugging his shoulders:

"A common trick. When the actual revelations come they usually disappoint the cravers after sensation badly."

Ferrier said dryly: "These will not disappoint them."

Hercule Poirot asked:

"You know then, what these revelations are going to be?"

"With a fair amount of accuracy."

Edward Ferrier paused a minute, then he began speaking. Carefully, methodically, he outlined the story.

It was not an edifying story. Accusations of shameless chicanery, of share juggling, of a gross misuse of Party Funds.

The charges were levelled against the late Prime Minister, John Hammett. They showed him to be a dishonest rascal, a gigantic confidence trickster, who had used his position to amass for himself a vast private fortune.

The Prime Minister's quiet voice stopped at last. The Home Secretary groaned. He spluttered out :

" It's monstrous—*monstrous !* This fellow, Perry, who edits the rag, ought to be shot ! "

Hercule Poirot said :

" These so-called revelations are to appear in the *X-ray News* ? "

" Yes."

" What steps do you propose to take about them ? "

Ferrier said slowly :

" They constitute a private attack on John Hammett. It is open to him to sue the paper for libel."

" Will he do that ? "

" No."

" Why not ? "

Ferrier said :

" It is probable that there is nothing the *X-ray News* would like better. The publicity given them would be enormous. Their defence would be fair comment and that the statements complained of were true. The whole business would be exhaustively held up to view in a blaze of limelight."

" Still, if the case went against them, the damages would be extremely heavy ."

Ferrier said slowly :  " It might not go against them."

" Why ? "

Sir George said primly, " I really think that——"

But Edward Ferrier was already speaking.

" Because what they intend to print is—the truth."

A groan burst from Sir George Conway, outraged at such un-Parliamentary frankness. He cried out :

" Edward, my dear fellow. We don't admit, surely——"

The ghost of a smile passed over Edward Ferrier's tired face. He said :

" Unfortunately, George, there are times when the stark truth has got to be told. This is one of them."

Sir George exclaimed :

" You understand, M.Poirot, all this is strictly in confidence. Not one word——"

Ferrier interrupted him. He said :

" M. Poirot understands that." He went on slowly, " What he may not understand is this : the whole future of the People's Party is at stake. John Hammett, M. Poirot, *was* the People's Party. He stood for what it represents to the people of England—he stood for Decency and Honesty. No one has ever thought us brilliant. We have muddled and blundered. But we *have* stood for the tradition of doing one's best—and we have stood, too, for fundamental honesty. Our disaster is this—that the man who was our figurehead, the Honest Man of the People, *par excellence*—turns out to have been one of the worst crooks of this generation."

Another groan burst from Sir George.

Poirot asked :

" *You* knew nothing of all this ? "

Again the smile flashed across the weary face. Ferrier said :

" You may not believe me, M. Poirot, but like everyone else, I was completely deceived. I never understood my wife's curious attitude of reserve towards her father. I understand it now. She knew his essential character."

He paused and then said :

" When the truth began to leak out, I was horrified, incredulous. We insisted on my father-in-law's resignation on the grounds of ill-health and we set to work to—to clean up the mess, shall I say ? "

Sir George groaned.

" The Augean Stables ! "

Poirot started.

Ferrier said :

" It will prove, I fear, too Herculean a task for us. Once the facts become public, there will be a wave of reaction all over the country. The Government will fall. There will be a General Election and in all probability Everhard and his party will be returned to power. You know Everhard's policy."

Sir George spluttered.

" A firebrand—a complete firebrand."

Ferrier said gravely :

" Everhard has ability—but he is reckless, belligerent and utterly tactless. His supporters are inept and vacillating— it would be practically a Dictatorship."

Hercule Poirot nodded.

Sir George bleated out :

" If only the whole thing can be hushed up. . . ."

Slowly, the Premier shook his head. It was a movement of defeat.

Poirot said :

" You do not believe that it can be hushed up ? "

Ferrier said :

" I sent for you, M. Poirot, as a last hope. In my opinion this business is too big, too many people know about it, for it to be successfully concealed. The only two methods open to us which are, to put it bluntly, the use of force, or the adoption of bribery—cannot really hope to succeed. The Home Secretary compared our troubles with the cleansing of the Augean Stables. It needs, M. Poirot, the violence of a river in spate, the disruption of the great natural forces of Nature—nothing less, in fact, than a miracle."

" It needs, in fact, a Hercules," said Poirot, nodding his head with a pleased expression.

He added : " My name, remember, is Hercule. . . ."

Edward Ferrier said :

" Can you perform miracles, M. Poirot ? "

" It is why you sent for me, is it not ? Because you thought that I might ? "

" That is true. . . . I realised that if salvation was to be achieved, it could only come through some fantastic and completely unorthodox suggestion."

He paused a minute, then he said :

" But perhaps, M. Poirot, you take an ethical view of the situation ? John Hammett was a crook, the legend of John Hammett must be exploded. Can one build an honest house on dishonest foundations ? I do not know. But I do know that I want to try." He smiled with a sudden sharp bitterness. " The politician wants to remain in office—as usual from the highest motives."

Hercule Poirot rose. He said :

" Monsieur, my experience in the police force has not,

perhaps, allowed me to think very highly of politicians. If
John Hammett were in office—I would not lift a finger—no,
not a little finger. But I know something about you. I have
been told, by a man who is really great, one of the greatest
scientists and brains of the day, that you are—*a sound man.*
I will do what I can."

He bowed and left the room.

Sir George burst out :

" Well, of all the damned cheek——"

But Edward Ferrier still smiling said :

" It was a compliment."


## II


On his way downstairs, Hercule Poirot was intercepted by
a tall, fair-haired woman. She said :

" Please come into my sitting-room, M. Poirot."

He bowed and followed her.

She shut the door, motioned him to a chair, and offered him
a cigarette. She sat down opposite him. She said quietly :

" You have just seen my husband—and he has told you—
about my father."

Poirot looked at her with attention. He saw a tall woman,
still handsome, with character and intelligence in her face.
Mrs. Ferrier was a popular figure. As the wife of the Prime
Minister she naturally came in for a good share of the limelight. As the daughter of her father, her popularity was even
greater. Dagmar Ferrier represented the popular ideal of
English womanhood.

She was a devoted wife, a fond mother, she shared her
husband's love of country life. She interested herself in just
those aspects of public life which were generally felt to be
proper spheres of womanly activity. She dressed well, but
never in an ostentatiously fashionable manner. She devoted
much of her time and activity to large scale charities, she had
inaugurated special schemes for the relief of the wives of
unemployed men. She was looked up to by the whole nation
and was a most valuable asset to the Party.

Hercule Poirot said :

" You must be terribly worried, Madame."

" Oh I am—you don't know how much. For years I have been dreading—something."

Poirot said :

" You had no idea of what was going on actually ? "

She shook her head.

" No—not in the least. I only knew that my father was not —was not what everyone thought him. I realised, from the time that I was a child, that he was a—a humbug."

Her voice was deep and bitter. She said :

" It is through marrying me that Edward—that Edward will lose everything."

Poirot said in a quiet voice :

" Have you any enemies, Madame ? "

She looked up at him, surprised.

" Enemies ? I don't think so."

Poirot said thoughtfully :

" I think you have. . . ."

He went on :

" Have you courage, Madame ? There is a great campaign afoot—against your husband—and against yourself. You must prepare to defend yourself."

She cried :

" But it doesn't matter about *me*. Only about Edward ! "

Poirot said : " The one includes the other. Remember, Madame, you are Cæsar's wife."

He saw her colour ebb. She leaned forward. She said :

" What is it you are trying to tell me ? "


III


Percy Perry, editor of the *X-ray News*, sat behind his desk smoking.

He was a small man with a face like a weasel.

He was saying in a soft, oily voice :

" We'll give 'em the dirt, all right. Lovely—lovely ! Oh boy ! "

His second-in-command, a thin, spectacled youth, said un-easily :

" You're not nervous ? "

" Expecting strong arm stuff ? Not them. Haven't got the nerve. Wouldn't do them any good, either. Not the way we've got it farmed out—in this country and on the Continent and America."

The other said :

" They must be in a pretty good stew. Won't they do anything ? "

" They'll send someone to talk pretty——"

A buzzer sounded. Percy Perry picked up a receiver. He said : " Who do you say ? Right, send him up."

He put the receiver down—grinned.

" They've got that high-toned Belgian dick on to it. He's coming up now to do his stuff. Wants to know if we'll play ball."

Hercule Poirot came in. He was immaculately dressed—a white camelia in his buttonhole.

Percy Perry said :

" Pleased to meet you, M. Poirot. On your way to the Royal Enclosure at Ascot ? No ? My mistake."

Hercule Poirot said :

" I am flattered. One hopes to present a good appearance. It is even more important," his eyes roamed innocently over the editor's face and somewhat slovenly attire, " when one has few natural advantages."

Perry said shortly :

" What do you want to see me about ? "

Poirot leaned forward, tapped him on the knee, and said with a beaming smile :

" Blackmail."

" What the devil do you mean, blackmail ? "

" I have heard—the little bird has told me—that on occasions you have been on the point of publishing certain very damaging statements in your so *spirituel* paper—then, there has been a pleasant little increase in your bank balance—and after all, those statements have not been published."

Poirot leaned back and nodded his head in a satisfied sort of way.

" Do you realise that what you're suggesting amounts to slander ? "

Poirot smiled confidently.

" I am sure you will not take offence."

" I do take offence ! As to blackmail there is no evidence of my ever having blackmailed anybody."

" No, no, I am quite sure of that. You misunderstand me. I was not threatening you. I was leading up to a simple question. *How much ?* "

" I don't know what you're talking about," said Percy Perry.

" A matter of National importance, M. Perry."

They exchanged a significant glance.

Percy Perry said :

" I'm a reformer, M. Poirot. I want to see politics cleaned up. I'm opposed to corruption. Do you know what the state of politics is in this country ? The Augean Stables, no more, no less."

" *Tiens !* " said Hercule Poirot. " You, too, use that phrase."

" And what is needed," went on the editor, " to cleanse those stables is the great purifying flood of Public Opinion."

Hercule Poirot got up. He said :

" I applaud your sentiments."

He added :

" It is a pity that you do not feel in need of money."

Percy Perry said hurriedly :

" Here, wait a sec—I didn't say that exactly. . . ."

But Hercule Poirot had gone through the door.

His excuse for later events is that he does not like blackmailers.

IV

Everitt Dashwood, the cheery young man on the staff of *The Branch*, clapped Hercule Poirot affectionately on the back.

He said : " There's dirt and dirt, my boy. *My* dirt's clean dirt—that's all."

" I was not suggesting that you were on a par with Percy Perry."

" Damned little bloodsucker. He's a blot on our profession. We'd all down him if we could."

" It happens," said Hercule Poirot, " that I am engaged at the moment on a little matter of clearing up a political scandal."

" Cleaning out the Augean Stables, eh ? " said Dashwood. " Too much for you, my boy. Only hope is to divert the Thames and wash away the Houses of Parliament."

" You are cynical," said Hercule Poirot, shaking his head.

" I know the world, that's all."

Poirot said : " You, I think, are just the man I seek. You have a reckless disposition, you are the good sport, you like something that is out of the usual."

" And granting all that ? "

" I have a little scheme to put into action. If my ideas are right, there is a sensational plot to unmask. That, my friend, shall be a scoop for your paper."

" Can do," said Dashwood cheerfully.

" It will concern a scurrilous plot against a woman."

" Better and better. Sex stuff always goes."

" Then sit down and listen."

v

People were talking.

In the Goose and Feathers at Little Wimplington.

" Well, I don't believe it. John Hammett, he was always an honest man, he was. Not like some of these political folk."

" That's what they say about all swindlers before they're found out."

" Thousands, they say he made, out of that Palestine Oil business. Just a crook deal, it was."

" Whole lot of 'em tarred with the same brush. Dirty crooks, every one of 'em."

" You wouldn't find Everhard doing that. He's one of the old school."

" Eh, but I can't believe as John Hammett was a wrong 'un. You can't believe all these papers say."

"Ferrier's wife was 'is daughter. Have you seen what it says about *her* ? "

They poured over a much thumbed copy of the *X-ray News* :

*Cæsar's wife ? We hear that a certain highly placed political lady was seen in very strange surroundings the other day. Complete with her gigolo. Oh Dagmar, Dagmar, how could you be so naughty ?*

A rustic voice said slowly :

" Mrs. Ferrier's not that kind. Gigolo ? That's one of these dago skunks."

Another voice said :

" You never can tell with women. The whole bunch of 'em wrong 'uns if you ask me."


## VI

People were talking.

" But, darling, I believe it's absolutely *true*. Naomi had it from Paul and he had it from Andy. She's absolutely *depraved*."

" But she was always so terribly dowdy and proper and opening Bazaars."

" Just camouflage, darling. They say she's a nympho-maniac. Well, I *mean !* It's all in the *X-ray News*. Oh, not right out, but you can read between the lines. I don't know how they get hold of these things."

" What do you think of all this political scandal touch ? They say her father embezzled the Party funds."


## VII

People were talking.

" I don't like to think of it, and that's a fact, Mrs. Rogers. I mean, I always thought Mrs. Ferrier was a really *nice* woman."

" Do you think all these awful things are true ? "

" As I say, I don't like to think it of her. Why, she opened a Bazaar in Pelchester only last June. I was as near to her as I am to that sofa. And she had such a pleasant smile."

"Yes, but what I say is there's no smoke without fire."

"Well, of course *that's* true. Oh dear, it seems as though you can't believe in *any one!*"


## VIII

Edward Ferrier, his face white and strained, said to Poirot :

"These attacks on my wife! They're scurrilous—absolutely scurrilous! I'm bringing an action against that vile rag."

Hercule Poirot said : "I do not advise you to do so."

"But these damned lies have got to be stopped."

"Are you sure they *are* lies ?"

"God damn you, *yes!*"

Poirot said, his head held a little on one side:

"What does your wife say ?"

For a moment Ferrier looked taken aback.

"She says it is best to take no notice. . . . But I can't do that—everybody is talking."

Hercule Poirot said : "Yes, everybody is talking."


## IX

And then came the small bald announcement in all the papers.

*Mrs. Ferrier has had a slight nervous breakdown. She has gone to Scotland to recuperate.*

Conjectures, rumours—positive information that Mrs. Ferrier was *not* in Scotland, had never been to Scotland.

Stories, scandalous stories, of where Mrs. Ferrier *really* was. . . .

And again, people talking.

"I tell you Andy *saw* her. At that frightful place! She was drunk or doped and with an awful Argentine gigolo—Ramon. *You* know!"

More talking.

Mrs. Ferrier had gone off with an Argentine dancer. She had been seen in Paris, doped. She had been taking drugs for years. She drank like a fish.

Slowly the righteous mind of England, at first unbelieving, had hardened against Mrs. Ferrier. Seemed as though there must be something in it! *That* wasn't the sort of woman to be the Prime Minister's wife. "A Jezebel, that's what she is, nothing better than a Jezebel!"

And then came the camera records.

Mrs. Ferrier, photographed in Paris—lying back in a Night Club, her arm twined familiarly over the shoulder of a dark, olive-skinned vicious-looking young man.

Other snapshots—half-naked on a beach—her head on the lounge lizard's shoulder.

And underneath:

" *Mrs. Ferrier has a good time.* . . . "

Two days later an action for libel was brought against the *X-ray News*.

## x

The case for the prosecution was opened by Sir Mortimer Inglewood, K.C. He was dignified and full of righteous indignation. Mrs. Ferrier was the victim of an infamous plot—a plot only to be equalled by the famous case of the Queen's Necklace familiar to readers of Alexandre Dumas. That plot had been engineered to lower Queen Marie Antoinette in the eyes of the populace. This plot, also, had been engineered to discredit a noble and virtuous lady who was in this country in the position of Cæsar's wife. Sir Mortimer spoke with bitter disparagement of Fascists and Communists both of whom sought to undermine Democracy by every unfair machination known. He then proceeded to call witnesses.

The first was the Bishop of Northumbria.

Dr. Henderson, the Bishop of Northumbria was one of the best-known figures in the English church, a man of great saintliness and integrity of character. He was broadminded, tolerant, and a fine preacher. He was loved and revered by all who knew him.

He went into the box and swore that between the dates mentioned Mrs. Edward Ferrier had been staying in the Palace with himself and his wife. Worn out by her activities in good works, she had been recommended a thorough rest. Her visit had been kept a secret so as to obviate any worry from the Press.

An eminent doctor followed the Bishop and deposed to having ordered Mrs. Ferrier rest and complete absence from worry.

A local general practitioner gave evidence to the effect that he had attended Mrs. Ferrier at the Palace.

The next witness called was Thelma Andersen.

A thrill went round the Court when she entered the witness-box. Everyone realised at once what a strong resemblance the woman bore to Mrs. Edward Ferrier.

" Your name is Thelma Andersen ? "

" Yes."

" You are a Danish subject ? "

" Yes. Copenhagen is my home."

" And you formerly worked at a café there ? "

" Yes, sir."

" Please tell us in your own words what happened on the 18th March last."

" There is a gentleman who comes to my table there—an English gentleman. He tells me he works for an English paper—the *X-ray News.*"

" You are sure he mentioned that name—*X-ray News* ? "

" Yes, I am sure—because, you see, I think at first it must be a medical paper. But no, it seems not so. Then he tells me there is an English film actress who wants to find a ' stand-in ', and that I am just the type. I do not go to the pictures much, and I do not recognise the name he says, but he tells me, yes, she is very famous, and that she has not been well and so she wants someone to appear as her in public places, and for that she will pay very much money."

" How much money did this gentleman offer you ? "

" Five hundred pounds in English money. I do not at first believe—I think it is some trick, but he pays me at once half the money. So then, I give in my notice where I work."

The tale went on. She had been taken to Paris, supplied

with smart clothes, and had been provided with an " escort ".
" A very nice Argentinian gentleman—very respectful, very
polite."

It was clear that the woman had thoroughly enjoyed herself.
She had flown over to London and been taken there to certain
" Night Clubs " by her olive-skinned cavalier. She had been
photographed in Paris with him. Some of the places to which
she had gone were not, she admitted, quite nice. . . . Indeed,
they were not respectable ! And some of the photographs
taken, they too, had not been very nice. But these things,
they had told her, were necessary for " advertisement "—
and Señor Ramon himself had always been most respectful.

In answer to questioning she declared that the name of
Mrs. Ferrier had never been mentioned and that she had had
no idea that it was that lady she was supposed to be under-
studying. She had meant no harm. She identified certain
photographs which were shown to her as having been taken
of her in Paris and on the Riviera.

There was the hall mark of absolute honesty about Thelma
Andersen. She was quite clearly a pleasant, but slightly stupid
woman. Her distress at the whole thing, now that she understood it, was patent to everyone.

The defence was unconvincing. A frenzied denial of having
had any dealings with the woman Andersen. The photos
in question had been brought to the London office and had
been believed to be genuine. Sir Mortimer's closing speech
roused enthusiasm. He described the whole thing as a das-
tardly political plot, formed to discredit the Prime Minister
and his wife. All sympathy would be extended to the unfortunate Mrs. Ferrier.

The verdict, a foregone conclusion, was given amidst unpar-
alleled scenes. Damages were assessed at an enormous figure.
As Mrs. Ferrier and her husband and father left the court
they were greeted by the appreciative roars of a vast crowd.

XI

Edward Ferrier grasped Poirot warmly by the hand.
He said :

" I thank you, M. Poirot, a thousand times. Well, that finishes the *X-ray News*. Dirty little rag. They're wiped out completely. Serves them right for cooking up such a scurrilous plot. Against Dagmar, too, the kindliest creature in the world. Thank goodness you managed to expose the whole thing for the wicked ramp it was. . . . What put you on to the idea that they might be using a double ? "

" It is not a new idea," Poirot reminded him. " It was employed successfully in the case of Jeanne de la Motte when she impersonated Marie Antoinette."

" I know. I must re-read *The Queen's Necklace*. But how did you actually *find* the woman they were employing ? "

" I looked for her in Denmark, and I found her there."

" But why Denmark ? "

" Because Mrs. Ferrier's grandmother was a Dane, and she herself is a markedly Danish type. And there were other reasons."

" The resemblance is certainly striking. What a devilish idea ! I wonder how the little rat came to think of it ? "

Poirot smiled.

" But he did not."

He tapped himself on the chest.

" I thought of it ! "

Edward Ferrier stared.

" I don't understand. What do you mean ? "

Poirot said :

" We must go back to an older story than that of *The Queen's Necklace*—to the cleansing of the Augean Stables. What Hercules used was a river—that is to say one of the great forces of Nature. Modernise that ! What is a great force of Nature ? Sex, is it not ? It is the sex angle that sells stories, that makes news. Give people scandal allied to sex and it appeals far more than any mere political chicanery or fraud.

" *Eh bien, that* was my task ! First to put my own hands in the mud like Hercules to build up a dam that should turn the course of that river. A journalistic friend of mine aided me. He searched Denmark until he found a suitable person to attempt the impersonation. He approached her, casually mentioned the *X-ray News* to her, hoping she would remember it. She did.

"And so, what happened? *Mud*—a great deal of mud! Cæsar's wife is bespattered with it. Far more interesting to everybody than any political scandal. And the result—the *dénouement*? Why, Reaction! Virtue vindicated! The pure woman cleared! A great tide of Romance and Sentiment sweeping through the Augean Stables.

"If all the newspapers in the country publish the news of John Hammett's defalcations now, no one will believe it. It will be put down as another politcal plot to discredit the Government."

Edward Ferrier took a deep breath. For a moment Hercule Poirot came nearer to being physically assaulted than at any other time in his career.

"My wife! You dared to use her——"

Fortunately, perhaps, Mrs. Ferrier herself entered the room at this moment.

"Well," she said. "That went off very well."

"Dagmar, did you—know all along?"

"Of course, dear," said Dagmar Ferrier.

And she smiled, the gentle, maternal smile of a devoted wife.

"And you never told me!"

"But, Edward, you would never have let M. Poirot do it."

"Indeed I would not!"

Dagmar smiled.

"That's what we thought."

"We?"

"I and M. Poirot."

She smiled at Hercule Poirot and at her husband.

She added:

"I had a very restful time with the dear Bishop—I feel full of energy now. They want me to christen the new battleship at Liverpool next month—I think it would be a popular thing to do."

# THE STYMPHALEAN BIRDS

I

HAROLD WARING noticed Them first walking up the path from the lake. He was sitting outside the hotel on the terrace. The day was fine, the lake was blue, and the sun shone. Harold was smoking a pipe and feeling that the world was a pretty good place.

His political career was shaping well. An under-secretaryship at the age of thirty was something to be justly proud of. It had been reported that the Prime Minister had said to someone that " young Waring would go far." Harold was, not unnaturally, elated. Life presented itself to him in rosy colours. He was young, sufficiently good-looking, in first-class condition, and quite unencumbered with romantic ties.

He had decided to take a holiday in Herzoslovakia so as to get right off the beaten track and have a real rest from everyone and everything. The hotel at Lake Stempka, though small, was comfortable and not overcrowded. The few people there were mostly foreigners. So far the only other English people were an elderly woman, Mrs. Rice, and her married daughter, Mrs. Clayton. Harold liked them both. Elsie Clayton was pretty in a rather old-fashioned style. She made up very little, if at all, and was gentle and rather shy. Mrs. Rice was what is called a woman of character. She was tall, with a deep voice and a masterful manner, but she had a sense of humour and was good company. Her life was clearly bound up in that of her daughter.

Harold had spent some pleasant hours in the company of mother and daughter, but they did not attempt to monopolise him and relations remained friendly and unexacting between them.

The other people in the hotel had not aroused Harold's notice. Usually they were hikers, or members of a motorcoach tour. They stayed a night or two and then went on. He had hardly noticed any one else—until this afternoon.

*They* came up the path from the lake very slowly and it just happened that at the moment when Harold's attention was attracted to them, a cloud came over the sun. He shivered a little.

Then he stared. Surely there was something odd about these two women? They had long, curved noses, like birds, and their faces, which were curiously alike, were quite immobile. Over their shoulders they wore loose cloaks that flapped in the wind like the wings of two big birds.

Harold thought to himself.

" They *are* like birds—" he added almost without volition, " *birds of ill omen.*"

The women came straight up on the terrace and passed close by him. They were not young—perhaps nearer fifty than forty, and the resemblance between them was so close that they were obviously sisters. Their expression was forbidding. As they passed Harold the eyes of both of them rested on him for a minute. It was a curious, appraising glance—almost inhuman.

Harold's impression of evil grew stronger. He noticed the hand of one of the two sisters, a long claw-like hand. . . . Although the sun had come out, he shivered once again. He thought :

" Horrible creatures. Like birds of prey. . . ."

He was distracted from these imaginings by the emergence of Mrs. Rice from the hotel. He jumped up and drew forward a chair. With a word of thanks she sat down and, as usual, began to knit vigorously.

Harold asked :

" Did you see those two women who just went into the hotel ? "

" With cloaks on ? Yes, I passed them."

" Extraordinary creatures, didn't you think ? "

" Well—yes, perhaps they are rather odd. They only arrived yesterday, I think. Very alike—they must be twins."

Harold said :

" I may be fanciful, but I distinctly felt there was something evil about them."

"How curious. I must look at them more closely and see if I agree with you."

She added: "We'll find out from the concierge who they are. Not English, I imagine?"

"Oh no."

Mrs. Rice glanced at her watch. She said:

"Tea-time. I wonder if you'd mind going in and ringing the bell, Mr. Waring?"

"Certainly, Mrs. Rice."

He did so and then as he returned to his seat he asked:

"Where's your daughter this afternoon?"

"Elsie? We went for a walk together. Part of the way round the lake and then back through the pinewoods. It really was lovely."

A waiter came out and received orders for tea. Mrs. Rice went on, her needles flying vigorously:

"Elsie had a letter from her husband. She mayn't come down to tea."

"Her husband?" Harold was surprised. "Do you know, I always thought she was a widow."

Mrs. Rice shot him a sharp glance. She said dryly:

"Oh no, Elsie isn't a widow." She added with emphasis: "Unfortunately!"

Harold was startled.

Mrs. Rice, nodding her head grimly, said:

"Drink is responsible for a lot of unhappiness, Mr. Waring."

"Does he drink?"

"Yes. And a good many other things as well. He's insanely jealous and has a singularly violent temper." She sighed. "It's a difficult world, Mr. Waring. I'm devoted to Elsie, she's my only child—and to see her unhappy isn't an easy thing to bear."

Harold said with real emotion:

"She's such a gentle creature."

"A little too gentle, perhaps."

"You mean—"

Mrs. Rice said slowly:

"A happy creature is more arrogant. Elsie's gentleness comes, I think, from a sense of defeat. Life has been too much for her."

Harold said with some slight hesitation :

" How—did she come to marry this husband of hers ? "

Mrs. Rice answered :

" Philip Clayton was a very attractive person.  He had
(still has) great charm, he had a certain amount of money—
and there was no one to advise us of his real character.   I
had been a widow for many years.   Two women, living
alone, are not the best judges of a man's character."

Harold said thoughtfully :

" No, that's true."

He felt a wave of indignation and pity sweep over him.
Elsie Clayton could not be more than twenty-five at the most.
He recalled the clear friendliness of her blue eyes, the soft
droop of her mouth.  He realised, suddenly, that his interest
in her went a little beyond friendship.

And she was tied to a brute. . . .


## II


That evening, Harold joined mother and daughter after
dinner.  Elsie Clayton was wearing a soft dull pink dress.
Her eyelids, he noticed, were red.  She had been crying.

Mrs. Rice said briskly :

" I've found out who your two harpies are, Mr. Waring.
Polish ladies—of very good family, so the concierge says."

Harold looked across the room to where the Polish ladies
were sitting.  Elsie said with interest :

" Those two women over there ?  With the henna-dyed
hair ?  They look rather horrible somehow—I don't know
why."

Harold said triumphantly :

" That's just what I thought."

Mrs. Rice said with a laugh :

" I think you are both being absurd.  You can't possibly
tell what people are like just by looking at them."

Elsie laughed.

She said :

" I suppose one can't.  All the same *I* think they're vul-
tures ! "

" Picking out dead men's eyes ! " said Harold.

" Oh, don't," cried Elsie.

Harold said quickly :

" Sorry."

Mrs. Rice said with a smile :

" Anyway they're not likely to cross *our* path."

Elsie said :

" *We* haven't got any guilty secrets ! "

" Perhaps Mr. Waring has," said Mrs. Rice with a twinkle.

Harold laughed, throwing his head back.

He said :

" Not a secret in the world.  My life's an open book."

And it flashed across his mind :

" What fools people are who leave the straight path.  A clear conscience—that's all one needs in life.  With that you can face the world and tell everyone who interferes with you to go to the devil ! "

He felt suddenly very much alive—very strong—very much master of his fate !


### III


Harold Waring, like many other Englishmen, was a bad linguist.  His French was halting and decidedly British in intonation.  Of German and Italian he knew nothing.

Up to now, these linguistic disabilities had not worried him.  In most hotels on the Continent, he had always found, everyone spoke English, so why worry ?

But in this out-of-the-way spot, where the native language was a form of Slovak and even the concierge only spoke German it was sometimes galling to Harold when one of his two women friends acted as interpreter for him.  Mrs. Rice, who was fond of languages, could even speak a little Slovak.

Harold determined that he would set about learning German. He decided to buy some text books and spend a couple of hours each morning in mastering the language.

The morning was fine and after writing some letters, Harold looked at his watch and saw there was still time for an hour's stroll before lunch.  He went down towards the lake and then turned aside into the pine woods. He had walked there for perhaps five minutes when he heard an unmistakable sound. Somewhere not far away a woman was sobbing her heart out.

Harold paused a minute, then he went in the direction of the sound. The woman was Elsie Clayton and she was sitting on a fallen tree with her face buried in her hands and her shoulders quivering with the violence of her grief.

Harold hesitated a minute, then he came up to her. He said gently :

" Mrs. Clayton—Elsie ? "

She started violently and looked up at him. Harold sat down beside her.

He said with real sympathy :

" Is there anything I can do ? Anything at all ? "

She shook her head.

" No—no—you're very kind. But there's nothing that any one can do for me."

Harold said rather diffidently :

" Is it to do with—your husband ? "

She nodded. Then she wiped her eyes and took out her powder compact, struggling to regain command of herself. She said in a quavering voice :

" I didn't want Mother to worry. She's so upset when she sees me unhappy. So I came out here to have a good cry. It's silly, I know. Crying doesn't help. But—sometimes— one just feels that life is quite unbearable."

Harold said :

" I'm terribly sorry."

She threw him a grateful glance. Then she said hurriedly :

" It's my own fault, of course. I married Philip of my own free will. It—it's turned out badly, I've only myself to blame."

Harold said :

" It's very plucky of you to put it like that."

Elsie shook her head.

" No, I'm not plucky. I'm not brave at all. I'm an awful coward. That's partly the trouble with Philip. I'm terrified of him—absolutely terrified—when he gets in one of his rages."

Harold said with feeling :

" You ought to leave him ! "

" I daren't. He—he wouldn't let me."

"Nonsense! What about a divorce?"

She shook her head slowly.

"I've no grounds." She straightened her shoulders. "No, I've got to carry on. I spend a fair amount of time with Mother, you know. Philip doesn't mind that. Especially when we go somewhere off the beaten track like this." She added, the colour rising in her cheeks, "You see, part of the trouble is that he's insanely jealous. If—if I so much as speak to another man he makes the most frightful scenes."

Harold's indignation rose. He had heard many women complain of the jealousy of a husband, and whilst professing sympathy, had been secretly of the opinion that the husband was amply justified. But Elsie Clayton was not one of those women. She had never thrown him so much as a flirtatious glance.

Elsie drew away from him with a slight shiver. She glanced up at the sky.

"The sun's gone in. It's quite cold. We'd better get back to the hotel. It must be nearly lunch time."

They got up and turned in the direction of the hotel. They had walked for perhaps a minute when they overtook a figure going in the same direction. They recognised her by the flapping cloak she wore. It was one of the Polish sisters.

They passed her, Harold bowing slightly. She made no response but her eyes rested on them both for a minute and there was a certain appraising quality in the glance which made Harold feel suddenly hot. He wondered if the woman had seen him sitting by Elsie on the tree trunk. If so, she probably thought . . .

Well, she looked as though she thought. . . . A wave of indignation overwhelmed him! What foul minds some women had!

Odd that the sun had gone in and that they should both have shivered—perhaps just at the moment that that woman was watching them. . . .

Somehow, Harold felt a little uneasy.

IV

That evening, Harold went to his room a little after ten.
The English mail had arrived and he had received a number
of letters, some of which needed immediate answers.

He got into his pyjamas and a dressing-gown and sat down
at the desk to deal with his correspondence. He had written
three letters and was just starting on the fourth when the door
was suddenly flung open and Elsie Clayton staggered into the
room.

Harold jumped up, startled. Elsie had pushed the door
to behind her and was standing clutching at the chest of
drawers. Her breath was coming in great gasps, her face was
the colour of chalk. She looked frightened to death.

She gasped out : "It's my husband! He arrived unexpectedly. I—I think he'll kill me. He's mad—quite mad.
I came to you. Don't—don't let him find me."

She took a step or two forward, swaying so much that she
almost fell. Harold put out an arm to support her.

As he did so, the door was flung open and a man stood in
the doorway. He was of medium height with thick eyebrows
and a sleek, dark head. In his hand he carried a heavy car
spanner. His voice rose high and shook with rage. He almost
screamed the words.

"So that Polish woman was right! You *are* carrying on
with this fellow!"

Elsie cried :

"No, no, Phillip. It's not true. You're wrong."

Harold thrust the girl swiftly behind him, as Philip Clayton
advanced on them both. The latter cried :

"Wrong, am I? When I find you here in his room? You
she-devil, I'll kill you for this."

With a swift, sideways movement he dodged Harold's arm.
Elsie, with a cry, ran round the other side of Harold, who
swung round to fend the other off.

But Philip Clayton had only one idea, to get at his wife.
He swerved round again. Elsie, terrified, rushed out of the
room. Philip Clayton dashed after her, and Harold, with not
a moment's hesitation, followed him.

Elsie had darted back into her own bedroom at the end of the corridor. Harold could hear the sound of the key turning in the lock, but it did not turn in time. Before the lock could catch Philip Clayton wrenched the door open. He disappeared into the room and Harold heard Elsie's frightened cry. In another minute Harold burst in after them.

Elsie was standing at bay against the curtains of the window. As Harold entered Philip Clayton rushed at her brandishing the spanner. She gave a terrified cry, then snatching up a heavy paper-weight from the desk beside her, she flung it at him.

Clayton went down like a log. Elsie screamed. Harold stopped petrified in the doorway. The girl fell on her knees beside her husband. He lay quite still where he had fallen.

Outside in the passage, there was the sound of the bolt of one of the doors being drawn back. Elsie jumped up and ran to Harold.

"Please—please——" Her voice was low and breathless. "Go back to your room. They'll come—they'll find you here."

Harold nodded. He took in the situation like lightning. For the moment, Philip Clayton was *hors de combat*. But Elsie's scream might have been heard. If he were found in her room it could only cause embarrassment and misunderstanding. Both for her sake and his own there must be no scandal.

As noiselessly as possible, he sprinted down the passage and back into his room. Just as he reached it, he heard the sound of an opening door.

He sat in his room for nearly half an hour, waiting. He dared not go out. Sooner or later, he felt sure, Elsie would come.

There was a light tap on his door. Harold jumped up to open it.

It was not Elsie who came in but her mother and Harold was aghast at her appearance. She looked suddenly years older. Her grey hair was dishevelled and there were deep black circles under her eyes.

He sprang up and helped her to a chair. She sat down, her breath coming painfully. Harold said quickly:

"You look all in, Mrs. Rice. Can I get you something?"

She shook her head.

" No. Never mind me. I'm all right, really. It's only the shock. Mr. Waring, a terrible thing has happened."

Harold asked :

" Is Clayton seriously injured ? "

She caught her breath.

" Worse than that. *He's dead. . . .*"

v

The room spun round.

A feeling as of icy water trickling down his spine rendered Harold incapable of speech for a moment or two.

He repeated dully :

" *Dead ?* "

Mrs. Rice nodded.

She said, and her voice had the flat level tones of complete exhaustion :

" The corner of that marble paper-weight caught him right on the temple and he fell back with his head on the iron fender. I don't know which it was that killed him—but he is certainly dead. I have seen death often enough to know."

Disaster—that was the word that rang insistently in Harold's brain. Disaster, disaster, disaster. . . .

He said vehemently :

" It was an accident. . . . I saw it happen."

Mrs. Rice said sharply :

" Of course it was an accident. *I* know that. But—but— is any one else going to think so ? I'm—frankly, I'm frightened, Harold ! This isn't England."

Harold said slowly :

" I can confirm Elsie's story."

Mrs. Rice said :

" Yes, and she can confirm yours. That—that is just it ! "

Harold's brain, naturally a keen and cautious one, saw her point. He reviewed the whole thing and appreciated the weakness of their position.

He and Elsie had spent a good deal of their time together. Then there was the fact that they had been seen together in the pinewoods by one of the Polish women under rather compromising circumstances. The Polish ladies apparently spoke no English, but they might nevertheless understand it a little. The woman might have known the meaning of words like " jealously " and " husband " if she had chanced to overhear their conversation. Anyway it was clear that it was something she had said to Clayton that had aroused his jealousy. And now—his death. When Clayton had died, he, Harold, *had been in Elsie Clayton's room.* There was nothing to show that he had not deliberately assaulted Philip Clayton with the paper-weight. Nothing to show that the jealous husband had not actually found them together. There was only his word and Elsie's. Would they be believed ?

A cold fear gripped him.

He did not imagine—no, he really did *not* imagine—that either he or Elsie was in danger of being condemned to death for a murder they had not committed. Surely, in any case, it could be only a charge of manslaughter brought against them. (Did they have manslaughter in these foreign countries ? ) But even if they were acquitted of blame there would have to be an inquiry—it would be reported in all the papers. *An English man and woman accused—jealous husband— rising politician.* Yes, it would mean the end of his political career. It would never survive a scandal like that.

He said on an impulse :

" Can't we get rid of the body somehow ? Plant it somewhere ? "

Mrs. Rice's astonished and scornful look made him blush. She said incisively :

" My dear Harold, this isn't a detective story ! To attempt a thing like that would be quite crazy."

" I suppose it would." He groaned. " What can we do ? My God, what can we do ? "

Mrs. Rice shook her head despairingly. She was frowning, her mind working painfully.

Harold demanded :

" Isn't there anything we can do ? Anything to avoid this frightful disaster ? "

There, it was out—disaster ! Terrible—unforeseen—utterly damning.

They stared at each other. Mrs. Rice said hoarsely :

" Elsie—my little girl. I'd do anything. . . . It will kill her if she has to go through a thing like this." And she added : " You too, your career—everything."

Harold managed to say :

" Never mind me."

But he did not really mean it.

Mrs. Rice went on bitterly :

" And all so unfair—so utterly untrue ! It's not as though there had ever been anything between you. *I* know that well enough."

Harold suggested, catching at a straw :

" You'll be able to say that at least—that it was all perfectly all right."

Mrs. Rice said bitterly :

" Yes, if they believe me. But you know what these people out here are like ! "

Harold agreed gloomily. To the Continental mind, there would undoubtedly be a guilty connection between himself and Elsie, and all Mrs. Rice's denials would be taken as a mother lying herself black in the face for her daughter.

Harold said gloomily :

" Yes, we're not in England, worse luck."

" Ah ! " Mrs. Rice lifted her head. " *That's* true. . . . It's not England. I wonder now if something *could* be done——"

" Yes ? " Harold looked at her eagerly.

Mrs. Rice said abruptly :

" How much money have you got ? "

" Not much with me." He added : " I could wire for money, of course."

Mrs. Rice said grimly :

" We may need a good deal. But I think it's worth trying."

Harold felt a faint lifting of despair. He said :

" What is your idea ? "

Mrs. Rice spoke decisively.

" We haven't a chance of concealing the death *ourselves*, but I do think there's just a chance of hushing it up *officially* ! "

" You really think so ? " Harold was hopeful but slightly incredulous.

"Yes, for one thing the manager of the hotel will be on
our side. He'd much rather have the thing hushed up. It's
my opinion that in these out of the way curious little Balkan
countries you can bribe anyone and everyone—and the police
are probably more corrupt than anyone else!"

Harold said slowly :

"Do you know, I believe you're right."

Mrs. Rice went on :

"Fortunately, I don't think anyone in the hotel *heard*
anything."

"Who has the room next to Elsie's on the other side from
yours ? "

"The two Polish ladies. They didn't hear anything. They'd
have come out into the passage if they had. Philip arrived
late, nobody saw him but the night porter. Do you know,
Harold, I believe it will be possible to hush the whole thing up
and get Philip's death certified as due to natural causes!
It's just a question of bribing high enough—and finding the
right man—probably the Chief of Police !"

Harold smiled faintly. He said :

"It's rather Comic Opera, isn't it ? Well, after all, we
can but try."


## VI


Mrs. Rice was energy personified. First the manager was
summoned. Harold remained in his room, keeping out of it.
He and Mrs. Rice had agreed that the story told had better
be that of a quarrel between husband and wife. Elsie's youth
and prettiness would command more sympathy.

On the following morning various police officials arrived
and were shown up to Mrs. Rice's bedroom. They left at mid-
day. Harold had wired for money but otherwise had taken
no part in the proceedings—indeed he would have been unable
to do so since none of these official personages spoke English.

At twelve o'clock Mrs. Rice came to his room. She looked
white and tired, but the relief on her face told its own story.
She said simply :

"*It's worked !*"

" Thank heaven ! You've really been marvellous ! It seems incredible ! "

Mrs. Rice said thoughtfully :

" By the ease with which it went, you might almost think it was quite normal. They practically held out their hands right away. It's—it's rather disgusting, really ! "

Harold said dryly :

" This isn't the moment to quarrel with the corruption of the public services. How much ? "

" The tariff's rather high."

She read out a list of figures.

> The Chief of Police.
> The *Commissaire*.
> The *Agent*.
> The Doctor.
> The Hotel Manager.
> The Night Porter.

Harold's comment was merely :

" The night porter doesn't get much, does he ? I suppose it's mostly a question of gold lace."

Mrs. Rice explained :

" The manager stipulated that the death should not have taken place in his hotel at all. The official story will be that Philip had a heart attack in the train. He went along the corridor for air—you know how they always leave those doors open—and he fell out on the line. It's wonderful what the police can do when they try ! "

" Well," said Harold. " Thank God *our* police force isn't like that."

And in a British and superior mood he went down to lunch.

VII

After lunch Harold usually joined Mrs. Rice and her daughter for coffee. He decided to make no change in his usual behaviour.

This was the first time he had seen Elsie since the night

before. She was very pale and was obviously still suffering from shock, but she made a gallant endeavour to behave as usual, uttering small commonplaces about the weather and the scenery.

They commented on a new guest who had just arrived, trying to guess his nationality. Harold thought a moustache like that must be French—Elsie said German—and Mrs. Rice thought he might be Spanish.

There was no one else but themselves on the terrace with the exception of the two Polish ladies who were sitting at the extreme end, both doing fancy-work.

As always when he saw them, Harold felt a queer shiver of apprehension pass over him. Those still faces, those curved beaks of noses, those long claw-like hands. . . .

A page boy approached and told Mrs. Rice she was wanted. She rose and followed him. At the entrance to the hotel they saw her encounter a police official in full uniform.

Elsie caught her breath.

" You don't think—anything's gone wrong ? "

Harold reassured her quickly.

" Oh no, no, nothing of that kind."

But he himself knew a sudden pang of fear.

He said :

" Your mother's been wonderful ! "

" I know. Mother is a great fighter. She'll never sit down under defeat." Elsie shivered. " But it is all horrible, isn't it ? "

" Now, don't dwell on it. It's all over and done with."

Elsie said in a low voice :

" I can't forget that—that it was *I* who killed him."

Harold said urgently :

" Don't think of it that way. It was an accident. You know that really."

Her face grew a little happier. Harold added :

" And anyway it's past. The past is the past. Try never to think of it again."

Mrs. Rice came back. By the expression on her face they saw that all was well.

" It gave me quite a fright," she said almost gaily. " But it was only a formality about some papers. Everything's all right, my children. We're out of the shadow. I think we might order ourselves a liqueur on the strength of it."

The liqueur was ordered and came. They raised their glasses.

Mrs. Rice said: "To the Future!"

Harold smiled at Elsie and said:

"To your happiness!"

She smiled back at him and said as she lifted her glass:

"And to you—to your success! I'm sure you're going to be a very great man."

With the reaction from fear they felt gay, almost light-headed. The shadow had lifted! All was well . . .

From the far end of the terrace the two bird-like women rose. They rolled up their work carefully. They came across the stone flags.

With little bows they sat down by Mrs. Rice. One of them began to speak. The other one let her eyes rest on Elsie and Harold. There was a little smile on her lips. It was not, Harold thought, a nice smile. . . .

He looked over at Mrs. Rice. She was listening to the Polish woman and though he couldn't understand a word, the expression on Mrs. Rice's face was clear enough. All the old anguish and despair came back. She listened and occasionally spoke a brief word.

Presently the two sisters rose, and with stiff little bows went into the hotel.

Harold leaned forward. He said hoarsely:

"What is it?"

Mrs. Rice answered him in the quiet hopeless tones of despair.

"*Those women are going to blackmail us. They heard every-thing last night. And now we've tried to hush it up, it makes the whole thing a thousand times worse. . . .*"


VIII


Harold Waring was down by the lake. He had been walking feverishly for over an hour, trying by sheer physical energy to still the clamour of despair that had attacked him.

He came at last to the spot where he had first noticed the two grim women who held his life and Elsie's in their evil talons. He said aloud :

" Curse them ! Damn them for a pair of devilish blood-sucking harpies ! "

A slight cough made him spin round. He found himself facing the luxuriantly moustached stranger who had just come out from the shade of the trees.

Harold found it difficult to know what to say. This little man must have almost certainly overheard what he had just said.

Harold, at a loss, said somewhat ridiculously :

" Oh—er—good afternoon."

In perfect English the other replied :

" But for you, I fear, it is not a good afternoon ? "

" Well—er—I——" Harold was in difficulties again.

The little man said :

" You are, I think, in trouble, Monsieur ? Can I be of any assistance to you ? "

" Oh no thanks, no thanks ! Just blowing off steam, you know."

The other said gently :

" But I think, you know, that I *could* help you. I am correct, am I not, in connecting your troubles with two ladies who were sitting on the terrace just now ? "

Harold stared at him.

" Do you know anything about them ? " He added : " Who are you, anyway ? "

As though confessing to royal birth the little man said modestly :

" *I am Hercule Poirot.* Shall we walk a little way into the wood and you shall tell me your story ? As I say, I think I can aid you."

To this day, Harold is not quite certain what made him suddenly pour out the whole story to a man to whom he had only spoken a few minutes before. Perhaps it was overstrain. Anyway, it happened. He told Hercule Poirot the whole story.

The latter listened in silence. Once or twice he nodded his head gravely. When Harold came to a stop the other spoke dreamily.

" The Stymphalean Birds, with iron beaks, who feed on human flesh and who dwell by the Stymphalean Lake. . . . Yes, it accords very well."

" I beg your pardon," said Harold staring.

Perhaps, he thought, this curious-looking little man was mad !

Hercule Poirot smiled.

" I reflect, that is all. I have my own way of looking at things, you understand. Now as to this business of yours. You are very unpleasantly placed."

Harold said impatiently :

" I don't need you to tell me that ! "

Hercule Poirot went on :

" It is a serious business, blackmail. These harpies will force you to pay—and pay—and pay again ! And if you defy them, well, what happens ? "

Harold said bitterly :

" The whole thing comes out. My career's ruined, and a wretched girl who's never done anyone any harm will be put through hell, and God knows what the end of it all will be ! "

" Therefore," said Hercule Poirot, " something must be done ! "

Harold said baldly : " What ? "

Hercule Poirot leaned back, half-closing his eyes. He said (and again a doubt of his sanity crossed Harold's mind) :

" It is the moment for the castanets of bronze."

Harold said :

" Are you quite mad ? "

The other shook his head. He said :

" *Mais non !* I strive only to follow the example of my great predecessor, Hercules. Have a few hours' patience, my friend. By to-morrow I may be able to deliver you from your persecutors."


IX


Harold Waring came down the following morning to find Hercule Poirot sitting alone on the terrace. In spite of himself Harold had been impressed by Hercule Poirot's promises.

He came up to him now and asked anxiously :

" Well ? "

Hercule Poirot beamed upon him.

" It is well."

" What do you mean ? "

" Everything has settled itself satisfactorily."

" But what has *happened* ? "

Hercule Poirot replied dreamily :

" I have employed the castanets of bronze. Or, in modern parlance, I have caused metal wires to hum—in short I have employed the telegraph ! Your Stymphalean Birds, Monsieur, have been removed to where they will be unable to exercise their ingenuity for some time to come."

" They were wanted by the police ? They have been arrested ? "

" Precisely."

Harold drew a deep breath.

" How marvellous ! I never thought of that." He got up. " I must find Mrs. Rice and Elsie and tell them."

" They know."

"Oh good." Harold sat down again. "Tell me just what——" He broke off.

*Coming up the path from the lake were two figures with flapping cloaks and profiles like birds.*

He exclaimed :

" I thought you said they had been taken away ! "

Hercule Poirot followed his glance.

" Oh, those ladies ? They are very harmless ; Polish ladies of good family, as the porter told you. Their appearance is, perhaps, not very pleasing but that is all."

" But I don't *understand* ! "

" No, you do not understand ! It is the *other* ladies who were wanted by the police—the resourceful Mrs. Rice and the lachrymose Mrs. Clayton ! It is *they* who are well-known birds of prey. Those two, they make their living by blackmail, *mon cher*."

Harold had a sensation of the world spinning round him. He said faintly :

" But the man—the man who was killed ? "

" No one was killed. There was no man ! "

"But I *saw* him!"

"Oh no. The tall deep-voiced Mrs. Rice is a very successful male impersonator. It was she who played the part of the husband—without her grey wig and suitably made up for the part."

He leaned forward and tapped the other on the knee.

"You must not go through life being too credulous, my friend. The police of a country are not so easily bribed—they are probably not to be bribed at all—certainly not when it is a question of murder! These women trade on the average Englishman's ignorance of foreign languages. Because she speaks French or German, it is always this Mrs. Rice who interviews the manager and takes charge of the affair. The police arrive and go to *her* room, yes! But what actually passes? *You* do not know. Perhaps she says she has lost a brooch—something of that kind. Any excuse to arrange for the police to come *so that you shall see them*. For the rest, what actually happens? You wire for money, a lot of money, and you hand it over to Mrs. Rice who is in charge of all the negotiations! And that is that! But they are greedy, these birds of prey. They have seen that you have taken an unreasonable aversion to these two unfortunate Polish ladies. The ladies in question come and hold a perfectly innocent conversation with Mrs. Rice and she cannot resist repeating the game. She knows you cannot understand what is being said.

"So you will have to send for more money which Mrs. Rice will pretend to distribute to a fresh set of people."

Harold drew a deep breath. He said :

"And Elsie—Elsie?"

Hercule Poirot averted his eyes.

"She played her part very well. She always does. A most accomplished little actress. Everything is very pure—very innocent. She appeals, not to sex, but to chivalry."

Hercule Poirot added dreamily :

"That is always successful with Englishmen."

Harold Waring drew a deep breath. He said crisply :

"I'm going to set to work and learn every European language there is! Nobody's going to make a fool of me a second time!"

# THE CRETAN BULL

### I

Hercule Poirot looked thoughtfully at his visitor.

He saw a pale face with a determined looking chin, eyes that were more grey than blue, and hair that was of that real blue-black shade so seldom seen—the hyacinthine locks of ancient Greece.

He noted the well-cut, but also well-worn, country tweeds, the shabby handbag, and the unconscious arrogance of manner that lay behind the girl's obvious nervousness. He thought to himself :

" Ah yes, she is ' the County '—but no money ! And it must be something quite out of the way that would bring her to me."

Diana Maberly said, and her voice shook a little :

" I—I don't know whether you can help me or not, M. Poirot. It's—it's a very extraordinary position."

Poirot said :

" But yes ? Tell me ? "

Diana Maberly said :

" I've come to you because I don't know *what* to do ! I don't even know if there *is* anything to do ! "

" Will you let me be the judge of that ? "

The colour surged suddenly into the girl's face. She said rapidly and breathlessly :

" I've come to you because the man I've been engaged to for over a year has broken off our engagement."

She stopped and eyed him defiantly.

" You must think," she said, " that I'm completely mental."

Slowly, Hercule Poirot shook his head.

" On the contrary, Mademoiselle, I have no doubt whatever but that you are extremely intelligent. It is certainly not my *métier* in life to patch up the lovers' quarrels, and I know very well that you are quite aware of that. It is, therefore, that there is something unusual about the breaking of this engagement. That is so, is it not ? "

The girl nodded. She said in a clear, precise voice.

" Hugh broke off our engagement because he thinks he is going mad. He thinks people who are mad should not marry."

Hercule Poirot's eyebrows rose a little.

" And do you not agree ? "

" I don't know. . . . What *is* being mad, after all ? Everyone is a little mad."

" It has been said so," Poirot agreed cautiously.

" It's only when you begin thinking you're a poached egg or something that they have to shut you up."

" And your fiancé has not reached that stage ? "

Diana Maberly said :

" I can't see that there's anything wrong with Hugh at all. He's, oh, he's the sanest person I know. Sound—dependable——"

" Then why does he think he is going mad ? "

Poirot paused a moment before going on.

" Is there, perhaps, madness in his family ? "

Reluctantly Diana jerked her head in assent. She said :

" His grandfather was mental, I believe—and some great-aunt or other. But what I say is, that *every* family has got someone queer in it. You know, a bit half-witted or extra clever or *something* ! "

Her eyes were appealing.

Hercule Poirot shook his head sadly. He said :

" I am very sorry for you, Mademoiselle."

Her chin shot out. She cried :

" I don't want you to be sorry for me ! I want you to *do* something ! "

" What do you want me to do ? "

" I don't know—*but there's something wrong.*"

" Will you tell me Mademoiselle, all about your fiancé ? "

Diana spoke rapidly :

" His name's Hugh Chandler. He's twenty-four. His father is Admiral Chandler. They live at Lyde Manor. It's been in the Chandler family since the time of Elizabeth. Hugh's the only son. He went into the Navy—all the Chandlers are sailors—it's a sort of tradition—ever since Sir Gilbert Chandler sailed with Sir Walter Raleigh in fifteen-something-or-other. Hugh went into the Navy as a matter of course. His father wouldn't have heard of anything else. And yet—and yet, it was his *father* who insisted on getting him out of it !"

" When was that ? "

" Nearly a year ago. Quite suddenly."

" Was Hugh Chandler happy in his profession ? "

" Absolutely."

" There was no scandal of any kind ? "

" About Hugh ? Absolutely nothing. He was getting on splendidly. He—he couldn't understand his father."

" What reason did Admiral Chandler himself give ? "

Diana said slowly :

" He never really gave a reason. Oh ! he said it was necessary Hugh should learn to manage the estate—but—but that was only a pretext. Even George Frobisher realised that."

" Who is George Frobisher ? "

" Colonel Frobisher. He's Admiral Chandler's oldest friend and Hugh's godfather. He spends most of his time down at the Manor."

" And what did Colonel Frobisher think of Admiral Chandler's determination that his son should leave the Navy ? "

" He was dumbfounded. He couldn't understand it at all. Nobody could."

" Not even Hugh Chandler himself ? "

Diana did not answer at once. Poirot waited a minute, then he went on :

" At the time, perhaps, he, too, was astonished. But now ? Has he said nothing—nothing at all ? "

Diana murmured reluctantly :

" He said—about a week ago—that—that his father was right—that it was the only thing to be done."

" Did you ask him why ? "

" Of course. But he wouldn't tell me."

Hercule Poirot reflected for a minute or two. Then he said :

" Have there been any unusual occurrences in your part of the world ? Starting, perhaps, about a year ago ? Something that has given rise to a lot of local talk and surmise ? "

She flashed out : " I don't know what you mean ! "
Poirot said quietly, but with authority in his voice :
" You had better tell me."
" There wasn't anything—nothing of the kind you mean."
" Of what kind then ? "
" I think you're simply odious ! Queer things often happen
on farms. It's revenge—or the village idiot or somebody."
" *What happened ?* "
She said reluctantly :
" There was a fuss about some sheep. . . . Their throats
were cut. Oh ! it was horrid ! But they all belonged to one
farmer and he's a very hard man. The police thought it was
some kind of spite against him."
" But they didn't catch the person who had done it ? "
" No."
She added fiercely. " But if you think——"
Poirot held up his hand. He said :
" You do not know in the least what I think. Tell me this,
has your fiancé consulted a doctor ? "
" No, I'm sure he hasn't."
" Wouldn't that be the simplest thing for him to do ? "
Diana said slowly :
" He won't. He—he hates doctors."
" And his father ? "
" I don't think the Admiral believes much in doctors either.
Says they're a lot of humbug merchants."
" How does the Admiral seem himself ? Is he well ?
Happy ? "
Diana said in a low voice :
" He's aged terribly in—in——"
" In the last year ? "
" Yes. He's a wreck—a sort of shadow of what he used to
be."
Poirot nodded thoughtfully. Then he said :
" Did he approve of his son's engagement ? "
" Oh yes. You see, my people's land adjoins his. We've
been there for generations. He was frightfully pleased when
Hugh and I fixed it up."
" And now ? What does he say to your engagement being
broken off ? "

The girl's voice shook a little. She said :

" I met him yesterday morning. He was looking ghastly. He took my hand in both of his. He said : ' *It's hard on you, my girl. But the boy's doing the right thing—the only thing he can do.*"

" And so," said Hercule Poirot, " you came to me ? "

She nodded. She asked : " Can you do anything ? "

Hercule Poirot replied :

" I do not know. But I can at least come down and see for myself."

## II

It was Hugh Chandler's magnificent physique that impressed Hercule Poirot more than anything else. Tall, magnificently proportioned, with a terrific chest and shoulders, and a tawny head of hair. There was a tremendous air of strength and virility about him.

On their arrival at Diana's house, she had at once rung up Admiral Chandler, and they had forthwith gone over to Lyde Manor where they had found tea waiting on the long terrace. And with the tea, three men. There was Admiral Chandler, white haired, looking older than his years, his shoulders bowed as though by an over-heavy burden, and his eyes dark and brooding. A contrast to him was his friend Colonel Frobisher, a dried-up, tough, little man with reddish hair turning grey at the temples. A restless, irascible, snappy, little man, rather like a terrier—but the possessor of a pair of extremely shrewd eyes. He had a habit of drawing down his brows over his eyes and lowering his head, thrusting it forward, whilst those same shrewd little eyes studied you piercingly. The third man was Hugh.

" Fine specimen, eh ? " said Colonel Frobisher.

He spoke in a low voice, having noted Poirot's close scrutiny of the young man.

Hercule Poirot nodded his head. He and Frobisher were sitting close together. The other three had their chairs on the far side of the tea-table and were chatting together in an animated but slightly artificial manner.

Poirot murmured : " Yes, he is magnificent—magnificent.
He is the young Bull—yes, one might say the Bull dedicated
to Poseidon. . . . A perfect specimen of healthy manhood."

" Looks fit enough, doesn't he ? "

Frobisher sighed. His shrewd little eyes stole sideways,
considering Hercule Poirot. Presently he said :

" I know who you are, you know."

" Ah that, it is no secret ! "

Poirot waved a royal hand. He was not *incognito*, the gesture
seemed to say. He was travelling as Himself.

After a minute or two Frobisher asked : " Did the girl get
you down—over this business ? "

" The business——? "

" The business of young Hugh. . . . Yes, I see you know
all about it. But I can't quite see why she went to *you*. . . .
Shouldn't have thought this sort of thing was in your line—
meantersay it's more a medical show."

" All kinds of things are in my line. . . . You would be
surprised."

" I mean I can't see quite what she expected you could *do*."

" Miss Maberly," said Poirot, " is a fighter."

Colonel Frobisher nodded a warm assent.

" Yes, she's a fighter all right. She's a fine kid. She won't
give up. All the same, you know, there are some things that
you *can't* fight. . . ."

His face looked suddenly old and tired.

Poirot dropped his voice still lower. He murmured discreetly :

" There is—insanity, I understand, in the family ? "

Frobisher nodded.

" Only crops up now and again," he murmured. " Skips
a generation or two. Hugh's grandfather was the last."

Poirot threw a quick glance in the direction of the other
three. Diana was holding the conversation well, laughing and
bantering Hugh. You would have said that the three of them
had not a care in the world.

" What form did the madness take ? " Poirot asked softly.

" The old boy became pretty violent in the end. He was
perfectly all right up to thirty—normal as could be. Then he
began to go a bit queer. It was some time before people noticed

it. Then a lot of rumours began going around. People started talking properly. Things happened that were hushed up. But—well," he raised his shoulders " ended up as mad as a hatter, poor devil ! Homicidal ! Had to be certified."

He paused for a moment and then added :

" He lived to be quite an old man, I believe. . . . That's what Hugh is afraid of, of course. That's why he doesn't want to see a doctor. He's afraid of being shut up and living shut up for years. Can't say I blame him. I'd feel the same."

" And Admiral Chandler, how does he feel ? "

" It's broken him up completely," Frobisher spoke shortly.

" He is very fond of his son ? "

" Wrapped up in the boy. You see, his wife was drowned in a boating accident when the boy was only ten years old. Since then he's lived for nothing but the child."

" Was he very devoted to his wife ? "

" Worshipped her. Everybody worshipped her. She was— she was one of the loveliest women I've ever known." He paused a moment and then said jerkily, " Care to see her portrait ? "

" I should like to see it very much."

Frobisher pushed back his chair and rose. Aloud he said :

" Going to show M. Poirot one or two things, Charles. He's a bit of a connoisseur."

The Admiral raised a vague hand. Frobisher tramped along the terrace and Poirot followed him. For a moment Diana's face dropped its mask of gaiety and looked an agonised question. Hugh, too, raised his head, and looked steadily at the small man with the big black moustache.

Poirot followed Frobisher into the house. It was so dim at first coming in out of the sunlight that he could hardly distinguish one article from another. But he realised that the house was full of old and beautiful things.

Colonel Frobisher led the way to the Picture Gallery. On the panelled walls hung portraits of dead and gone Chandlers, Faces stern and gay, men in court dress or in Naval uniform. Women in satin and pearls.

Finally Frobisher stopped under a portrait at the end of the gallery.

" Painted by Orpen," he said gruffly.

They stood looking up at a tall woman, her hand on a greyhound's collar. A woman with auburn hair and an expression of radiant vitality.

"Boy's the spitting image of her," said Frobisher. "Don't you think so?"

"In some things, yes."

"He hasn't got her delicacy—her femininity, of course. He's a masculine edition—but in all the essential things——" He broke off. "Pity he inherited from the Chandlers the one thing he could well have done without. . . ."

They were silent. There was melancholy in the air all around them—as though dead and gone Chandlers sighed for the taint that lay in their blood and which, remorselessly, from time to time, they passed on. . . .

Hercule Poirot turned his head to look at his companion. George Frobisher was still gazing up at the beautiful woman on the wall above him. And Poirot said softly :

"You knew her well. . . ."

Frobisher spoke jerkily.

"We were boy and girl together. I went off as a subaltern to India when she was sixteen. . . . When I got back—she was married to Charles Chandler."

"You knew him well also?"

"Charles is one of my oldest friends. He's my best friend—always has been."

"Did you see much of them—after the marriage?"

"Used to spend most of my leaves here. Like a second home to me, this place. Charles and Caroline always kept my room here—ready and waiting. . . ." He squared his shoulders, suddenly thrust his head forward pugnaciously. "That's why I'm here now—to stand by in case I'm wanted. If Charles needs me—I'm here."

Again the shadow of tragedy crept over them.

"And what do you think—about all this?" Poirot asked.

Frobisher stood stiffly. His brows came down over his eyes.

"What I think is, the least said the better. And to be frank, I don't see what you're doing in the business, M. Poirot. I don't see why Diana roped you in and got you down here."

"You are aware that Diana Maberly's engagement to Hugh Chandler has been broken off?"

"Yes, I know that."

" And you know the reason for it ? "

Frobisher replied stiffly :

" I don't know anything about that. Young people manage these things between them. Not my business to butt in."

Poirot said :

" Hugh Chandler told Diana that it was not right that they should marry, because he was going out of his mind."

He saw the beads of perspiration break out on Frobisher's forehead. He said :

" Have we got to talk about the damned thing ? What do you think *you* can do ? Hugh's done the right thing, poor devil. It's not his fault, it's heredity—germ plasm—brain cells. . . . But once he *knew*, well, what else *could* he do but break the engagement ? It's one of those things that just has to be done."

" If I could be convinced of that——"

" You can take it from me."

" But you have told me nothing."

" I tell you I don't want to talk about it."

" Why did Admiral Chandler force his son to leave the Navy ? "

" Because it was the only thing to be done."

" Why ? "

Frobisher shook an obstinate head.

Poirot murmured softly :

" Was it to do with some sheep being killed ? "

The other man said angrily :

" So you've heard about that ? "

" Diana told me."

" That girl had far better keep her mouth shut."

" She did not think it was conclusive."

" She doesn't know."

" What doesn't she know ? "

Unwillingly, jerkily, angrily, Frobisher spoke :

" Oh well, if you must have it. . . . Chandler heard a noise that night. Thought it might be someone got in the house. Went out to investigate. Light in the boy's room. Chandler went in. Hugh asleep on bed—dead asleep—in his clothes. Blood on the clothes. Basin in the room full of blood. His father couldn't wake him. Next morning heard about sheep being found with their throats cut. Questioned Hugh. Boy didn't know anything about it. Didn't remember going out— and his shoes found by the side door caked in mud. Couldn't explain the blood in the basin. Couldn't explain anything. Poor devil didn't *know*, you understand.

"Charles came to me, talked it over. What was the best thing to be done? Then it happened again—three nights later. After that—well, you can see for yourself. The boy had got to leave the service. If he was here, under Charles' eye, Charles could watch over him. Couldn't afford to have a scandal in the Navy. Yes, it was the only thing to be done."

Poirot asked: "And since then?"

Frobisher said fiercely, "I'm not answering any more questions. Don't you think Hugh knows his own business best?"

Hercule Poirot did not answer. He was always loath to admit that anyone could know better than Hercule Poirot.

### III

As they came into the hall, they met Admiral Chandler coming in. He stood for a moment, a dark figure silhouetted against the bright light outside.

He said in a low, gruff voice:

"Oh there you both are. M. Poirot, I would like a word with you. Come into my study."

Frobisher went out through the open door, and Poirot followed the Admiral. He had rather the feeling of having been summoned to the quarter-deck to give an account of himself.

The Admiral motioned Poirot to take one of the big easy chairs and himself sat down in the other. Poirot, whilst with Frobisher, had been impressed by the other's restlessness, nervousness and irritability—all the signs of intense mental strain. With Admiral Chandler he felt a sense of hopelessness, of quiet, deep despair. . . .

With a deep sigh, Chandler said: "I can't help being sorry Diana has brought you into this. . . . Poor child, I know how hard it is for her. But—well—it is our own private tragedy, and I think you will understand, M. Poirot, that we don't want outsiders."

" I can understand your feeling, certainly."

" Diana, poor child, can't believe it. . . . _I_ couldn't at first. Probably wouldn't believe it now if I didn't know——"

He paused.

" Know what ? "

" That it's in the blood. The taint, I mean."

" And yet you agreed to the engagement ? "

Admiral Chandler flushed.

" You mean, I should have put my foot down then ? But at the time I'd no idea. Hugh takes after his mother—nothing about him to remind you of the Chandlers. I hoped he'd taken after her in every way. From his childhood upwards, there's never been a trace of abnormality about him until now. I couldn't know that—dash it all, there's a trace of insanity in nearly every old family ! "

Poirot said softly : " You have not consulted a doctor ? "

Chandler roared : " No, and I'm not going to ! The boy's safe enough here with me to look after him. They shan't shut him up between four walls like a wild beast. . . ."

" He is safe here, you say. But are _others_ safe ? "

" What do you mean by that ? "

Poirot did not reply. He looked steadily into Admiral Chandler's sad, dark eyes.

The Admiral said bitterly :

" Each man to his trade. You're looking for a criminal ! My boy's _not_ a criminal, M. Poirot."

" Not yet."

" What do you mean by ' not yet ' ? "

" These things increase. . . . Those sheep——"

" Who told you about the sheep ? "

" Diana Maberly. And also your friend Colonel Frobisher."

" George would have done better to keep his mouth shut."

" He is a very old friend of yours, is he not ? "

" My best friend," the Admiral said gruffly.

" And he was a friend of—your wife's, too ? "

Chandler smiled.

" Yes. George was in love with Caroline, I believe. When she was very young. He's never married. I believe that's the reason. Ah well, I was the lucky one—or so I thought. I carried her off—only to lose her."

He sighed and his shoulders sagged.

Poirot said : " Colonel Frobisher was with you when your wife was—drowned ? "

Chandler nodded.

" Yes, he was with us down in Cornwall when it happened. She and I were out in the boat together—he happened to stay at home that day. I've never understood how that boat came to capsize. . . . Must have sprung a sudden leak. We were right out in the bay—strong tide running. I held her up as long as I could. . . ." His voice broke. " Her body was washed up two days later. Thank the Lord we hadn't taken little Hugh out with us ! At least, that's what I thought at the time. Now—well—better for Hugh, poor devil, perhaps, if he *had* been with us. If it had all been finished and done for then. . . ."

Again there came that deep, hopeless sigh.

" We're the last of the Chandlers, M. Poirot. There will be no more Chandlers at Lyde after *we're* gone. When Hugh got engaged to Diana, I hoped—well, it's no good talking of that. Thank God, they didn't marry. That's all I can say ! "


IV


Hercule Poirot sat on a seat in the rose garden. Beside him sat Hugh Chandler. Diana Maberly had just left them.

The young man turned a handsome, tortured face towards his companion.

He said :

" You've got to make her understand, M. Poirot."

He paused for a minute and then went on :

" You see, Di's a fighter. She won't give in. She won't accept what she's darned well got to accept. She—she *will* go on believing that I'm—sane."

" While you yourself are quite certain that you are—pardon me—insane ? "

The young man winced. He said :

" I'm not actually hopelessly off my head yet—but it's getting worse. Diana doesn't know, bless her. She's only seen me when I am—all right."

" And when you are—all wrong, what happens ? "

Hugh Chandler took a long breath. Then he said :

" For one thing—I *dream*. And when I dream, I *am* mad. Last night, for instance—I wasn't a man any longer. I was first of all a bull—a mad bull—racing about in blazing sunlight—tasting dust and blood in my mouth—dust and blood. . . . And then I was a dog—a great slavering dog. I had hydrophobia—children scattered and fled as I came—men tried to shoot me—someone set down a great bowl of water for me and I couldn't drink. *I couldn't drink.* . . ."

He paused. " I woke up. *And I knew it was true.* I went over to the washstand. My mouth was parched—horribly parched—and dry. I was thirsty. But I couldn't drink, M. Poirot. . . . I couldn't swallow. . . . Oh, my God, *I wasn't able to drink.* . . ."

Hercule Poirot made a gentle murmur. Hugh Chandler went on. His hands were clenched on his knees. His face was thrust forward, his eyes were half closed as though he saw something coming towards him.

" And there are things that aren't dreams. Things that I see when I'm wide awake. Spectres, frightful shapes. They leer at me. And sometimes I'm able to fly, to leave my bed, and fly through the air, to ride the winds—and fiends bear me company ! "

" Tcha, tcha," said Hercule Poirot.

It was a gentle, deprecating little noise.

Hugh Chandler turned to him.

" Oh, there isn't any doubt. It's in my blood. It's my family heritage. I can't escape. Thank God I found it out in time ! Before I'd married Diana. Suppose we'd had a child and handed on this frightful thing to him ! "

He laid a hand on Poirot's arm.

" *You must make her understand.* You must tell her. She's got to forget. She's *got* to. There will be someone else someday. There's young Steve Graham—he's crazy about her and he's an awfully good chap. She'd be happy with him—and safe. I want her—to be happy. Graham's hard up, of course, and so are her people, but when I'm gone they'll be all right."

Hercule's voice interrupted him.

" Why will they be ' all right ' when you are gone ? "

Hugh Chandler smiled. It was a gentle, lovable smile. He said :

" There's my mother's money. She was an heiress, you know. It came to me. I've left it all to Diana."

Hercule Poirot sat back in his chair. He said : " Ah ! "

Then he said :

" But you may live to be quite an old man, Mr. Chandler."

Hugh Chandler shook his head. He said sharply :

" No, M. Poirot. I am not going to live to be an old man."

Then he drew back with a sudden shudder.

" My God ! Look ! " He stared over Poirot's shoulder. " *There*—standing by you. . . . it's a skeleton—it's bones are shaking. It's calling to me—beckoning——"

His eyes, the pupils widely dilated, stared into the sunshine. He leaned suddenly sideways as though collapsing.

Then, turning to Poirot, he said in an almost childlike voice :

" You didn't see—*anything* ? "

Slowly, Hercule Poirot shook his head.

Hugh Chandler said hoarsely :

" I don't mind this so much—seeing things. *It's the blood I'm frightened of.* The blood in my room—on my clothes. . . . We had a parrot. *One morning it was there in my room with its throat cut*—and I was lying on the bed with the razor in my hand wet with its blood ! "

He leant closer to Poirot.

" Even just lately things have been killed," he whispered. " All around—in the village—out on the downs. Sheep, young lambs—a collie dog. Father locks me in at night, but sometimes—sometimes—the door's open in the morning. I must have a key hidden somewhere but I don't know where I've hidden it. *I don't know.* It isn't *I* who do these things—it's someone else who comes into me—who takes possession of me —who turns me from a man into a raving monster who wants blood and who can't drink water. . . ."

Suddenly he buried his face in his hands.

After a minute or two, Poirot asked :

" I still do not understand why you have not seen a doctor ? "

Hugh Chandler shook his head. He said :

" Don't you really understand ? Physically I'm strong. I'm

as strong as a bull. I might live for years—years—shut up between four walls ! That I can't face ! It would be better to go out altogether. . . . There are ways, you know. An accident, cleaning a gun. . . . that sort of thing. Diana will understand. . . . I'd rather take my own way out ! ''

He looked defiantly at Poirot, but Poirot did not respond to the challenge. Instead he asked mildly :

" What do you eat and drink ? "

Hugh Chandler flung his head back. He roared with laughter.

" Nightmares after indigestion ? Is that your idea ? "

Poirot merely repeated gently :

" What do you eat and drink ? "

" Just what everybody else eats and drinks."

" No special medicine ? Cachets ? Pills ? "

" Good Lord, no. Do you really think patent pills would cure my trouble ? " He quoted derisively : " ' Canst thou then minister to a mind diseased ? ' "

Hercule Poirot said dryly :

" I am trying to. Does anyone in this house suffer with eye trouble ? "

Hugh Chandler stared at him. He said :

" Father's eyes give him a good deal of trouble. He has to go to an oculist fairly often."

" Ah ! " Poirot meditated for a moment or two. Then he said :

" Colonel Frobisher, I suppose, has spent much of his life in India ? "

" Yes, he was in the Indian Army. He's very keen on India—talks about it a lot—native traditions—and all that."

Poirot murmured " Ah ! " again.

Then he remarked :

" I see that you have cut your chin."

Hugh put his hand up.

" Yes, quite a nasty gash. Father startled me one day when I was shaving. I'm a bit nervy these days, you know. And I've had a bit of a rash over my chin and neck. Makes shaving difficult."

Poirot said :

" You should use a soothing cream."

" Oh, I do.  Uncle George gave me one."

He gave a sudden laugh.

" We're talking like a woman's beauty parlour.  Lotions, soothing creams, patent pills, eye trouble.  What does it all amount to ?  What are you getting at, M. Poirot ? "

Poirot said quietly :

" I am trying to do the best I can for Diana Maberly."

Hugh's mood changed.  His face sobered.  He laid a hand on Poirot's arm.

" Yes, do what you can for her.  Tell her she's got to forget. Tell her that it's no good hoping. . . . Tell her some of the things I've told you. . . . Tell her—oh, tell her for God's sake to keep away from me !  That's the only thing she can do for me now.  Keep away—and try to forget ! "

## V

" Have you courage, Mademoiselle ?  Great courage ?  You will need it."

Diana cried sharply :

" Then it's true.  It's true ?  He *is* mad ? "

Hercule Poirot said :

" I am not an alienist, Mademoiselle.  It is not I who can say, ' This man is mad.  This man is sane.' "

She came closer to him.

" Admiral Chandler thinks Hugh is mad.  George Frobisher thinks he is mad.  Hugh himself thinks he is mad——"

Poirot was watching her.

" And you, Mademoiselle ? "

" I ?  *I say he isn't mad !*  That's why——"

She stopped.

" That is why you came to me ? "

" Yes.  I couldn't have had any other reason for coming to you, could I ? "

" That," said Hercule Poirot, " is exactly what I have been asking myself, Mademoiselle ! "

" I don't understand you."

" Who is Stephen Graham ? "

She stared.

" Stephen Graham ?   Oh, he's—he's just someone."

She caught him by the arm.

" What's in your mind ?   What are you thinking about ?
You just stand there—behind that great moustache of yours—
blinking your eyes in the sunlight, and you don't tell me anything.  You're making me afraid—horribly afraid.  *Why* are
you making me afraid ? "

" Perhaps," said Poirot, " because I am afraid myself."

The deep grey eyes opened wide, stared up at him.  She said
in a whisper :

" What are you afraid of ? "

Hercule Poirot sighed—a deep sigh.  He said :

" It is much easier to catch a murderer than it is to prevent
a murder."

She cried out :  " Murder ?  Don't use that word."

" Nevertheless," said Hercule Poirot, " I do use it."

He altered his tone, speaking quickly and authoritatively.

" Mademoiselle, it is necessary that both you and I should
pass the night at Lyde Manor.  I look to you to arrange the
matter.  You can do that ? "

" I—yes—I suppose so.  But why——? "

" *Because there is no time to lose.*  You have told me that
you have courage.  Prove that courage now.  Do what I ask
and make no questions about it."

She nodded without a word and turned away.

Poirot followed her into the house after the lapse of a moment
or two.  He heard her voice in the library and the voices
of three men.  He passed up the broad staircase.  There was
no one on the upper floor.

He found Hugh Chandler's room easily enough.  In the
corner of the room was a fitted washbasin with hot and cold
water.  Over it, on a glass shelf, were various tubes and pots
and bottles.

Hercule Poirot went quickly and dexterously to work. . . .

What he had to do did not take him long. He was downstairs again in the hall when Diana came out of the library,
looking flushed and rebellious.

" It's all right," she said.

Admiral Chandler drew Poirot into the library and closed
the door.  He said :  " Look here, M. Poirot.  I don't like this."

" What don't you like, Admiral Chandler ? "

" Diana has been insisting that you and she should both spend the night here.    I don't want to be inhospitable——"

" It is not a question of hospitality."

" As I say, I don't like being inhospitable—but frankly, I don't like it, M. Poirot.    I—I don't want it.    And I don't understand the reason for it.    What good can it possibly do ? "

" Shall we say that it is an experiment I am trying ? "

" What kind of an experiment ? "

" That, you will pardon me, is my business. . . ."

" Now look here, M. Poirot, I didn't ask you to come here in the first place——"

Poirot interrupted.

" Believe me, Admiral Chandler, I quite understand and appreciate your point of view.    I am here simply and solely because of the obstinacy of a girl in love.    You have told me certain things.    Colonel Frobisher has told me certain things. Hugh himself has told me certain things.    Now—I want to see for myself."

" Yes, but see *what ?*    I tell you, there's nothing to see !    I lock Hugh into his room every night and that's that."

" And yet—sometimes—he tells me that the door is not locked in the morning ? "

" What's that ? "

" Have you not found the door unlocked yourself ? "

Chandler was frowning.

" I always imagined George had unlocked—what do you mean ? "

" Where do you leave the key—in the lock ? "

" No, I lay it on the chest outside.    I, or George, or Withers, the valet, take it from there in the morning.    We've told Withers it's because Hugh walks in his sleep. . . .    I daresay he knows more—but he's a faithful fellow, been with me for years."

" Is there another key ? "

" Not that I know of."

" One could have been made."

" But who——"

" Your son thinks that he himself has one hidden somewhere, although he is unaware of it in his waking state."

Colonel Frobisher, speaking from the far end of the room, said :

" I don't like it, Charles. . . . The girl——"

Admiral Chandler said quickly : " Just what I was thinking. The girl mustn't come back with you. Come back yourself, if you like."

Poirot said : " Why don't you want Miss Maberly here to-night ? "

Frobisher said in a low voice :

" It's too risky. In these cases——"

He stopped.

Poirot said : " Hugh is devoted to her. . . ."

Chandler cried : " That's just *why* ! Damn it all, man, everything's topsy-turvy where a madman's concerned. Hugh knows that himself. Diana mustn't come here."

" As to that," said Poirot, " Diana must decide for herself."

He went out of the library. Diana was waiting outside in the car. She called out, " We'll get what we want for the night and be back in time for dinner."

As they drove down the long drive, Poirot repeated to her the conversation he had just held with the Admiral and Colonel Frobisher. She laughed scornfully.

" Do they think Hugh would hurt *me* ? "

By way of reply, Poirot asked her if she would mind stopping at the chemist's in the village. He had forgotten, he said, to pack a toothbrush.

The chemist's shop was in the middle of the peaceful village street. Diana waited outside in the car. It struck her that Hercule Poirot was a long time choosing a toothbrush. . . .


## VI


In the big bedroom with the heavy Elizabethan, oak furniture, Hercule Poirot sat and waited. There was nothing to do but wait. All his arrangements were made.

It was towards early morning that the summons came.

At the sound of footsteps outside, Poirot drew back the bolt and opened the door. There were two men in the passage outside—two middle-aged men who looked older than their years. The Admiral was stern-faced and grim, Colonel Frobisher twitched and trembled.

Chandler said simply :

" Will you come with us, M. Poirot ? "

There was a huddled figure lying outside Diana Maberly's bedroom door. The light fell on a rumpled, tawny head. Hugh Chandler lay there breathing stertoriously. He was in his dressing-gown and slippers. In his right hand was a sharply-curved, shining knife. Not all of it was shining—here and there it was obscured by red glistening patches.

Hercule Poirot exclaimed softly :

" *Mon Dieu !* "

Frobisher said sharply :

" She's all right. He hasn't touched her." He raised his voice and called : " Diana ! It's us ! Let us in ! "

Poirot heard the Admiral groan and mutter under his breath :

" My boy. My poor boy."

There was a sound of bolts being drawn. The door opened and Diana stood there. Her face was dead white.

She faltered out :

" *What's happened ?* There was someone—trying to get in—I heard them—feeling the door—the handle—scratching on the panels—Oh ! it was awful. . . . *like an animal.* . . ."

Frobisher said sharply :

" Thank God your door was locked ! "

" M. Poirot told me to lock it."

Poirot said :

" Lift him up and bring him inside."

The two men stooped and raised the unconscious man. Diana caught her breath with a little gasp as they passed her.

" Hugh ? Is it Hugh ? What's that—on his hands ? "

Hugh Chandler's hands were sticky and wet with a brownish, red stain.

Diana breathed : " Is that blood ? "

Poirot looked inquiringly at the two men. The Admiral nodded. He said :

" Not human, thank God ! A cat ! I found it downstairs in the hall. Throat cut. Afterwards he must have come up here——"

" *Here ?* " Diana's voice was low with horror. " To *me ?* "

The man on the chair stirred—muttered. They watched him, fascinated. Hugh Chandler sat up. He blinked.

" Hallo," his voice was dazed—hoarse. " What's happened? Why am I——? "

He stopped. He was staring at the knife which he held still clasped in his hand.

He said in a slow, thick voice :

" *What have I done ?* "

His eyes went from one to the other. They rested at last on Diana shrinking back against the wall. He said quietly :

" Did I attack Diana ? "

His father shook his head. Hugh said :

" *Tell me what has happened ?* I've got to know ! "

They told him—told him unwillingly—haltingly. His quiet perseverance drew it out of them.

Outside the window the sun was coming up. Hercule Poirot drew a curtain aside. The radiance of the dawn came into the room.

Hugh Chandler's face was composed, his voice was steady.

He said :

" I see."

Then he got up. He smiled and stretched himself. His voice was quite natural as he said :

" Beautiful morning, what ? Think I'll go out in the woods and try to get a rabbit."

He went out of the room and left them staring after him.

Then the Admiral started forward. Frobisher caught him by the arm.

" No, Charles, no. It's the best way—for him, poor devil, if for nobody else."

Diana had thrown herself sobbing on the bed.

Admiral Chandler said, his voice coming unevenly :

" You're right, George—you're right, I know. The boy's got guts. . . ."

Frobisher said, and his voice, too, was broken :

" *He's a man. . . .*"

There was a moment's silence and then Chandler said :

" Damn it, where's that cursed foreigner ? "

## VII

In the gun-room, Hugh Chandler had lifted his gun from the rack and was in the act of loading it when Hercule Poirot's hand fell on his shoulder.

Hercule Poirot's voice said one word and said it with a strange authority. He said:

" *No!* "

Hugh Chandler stared at him. He said in a thick, angry voice: " Take your hands off me. Don't interfere. *There's going to be an accident,* I tell you. It's the only way out."

Again Hercule Poirot repeated that one word:

" *No.* "

" Don't you realise that if it hadn't been for the accident of her door being locked, I would have cut Diana's throat— Diana's! —with that knife? "

" I realise nothing of the kind. You would not have killed Miss Maberly."

" I killed the cat, didn't I ? "

" No, you did not kill the cat. You did not kill the parrot. You did not kill the sheep."

Hugh stared at him. He demanded :

" Are *you* mad, or am I ? "

Hercule Poirot replied :

" *Neither of us is mad.* "

It was at that moment that Admiral Chandler and Colonel Frobisher came in. Behind them came Diana.

Hugh Chandler said in a weak, dazed voice:

" This chap says I'm not mad. . . ."

Hercule Poirot said :

" I am happy to tell you that you are entirely and completely sane."

Hugh laughed. It was a laugh such as a lunatic might popularly be supposed to give.

" That's damned funny ! It's sane, is it, to cut the throats of sheep and other animals ? I was sane, was I, when I killed that parrot ? And the cat to-night ? "

" I tell you you did not kill the sheep—or the parrot—or the cat."

" Then who did ? "

" *Someone who has had at heart the sole object of proving you insane.* On each occasion you were given a heavy soporific and a blood-stained knife or razor was planted by you. It was someone else whose bloody hands were washed in your basin."

" But why ? "

" In order that you should do what you were just about to do when I stopped you."

Hugh stared. Poirot turned to Colonel Frobisher.

" Colonel Frobisher, you lived for many years in India. Did you never come across cases where persons were deliberately driven mad by the administration of drugs ? "

Colonel Frobisher's face lit up. He said :

" Never came across a case myself, but I've heard of them often enough. Datura poisoning. It ends by driving a person insane."

" Exactly. Well, the active principle of the datura is very closely allied to, if it is not actually, the alkaloid atropine—which is also obtained from belladonna or deadly nightshade. Belladonna preparations are fairly common and atropine sulphate itself is prescribed freely for eye treatments. By duplicating a prescription and getting it made up in different places a large quantity of the poison could be obtained without arousing suspicion. The alkaloid could be extracted from it and then introduced into, say—a soothing shaving cream. Applied externally it would cause a rash, this would soon lead to abrasions in shaving and thus the drug would be continually entering the system. It would produce certain symptoms —dryness of the mouth and throat, difficulty in swallowing, hallucinations, double vision—*all the symptoms, in fact, which Mr. Chandler has experienced.*"

He turned to the young man.

" And to remove the last doubt from your mind, I will tell you that that is not a supposition but a fact. *Your shaving cream was heavily impregnated with atropine sulphate.* I took a sample and had it tested."

White, shaking, Hugh asked :

" *Who did it ?* Why ? "

Hercule Poirot said :

" That is what I have been studying ever since I arrived

here. I have been looking for a motive for murder. Diana
Maberly gained financially by your death, but I did not consider her seriously——"

Hugh Chandler flashed out :

" I should hope not ! "

" I envisaged another possible motive. The eternal triangle ;
two men and a woman. Colonel Frobisher had been in love
with your mother, Admiral Chandler married her."

Admiral Chandler cried out :

" George ?  George !  I won't believe it."

Hugh said in an incredulous voice :

" Do you mean that hatred could go on—to a *son* ? "

Hercule Poirot said :

" Under certain circumstances, yes."

Frobisher cried out :

" It's a damned lie !  Don't believe him, Charles."

Chandler shrank away from him. He muttered to himself :

" The datura. . . . India—yes, I see. . . . And we'd never
suspect poison—not with madness in the family already. . . ."

" *Mais oui !* " Hercule Poirot's voice rose high and shrill.
" *Madness in the family*. A madman—bent on revenge—
cunning—as madmen are, concealing his madness for years."
He whirled round on Frobisher.  " *Mon Dieu*, you *must* have
known, you *must* have suspected, that Hugh was *your* son ?
Why did you never tell him so ? "

Frobisher stammered, gulped.

" I didn't know. I couldn't be sure. . . . You see, Caroline
came to me once—she was frightened of something—in great
trouble. I don't know, I never have known, what it was all
about. She—I—we lost our heads. Afterwards I went away
at once—it was the only thing to be done, we both knew we'd
got to play the game. I—well, I wondered, but I couldn't be
sure. Caroline never said anything that led me to think Hugh
*was* my son. And then when this—this streak of madness
appeared, it settled things definitely, I thought."

Poirot said :

" Yes, it settled things !  *You* could not see the way the
boy has of thrusting out his face and bringing down his brows—
a trick he inherited from *you*. *But Charles Chandler saw it*.
Saw it years ago—and learnt the truth from his wife. I think

she was afraid of him—he'd begun to show her the mad streak —that was what drove her into your arms—you whom she had always loved. Charles Chandler planned his revenge. His wife died in a boating accident. He and she were out in the boat alone and he knows how that accident came about. Then he settled down to feed his concentrated hatred against the boy who bore his name but who was not his son. Your Indian stories put the idea of datura poisoning into his head. Hugh should be slowly driven mad. Driven to the stage where he would take his own life in despair. The blood lust was Admiral Chandler's, not Hugh's. It was Charles Chandler who was driven to cut the throats of sheep in lonely fields. But it was Hugh who was to pay the penalty !

" Do you know when I suspected ? When Admiral Chandler was so averse to his son seeing a doctor. For Hugh to object was natural enough. But the father ! There might be treatment which would save his son—there were a hundred reasons why *he* should seek to have a doctor's opinion. But no, a doctor must not be allowed to see Hugh Chandler—in case a doctor should discover that *Hugh was sane* ! "

Hugh said very quietly :

" Sane . . . I *am* sane ? "

He took a step towards Diana. Frobisher said in a gruff voice :

" You're sane enough. There's no taint in *our* family."

Diana said :

" *Hugh* . . ."

Admiral Chandler picked up Hugh's gun. He said :

" All a lot of nonsense ! Think I'll go and see if I can get a rabbit——"

Frobisher started forward, but the hand of Hercule Poirot restrained him. Poirot said :

" You said yourself—just now—that it was the best way. . . ."

Hugh and Diana had gone from the room.

The two men, the Englishman and the Belgian, watched the last of the Chandlers cross the Park and go up into the woods.

Presently, they heard a shot. . . .

# VIII

# THE HORSES OF DIOMEDES

## I

THE TELEPHONE RANG.

" Hallo, Poirot, is that you ? "

Hercule Poirot recognised the voice as that of young Dr. Stoddart. He liked Michael Stoddart, liked the shy friendliness of his grin, was amused by his naïve interest in crime, and respected him as a hard-working and shrewd man in his chosen profession.

" I don't like bothering you——" the voice went on and hesitated.

" But something is bothering *you* ? " suggested Hercule Poirot acutely.

" Exactly." Michael Stoddart's voice sounded relieved. " Hit it in one ! "

" *Eh bien,* what can I do for you, my friend ? "

Stoddart sounded diffident. He stammered a little when he answered.

" I suppose it would be awful c-c-cheek if I asked you to come round at this time of night. . . . B-b-but I'm in a bit of a j-j-jam."

" Certainly I will come. To your house ? "

" No—as a matter of fact I'm at the Mews that runs along behind. Conningby Mews. The number is 17. Could you really come ? I'd be no end grateful."

" I arrive immediately," replied Hercule Poirot.

## II

Hercule Poirot walked along the dark Mews looking up at the numbers. It was past one o'clock in the morning and for the most part the Mews appeared to have gone to bed, though there were still lights in one or two windows.

As he reached 17, its door opened and Dr. Stoddart stood looking out.

"Good man!" he said. "Come up, will you?"

A small ladder-like stairway led to the upper floor. Here, on the right, was a fairly big room, furnished with divans, rugs, triangular silver cushions and large numbers of bottles and glasses.

Everything was more or less in confusion, cigarette ends were everywhere and there were many broken glasses.

"Ha!" said Hercule Poirot. "*Mon cher Watson*, I deduce that there has been here a party!"

"There's been a party all right," said Stoddart grimly. "Some party, I should say!"

"You did not, then, attend it yourself?"

"No, I'm here strictly in my professional capacity."

"What happened?"

Stoddart said:

"This place belongs to a woman called Patience Grace— Mrs. Patience Grace."

"It sounds," said Poirot, "a charming old-world name."

"There's nothing charming or old-world about Mrs. Grace. She's good-looking in a tough sort of way. She's got through a couple of husbands, and now she's got a boy friend whom she suspects of trying to run out on her. They started this party on drink and they finished it on dope—cocaine, to be exact. Cocaine is stuff that starts off making you feel just grand and with everything in the garden lovely. It peps you up and you feel you can do twice as much as you usually do. Take too much of it and you get violent mental excitement, delusions and delirium. Mrs. Grace had a violent quarrel with her boy friend, an unpleasant person by the name of Hawker. Result, he walked out on her then and there, and she leaned out of the window and took a pot-shot at him with a brand-new revolver that someone had been fool enough to give her."

Hercule Poirot's eyebrows rose.

"Did she hit him?"

"Not she! Bullet went several yards wide, I should say. What she *did* hit was a miserable loafer who was creeping along the Mews looking in the dustbins. Got him through the fleshy part of the arm. He raised Hell, of course, and the crowd hustled him in here quick, got the wind-up with all the blood that was spilling out of him and came round and got me."

" Yes ? "

" I patched him up all right. It wasn't serious. Then one or two of the men got busy on him and in the end he consented to accept a couple of five pound notes and say no more about it. Suited him all right, poor devil. Marvellous stroke of luck."

" And you ? "

" I had a bit more work to do. Mrs. Grace herself was in raving hysterics by that time. I gave her a shot of something and packed her off to bed. There was another girl who'd more or less passed out—quite young she was, and I attended to her too. By that time everyone was slinking off as fast as they could leave."

He paused.

" And then," said Poirot, " you had time to think over the situation."

" Exactly," said Stoddart. " If it was an ordinary drunken binge, well, that would be the end of it. But dope's different."

" You are quite sure of your facts ? "

" Oh, absolutely. No mistaking it. It's cocaine all right. I found some in a lacquer box—they snuff it up, you know. Question is, where does it come from ? I remembered that you'd been talking the other day about a big, new wave of drug-taking and the increase of drug addicts."

Hercule Poirot nodded. He said :

" The police will be interested in this party to-night."

Michael Stoddart said unhappily :

" That's just it. . . ."

Poirot looked at him with suddenly awakened interest. He said :

" But you—you are not very anxious that the police should be interested ? "

Michael Stoddart mumbled :

" Innocent people get mixed up in things. . . . hard lines on them."

" Is it Mrs. Patience Grace for whom you are so solicitous ? "

" Good Lord, no. She's as hard-boiled as they make them ! "

Hercule Poirot said gently :

" It is, then, the other one—the girl ? "

Dr. Stoddart said :

" Of course, she's hard-boiled, too, in a way. I mean, she'd *describe* herself as hard-boiled. But she's really just very young—a bit wild and all that—but it's just kid foolishness. She gets mixed up in a racket like this because she thinks it's smart or modern or something like that."

A faint smile came to Poirot's lips. He said softly :

" This girl, you have met her before to-night ? "

Michael Stoddart nodded. He looked very young and embarrassed.

" Ran across her in Mertonshire. At the Hunt Ball. Her father's a retired General—blood and thunder, shoot 'em down —pukka Sahib—all that sort of thing. There are four daughters and they are all a bit wild—driven to it with a father like that, I should say. And it's a bad part of the county where they live—armaments works nearby and a lot of money—none of the old-fashioned country feeling—a rich crowd and most of them pretty vicious. The girls have got in with a bad set."

Hercule Poirot looked at him thoughtfully for some minutes. Then he said :

" I perceive now why you desired my presence. You want me to take the affair in hand ? "

" Would you ? I feel I ought to do something about it —but I confess I'd like to keep Sheila Grant out of the limelight if I could."

" That can be managed, I fancy. I should like to see the young lady."

" Come along."

He led the way out of the room. A voice called fretfully from a door opposite.

" Doctor—for God's sake, doctor, I'm going crazy."

Stoddart went into the room. Poirot followed. It was a bedroom in a complete state of chaos—powder spilled on the floor—pots and jars everywhere, clothes flung about. On the bed was a woman with unnaturally blonde hair and a vacant, vicious face. She called out :

" I've got insects crawling all over me. . . . I have. I swear I have. I'm going mad. . . . For God's sake, give me a shot of something."

Dr. Stoddart stood by the bed, his tone was soothing—professional.

Hercule Poirot went quietly out of the room. There was another door opposite him. He opened that.

It was a tiny room—a mere slip of a room—plainly furnished. On the bed a slim, girlish figure lay motionless.

Hercule Poirot tip-toed to the side of the bed and looked down upon the girl.

Dark hair, a long, pale face—and—yes, young—very young. . . .

A gleam of white showed between the girl's lids. Her eyes opened, startled, frightened eyes. She stared, sat up, tossing her head in an effort to throw back the thick mane of blue-black hair. She looked like a frightened filly—she shrank away a little—as a wild animal shrinks when it is suspicious of a stranger who offers it food.

She said—and her voice was young and thin and abrupt :

" Who the hell are you ? "

" Do not be afraid, Mademoiselle."

" Where's Dr. Stoddart ? "

That young man came into the room at that minute. The girl said with a note of relief in her voice :

" Oh ! there you are ! Who's this ? "

" This is a friend of mine, Sheila. How are you feeling now ? "

The girl said :

" Awful. Lousy. . . . Why did I take that foul stuff ? "

Stoddart said dryly :

" I shouldn't do it again, if I were you."

" I—I shan't."

Hercule Poirot said :

" Who gave it to you ? "

Her eyes widened, her upper lip twitched a little. She said :

" It was here—at the party. We all tried it. It—it was wonderful at first."

Hercule Poirot said gently :

" But who brought it here ? "

She shook her head.

" I don't know. . . . It might have been Tony—Tony Hawker. But I don't really know anything about it."

Poirot said gently :

" Is it the first time you have taken cocaine, Mademoiselle ? "

She nodded.

" You'd better make it the last," said Stoddart brusquely.

" Yes—I suppose so—but it *was* rather marvellous."

" Now look here, Sheila Grant," said Stoddart. " I'm a doctor and I know what I'm talking about. Once start this drug-taking racket and you'll land yourself in unbelievable misery. I've seen some and I know. Drugs ruin people, body and soul. Drink's a gentle little picnic compared to drugs. Cut it right out from this minute. Believe me, it isn't funny ! What do you think your father would say to to-night's business ? "

" Father ? " Sheila Grant's voice rose. " Father ? " She began to laugh. " I can just see Father's face ! He mustn't know about it. He'd have seven fits ! "

" And quite right too," said Stoddart.

" Doctor—doctor——" the long wail of Mrs. Grace's voice came from the other room.

Stoddart muttered something uncomplimentary under his breath and went out of the room.

Sheila Grant stared at Poirot again. She was puzzled. She said :

" Who are you really ?  You weren't at the party."

" No, I was not at the party. I am a friend of Dr. Stoddart's."

" You're a doctor, too ?  You don't look like a doctor."

" My name," said Poirot, contriving as usual to make the simple statement sound like the curtain of the first act of a play, " my name is Hercule Poirot. . . ."

The statement did not fail of its effect. Occasionally Poirot was distressed to find that a callous younger generation had never heard of him.

But it was evident that Sheila Grant had heard of him. She was flabbergasted—dumbfounded. She stared and stared. . . .

## III

It has been said, with or without justification for the statement, that everyone has an aunt in Torquay.

It has also been said that everyone has at least a second
cousin in Mertonshire. Mertonshire is a reasonable distance
from London, it has hunting, shooting and fishing, it has
several very picturesque but slightly self-conscious villages,
it has a good system of railways and a new arterial road
facilitates motoring to and from the metropolis. Servants
object to it less than they do to other, more rural, portions
of the British Isles. As a result, it is practically impossible to
live in Mertonshire unless you have an income that runs into
four figures, and what with income-tax and one thing and another, five figures is better.

Hercule Poirot, being a foreigner, had no second cousins in
the county, but he had acquired by now a large circle of
friends and he had no difficulty in getting himself invited for
a visit in that part of the world. He had, moreover, selected
as hostess a dear lady whose chief delight was exercising her
tongue on the subject of her neighbours—the only drawback
being that Poirot had to submit to hearing a great deal about
people in whom he had no interest whatever, before coming
to the subject of the people he was interested in.

" The Grants ? Oh yes, there are four of them. Four girls.
I don't wonder the poor General can't control them. What
can a man do with four girls ? " Lady Carmichael's hands
flew up eloquently. Poirot said : " What indeed ? " and the
lady continued:

" Used to be a great disciplinarian in his regiment, so he
told me. But those girls defeat him. Not like when I was
young. Old Colonel Sandys was such a martinet, I remember,
that his poor daughters——"

(Long excursion into the trials of the Sandys girls and other
friends of Lady Carmichael's youth.)

" Mind you," said Lady Carmichael, reverting to her first
theme. " I don't say there's anything really wrong about
those girls. Just high spirits—and getting in with an undesirable set. It's not what it used to be down here. The oddest

people come here. There's no what you might call ' county '
left. It's all money, money, money nowadays. And you do
hear the oddest stories! Who did you say? Anthony Hawker?
Oh yes, I know him. What I call a very unpleasant young
man. But apparently rolling in money. He comes down here
to hunt—and he gives parties—very lavish parties—and rather
peculiar parties, too, if one is to believe all one is told—not
that I ever do, because I do think people are so ill-natured.
They always believe the worst. You know, it's become quite
a fashion to say a person drinks or takes drugs. Somebody
said to me the other day that young girls were natural in-
ebriates, and I really don't think that was a nice thing to say
at all. And if anyone's at all peculiar or vague in their manner,
everyone says ' drugs ' and that's unfair, too. They say it
about Mrs. Larkin and though I don't care for the woman, I
do really think it's nothing more than absent-mindedness.
She's a great friend of your Anthony Hawker, and that's
why, if you ask me, she's so down on the Grant girls—says
they're man-eaters! I dare say they do run after men a bit,
but why not? It's natural, after all. And they're good-
looking pieces, every one of them."

Poirot interjected a question.

" Mrs. Larkin? My dear man, it's no good asking me *who*
she is? Who's anybody nowadays? They say she rides well
and she's obviously well off. Husband was something in the
city. He's dead, not divorced. She's not been here very long,
came here just after the Grants did. I've always thought
she——"

Old Lady Carmichael stopped. Her mouth opened, her
eyes bulged. Leaning forward she struck Poirot a sharp blow
across the knuckles with a paper-cutter she was holding.
Disregarding his wince of pain she exclaimed excitedly:

" Why, of course! So *that's* why you're down here! You
nasty, deceitful creature, I insist on your telling me all about
it."

" But what is it I am to tell you all about? "

Lady Carmichael aimed another playful blow which Poirot
avoided deftly.

" Don't be an oyster, Hercule Poirot! I can see your
moustaches quivering. Of course, it's *crime* brings you down

here—and you're just pumping me shamelessly ! Now let me see, can it be murder ? Who's died lately ? Only old Louisa Gilmore and she was eighty-five and had dropsy too. Can't be her. Poor Leo Staverton broke his neck in the hunting-field and he's all done up in plaster—that can't be it. Perhaps it isn't murder. What a pity ! I can't remember any special jewel robberies lately. . . . Perhaps it's just a criminal you're tracking down. . . . Is it Beryl Larkin ? *Did* she poison her husband ? Perhaps it's remorse that makes her so vague."

"Madame, Madame," cried Hercule Poirot. "You go too fast."

"Nonsense. You're up to something, Hercule Poirot."

"Are you acquainted with the classics, Madame ? "

"What have the classics got to do with it ? "

"They have this to do with it. I emulate my great pre-decessor Hercules. One of the Labours of Hercules was the taming of the wild horses of Diomedes."

"Don't tell me you came down here to train horses—at your age—and always wearing patent-leather shoes ! You don't look to me as though you'd ever been on a horse in your life ! "

"The horses, Madame, are symbolic. They were the wild horses who ate human flesh."

"How very unpleasant of them. I always do think these ancient Greeks and Romans are very unpleasant. I can't think why clergymen are so fond of quoting from the classics —for one thing one never understands what they mean and it always seems to me that the whole subject matter of the classics is very unsuitable for clergymen. So much incest, and all those statues with nothing on—not that I mind that myself but you know what clergymen are—quite upset if girls come to church with no stockings on—let me see, where was I ? "

"I am not quite sure."

"I suppose, you wretch, you just won't tell me if Mrs. Larkin murdered her husband ? Or perhaps Anthony Hawker is the Brighton trunk murderer ? "

She looked at him hopefully, but Hercule Poirot's face remained impassive.

"It might be forgery," speculated Lady Carmichael. "I did see Mrs. Larkin in the bank the other morning and she'd

just cashed a fifty pound cheque to self—it seemed to me at
the time a lot of money to want in cash. Oh no, that's the
wrong way round—if she was a forger she would be paying it
in, wouldn't she ? Hercule Poirot, if you sit there looking like
an owl and saying nothing, I shall throw something at you."

"You must have a little patience," said Hercule Poirot.

IV

Ashley Lodge, the residence of General Grant, was not a
large house. It was situated on the side of a hill, had good
stables, and a straggling, rather neglected, garden.

Inside, it was what a house agent would have described as
"fully furnished." Cross-legged Buddhas leered down from
convenient niches, brass Benares trays and tables encumbered
the floor space. Processional elephants garnished the mantel-
pieces and more tortured brasswork adorned the walls.

In the midst of this Anglo-Indian home from home, General
Grant was ensconced in a large, shabby armchair with his leg,
swathed in bandages, reposing on another chair.

"Gout," he explained. "Ever had the gout, Mr.—er—
Poirot ? Makes a feller damned bad tempered ! All my
father's fault. Drank port all his life—so did my grandfather.
It's played the deuce with me. Have a drink ? Ring that
bell, will you, for that feller of mine ? "

A turbaned servant appeared. General Grant addressed
him as Abdul and ordered him to bring the whisky and soda.
When it came he poured out such a generous portion that
Poirot was moved to protest.

"Can't join you, I'm afraid, Mr. Poirot." The General
eyed the tantalus sadly. "My doctor wallah says it's poison
to me to touch the stuff. Don't suppose he knows for a minute.
Ignorant chaps doctors. Spoil-sports. Enjoy knocking a man
off his food and drink and putting him on some pap like
steamed fish. Steamed fish—pah ! "

In his indignation the General incautiously moved his bad
foot and uttered a yelp of agony at the twinge that ensued.

He apologised for his language.

"Like a bear with a sore head, that's what I am. My girls

give me a wide berth when I've got an attack of gout. Don't know that I blame them. You've met one of 'em, I hear."

" I have had that pleasure, yes. You have several daughters, have you not ? "

" Four," said the General gloomily. " Not a boy amongst 'em. Four blinking girls. Bit of a thought, these days."

" They are all four very charming, I hear ? "

" Not too bad—not too bad. Mind you, I never know what they're up to. You can't control girls nowadays. Lax times— too much laxity everywhere. What can a man do ? Can't lock 'em up, can I ? "

" They are popular in the neighbourhood, I gather."

" Some of the old cats don't like 'em," said General Grant. " A good deal of mutton dressed as lamb round here. A man's got to be careful. One of these blue-eyed widows nearly caught me—used to come round here purring like a kitten. ' *Poor General Grant—you must have had such an interesting life.*' " The General winked and placed one finger against his nose. " A little bit too obvious, Mr. Poirot. Oh well, take it all round, I suppose it's not a bad part of the world. A bit go ahead and noisy for my taste. I liked the country when it was the country—not all this motoring and jazz and that blasted, eternal radio. I won't have one here and the girls know it. A man's got a right to a little peace in his own home."

Gently Poirot led the conversation round to Anthony Hawker.

" Hawker ? Hawker ? Don't know him. Yes, I do, though. Nasty looking fellow with his eyes too close together. Never trust a man who can't look you in the face."

" He is a friend, is he not, of your daughter Sheila's ? "

" Sheila ? Wasn't aware of it. Girls never tell me any-thing." The bushy eyebrows came down over the nose—the piercing, blue eyes looked out of the red face straight into Hercule Poirot's. " Look here, Mr. Poirot, what's all this about ? Mind telling me what you've come to see me about ? "

Poirot said slowly :

" That would be difficult—perhaps I hardly know myself. I would say only this : your daughter Sheila—perhaps all your daughters—have made some undesirable friends."

" Got into a bad set, have they ? I was a bit afraid of that.

One hears a word dropped here and there." He looked patheti-
cally at Poirot. "But what am I to do, Mr. Poirot? What
am I to do?"

Poirot shook his head perplexedly.

General Grant went on :

"What's wrong with the bunch they're running with?"

Poirot replied by another question.

"Have you noticed, General Grant, that any of your
daughters have been moody, excited—then depressed—nervy
—uncertain in their tempers?"

"Damme, sir, you're talking like a patent medicine. No,
I haven't noticed anything of the kind."

"That is fortunate," said Poirot gravely.

"What the devil is the meaning of all this, sir?"

"Drugs!"

"WHAT!"

The word came in a roar.

Poirot said :

"An attempt is being made to induce your daughter Sheila
to become a drug addict. The cocaine habit is very quickly
formed. A week or two will suffice. Once the habit is formed,
an addict will pay anything, do anything, to get a further
supply of the drug. You can realise what a rich haul the person
who peddles that drug can make."

He listened in silence to the spluttering, wrathful blas-
phemies that poured from the old man's lips. Then, as the
fires died down, with a final choice description of exactly what
he, the General, would do to the blinkety blinkety son of a
blank when he got hold of him, Hercule Poirot said :

"We have first, as your so admirable Mrs. Beeton says,
to catch the hare. Once we have caught our drug pedlar, I
will turn him over to you with the greatest pleasure,
General."

He got up, tripped over a heavily-carved, small table, regained his balance with a clutch at the General, murmured :

"A thousand pardons, and may I beg of you, General—
you understand, *beg* of you—to say nothing whatever about
all this to your daughters."

"What? I'll have the truth out of them, that's what I'll
have!"

" That is exactly what you will not have. All you will get is a lie."

" But damme, sir——"

" I assure you, General Grant, you *must* hold your tongue. That is vital—you understand ?  *Vital !* "

" Oh well, have it your own way," growled the old soldier. He was mastered but not convinced.

Hercule Poirot picked his way carefully through the Benares brass and went out.


## v


Mrs. Larkin's room was full of people.

Mrs. Larkin herself was mixing cocktails at a side table. She was a tall woman with pale auburn hair rolled into the back of her neck. Her eyes were greenish-grey with big, black pupils. She moved easily, with a kind of sinister grace. She looked as though she were in the early thirties. Only a close scrutiny revealed the lines at the corners of the eyes and hinted that she was ten years older than her looks.

Hercule Poirot had been brought here by a brisk, middle-aged woman, a friend of Lady Carmichael's. He found himself given a cocktail and further directed to take one to a girl sitting in the window. The girl was small and fair—her face was pink and white and suspiciously angelic. Her eyes, Hercule Poirot noticed at once, were alert and suspicious.

He said :

" To your continued good health, Mademoiselle."

She nodded and drank. Then she said abruptly :

" You know my sister."

" Your sister ?  Ah, you are then one of the Miss Grants ? "

" I'm Pam Grant."

" And where is your sister to-day ? "

" She's out hunting. Ought to be back soon."

" I met your sister in London."

" I know."

" She told you ? "

Pam Grant nodded. She said abruptly :

" Was Sheila in a jam ? "

" So she did not tell you everything ? "

The girl shook her head. She asked :

" Was Tony Hawker there ? "

Before Poirot could answer, the door opened and Hawker and Sheila Grant came in. They were in hunting kit and Sheila had a streak of mud on her cheek.

" Hullo, people, we've come in for a drink. Tony's flask is dry."

Poirot murmured :

" Talk of the angels——"

Pam Grant snapped :

" Devils, you mean."

Poirot said sharply :

" Is it like that ? "

Beryl Larkin had come forward. She said :

" Here you are, Tony. Tell me about the run ? Did you draw Gelert's Copse ? "

She drew him away skilfully to a sofa near the fireplace. Poirot saw him turn his head and glance at Sheila before he went.

Sheila had seen Poirot. She hesitated a minute, then came over to the two in the window. She said abruptly :

" So it *was* you who came to the house yesterday ? "

" Did your father tell you ? "

She shook her head.

" Abdul described you. I—guessed."

Pam exclaimed : " You went to see Father ? "

Poirot said :

" Ah—yes. We have—some mutual friends."

Pam said sharply :

" I don't believe it."

" What do you not believe ? That your father and I could have a mutual friend ? "

The girl flushed.

" Don't be stupid. I meant—that wasn't really your reason——"

She turned on her sister.

" Why don't you say something, Sheila ? "

Sheila started. She said :

" It wasn't—it wasn't anything to do with Tony Hawker ? "

" Why should it be ? " asked Poirot.

Sheila flushed and went back across the room to the others.

Pam said with sudden vehemence but in a lowered voice :

" I don't like Tony Hawker. There—there's something sinister about him—and about her—Mrs. Larkin, I mean. Look at them now."

Poirot followed her glance.

Hawker's head was close to that of his hostess. He appeared to be soothing her. Her voice rose for a minute.

"—but I can't wait. I want it *now* ! "

Poirot said with a little smile :

" *Les femmes*—whatever it is—they always want it now, do they not ? "

But Pam Grant did not respond. Her face was cast down. She was nervously pleating and repleating her tweed skirt.

Poirot murmured conversationally :

" You are quite a different type from your sister, Mademoiselle."

She flung her head up, impatient of banalities. She said :

" M. Poirot. What's the stuff Tony's been giving Sheila ? What is it that's been making her—different ? "

He looked straight at her. He asked :

" Have you ever taken cocaine, Miss Grant ? "

She shook her head.

" Oh no ! So that's it ? Cocaine ? But isn't that very dangerous ? "

Sheila Grant had come over to them, a fresh drink in her hand. She said :

" What's dangerous ? "

Poirot said :

" We are talking of the effects of drug-taking. Of the slow death of the mind and spirit—the destroying of all that is true and good in a human being."

Sheila Grant caught her breath. The drink in her hand swayed and spilled on the floor. Poirot went on :

" Dr. Stoddart has, I think, made clear to you just what that death in life entails. It is so easily done—so hard to undo. The person who deliberately profits from the degradation and misery of other people is a vampire preying on flesh and blood."

He turned away. Behind him he heard Pam Grant's voice

say: "Sheila!" and caught a whisper—a faint whisper—from Sheila Grant. It was so low he hardly heard it.

"*The flask* . . ."

Hercule Poirot said good-bye to Mrs. Larkin and went out into the hall. On the hall table was a hunting flask lying with a crop and a hat. Poirot picked it up. There were initials on it: A. H.

Poirot murmured to himself:

"Tony's flask is empty?"

He shook it gently. There was no sound of liquor. He unscrewed the top.

Tony Hawker's flask was not empty. It was full—of white powder. . . .

## VI

Hercule Poirot stood on the terrace of Lady Carmichael's house and pleaded with a girl.

He said:

"You are very young, Mademoiselle. It is my belief that you have not known, not really known, what it is you and your sisters have been doing. You have been feeding, like the mares of Diomedes, on human flesh."

Sheila shuddered and gave a sob. She said:

"It sounds horrible, put like that. And yet it's true! I never realised it until that evening in London when Dr. Stoddart talked to me. He was so grave—so sincere. I saw then what an awful thing it was I had been doing. . . . Before that I thought it was—Oh! rather like drink after hours—something people would pay to get, but not something that really *mattered* very much!"

Poirot said:

"And now?"

Sheila Grant said:

"I'll do anything you say. I—I'll talk to the others," she added. . . . "I don't suppose Dr. Stoddart will ever speak to me again. . . ."

"On the contrary," said Poirot. "Both Dr. Stoddart and I are prepared to help you in every way in our power to start afresh. You can trust us. But one thing must be done. There is one person who must be destroyed—destroyed utterly, and only you and your sisters can destroy him. It is your evidence and your evidence alone that will convict him."

" You mean—my father ? "

" Not your father, Mademoiselle. Did I not tell you that Hercule Poirot knows everything ? Your photograph was easily recognised in official quarters. You are Sheila Kelly— a persistent young shoplifter who was sent to a reformatory some years ago. When you came out of that reformatory, you were approached by the man who calls himself General Grant and offered this post—the post of a ' daughter '. There would be plenty of money, plenty of fun, a good time. All you had to do was to introduce the ' snuff ' to your friends, always pretending that someone else had given it to you. Your ' sisters ' were in the same case as yourself."

He paused and said :

" Come now, Mademoiselle—this man must be exposed and sentenced. After that——"

" Yes, afterwards ? "

Poirot coughed. He said with a smile :

" You shall be dedicated to the service of the Gods. . . ."


## VII

Michael Stoddart stared at Poirot in amazement. He said :
" General Grant ? General *Grant* ? "

" Precisely, *mon cher*. The whole *mise en scène,* you know, was what you would call ' very bogus'. The Buddhas, the Benares brass, the Indian servant ! And the gout, too ! It is out of date, the gout. It is old, old gentlemen who have the gout—not the fathers of young ladies of nineteen.

" Moreover I made quite certain. As I go out, I stumble, I clutch at the gouty foot. So perturbed is the gentleman by what I have been saying that he did not even notice. Oh yes, he is very, very bogus, that General ! *Tout de même,* it is a smart idea. The retired Anglo-Indian General, the well-known comic figure with a liver and a choleric temper, he settles down—not amongst other retired Anglo-Indian Army officers

—oh no, he goes to a *milieu* far too expensive for the usual retired Army man. There are rich people there, people from London, an excellent field to market the goods. And who would suspect four lively, attractive, young girls ? If anything comes out, they will be considered as victims—that for a certainty ! "

" What was your idea exactly when you went to see the old devil ? Did you want to put the wind up him ? "

" Yes. I wanted to see *what would happen*. I had not long to wait. The girls had their orders. Anthony Hawker, actually one of their victims, was to be the scapegoat. Sheila was to tell me about the flask in the hall. She nearly could not bring herself to do so—but the other girl rapped out an angry ' Sheila ' at her and she just faltered it out."

Michael Stoddart got up and paced up and down. He said :

" You know, I'm not going to lose sight of that girl. I've got a pretty sound theory about those adolescent criminal tendencies. If you look into the home life, you nearly always find——"

Poirot interrupted him.

He said :

" *Mon cher*, I have the deepest respect for your science. I have no doubt that your theories will work admirably where Miss Sheila Kelly is concerned."

" The others, too."

" The others, perhaps. It may be. The only one I am sure about is the little Sheila. You will tame her, not a doubt of it ! In truth, she eats out of your hand already. . . ."

Flushing, Michael Stoddart said :

" What nonsense you talk, Poirot."

# IX

# THE GIRDLE OF HYPPOLITA

I

ONE THING leads to another, as Hercule Poirot is fond of saying without much originality.

He adds that this was never more clearly evidenced than in the case of the stolen Rubens.

He was never much interested in the Rubens. For one thing Rubens is not a painter he admires, and then the circumstances of the theft were quite ordinary. He took it up to oblige Alexander Simpson who was by way of being a friend of his and for a certain private reason of his own not unconnected with the classics!

After the theft, Alexander Simpson sent for Poirot and poured out all his woes. The Rubens was a recent discovery, a hitherto unknown masterpiece, but there was no doubt of its authenticity. It had been placed on display at Simpson's Galleries and it had been stolen in broad daylight. It was at the time when the unemployed were pursuing their tactics of lying down on street crossings and penetrating into the Ritz. A small body of them had entered Simpson's Galleries and lain down with the slogan displayed of "Art is a Luxury. Feed the Hungry." The police had been sent for, everyone had crowded round in eager curiosity, and it was not till the demonstrators had been forcibly removed by the arm of the law, that it was noticed that the new Rubens had been neatly cut out of its frame and removed also!

"It was quite a small picture, you see," explained Mr. Simpson "A man could put it under his arm and walk out while everyone was looking at those miserable idiots of unemployed."

The men in question, it was discovered, had been paid for their innocent part in the robbery. They were to demonstrate at Simpson's Galleries. But they had known nothing of the reason until afterwards.

Hercule Poirot thought that it was an amusing trick but did not see what he could do about it. The police, he pointed out, could be trusted to deal with a straightforward robbery.

Alexander Simpson said:

"Listen to me, Poirot. I know who stole the picture and where it is going."

According to the owner of Simpson's Galleries it had been stolen by a gang of international crooks on behalf of a certain millionaire who was not above acquiring works of art at a surprisingly low price—and no questions asked! The Rubens, said Simpson, would be smuggled over to France where it would pass into the millionaire's possession. The English and French police were on the alert, nevertheless Simpson was of the opinion that they would fail. "And once it has passed into this dirty dog's possession, it's going to be more difficult. Rich men have to be treated with respect. That's where *you* come in. The situation's going to be delicate. You're the man for that."

Finally, without enthusiasm, Hercule Poirot was induced to accept the task. He agreed to depart for France immediately. He was not very interested in his quest, but because of it, he was introduced to the case of the Missing Schoolgirl which interested him very much indeed.

He first heard of it from Chief Inspector Japp who dropped in to see him just as Poirot was expressing approval of his valet's packing.

"Ha," said Japp. "Going to France, aren't you?"

Poirot said:

"*Mon cher*, you are incredibly well informed at Scotland Yard."

Japp chuckled. He said:

"We have our spies! Simpson's got you on to this Rubens business. Doesn't trust us, it seems! Well, that's neither here nor there, but what I want you to do is something quite different. As you're going to Paris anyway, I thought you might as well kill two birds with one stone. Detective Inspector Hearn's over there co-operating with the Frenchies—you know Hearn? Good chap—but perhaps not very imaginative. I'd like your opinion on the business."

"What is this matter of which you speak?"

"Child's disappeared. It'll be in the papers this evening. Looks as though she's been kidnapped. Daughter of a Canon down at Cranchester. King, her name is, Winnie King."

He proceeded with the story.

Winnie had been on her way to Paris, to join that select and high-class establishment for English and American girls— Miss Pope's. Winnie had come up from Cranchester by the early train—had been seen across London by a member of Elder Sisters Ltd. who undertook such work as seeing girls from one station to another, had been delivered at Victoria to Miss Burshaw, Miss Pope's second-in-command, and had then, in company with eighteen other girls, left Victoria by the boat train. Nineteen girls had crossed the channel, had passed through the customs at Calais, had got into the Paris train, had lunched in the restaurant car. But when, on the outskirts of Paris, Miss Burshaw had counted heads, it was discovered that only *eighteen* girls could be found !

"Aha," Poirot nodded. "Did the train stop anywhere ? "

"It stopped at Amiens, but at that time the girls were in the restaurant car and they all say positively that Winnie was with them then. They lost her, so to speak, on the return journey to their compartments. That is to say, she did not enter her own compartment with the other five girls who were in it. They did not suspect anything was wrong, merely thought she was in one of the two other reserved carriages."

Poirot nodded.

"So she was last seen—when exactly ? "

"About ten minutes after the train left Amiens." Japp coughed modestly. "She was last seen—er—entering the Toilette."

Poirot murmured :

"Very natural." He went on : "There is nothing else ? "

"Yes, one thing." Japp's face was grim. "Her hat was found by the side of the line—at a spot approximately fourteen miles from Amiens."

"But no body ? "

"No body."

Poirot asked :

"What do you yourself think ? "

"Difficult to know *what* to think ! As there's no sign of her body—she can't have fallen off the train."

"Did the train stop at all after leaving Amiens ? "

"No. It slowed up once—for a signal, but it didn't stop, and I doubt if it slowed up enough for anyone to have jumped off without injury. You're thinking that the kid got a panic and tried to run away ? It was her first term and she might have been homesick, that's true enough, but all the same she was fifteen and a half—a sensible age, and she'd been in quite good spirits all the journey, chattering away and all that."

Poirot asked :

"Was the train searched ? "

"Oh yes, they went right through it before it arrived at the Nord station. The girl wasn't on the train, that's quite certain."

Japp added in an exasperated manner :

"She just disappeared—into thin air ! It doesn't make sense, M. Poirot. It's crazy ! "

"What kind of a girl was she ? "

"Ordinary, normal type as far as I can make out."

"I mean—what did she look like ? "

"I've got a snap of her here. She's not exactly a budding beauty."

He proffered the snapshot to Poirot who studied it in silence.

It represented a lanky girl with her hair in two limp plaits. It was not a posed photograph, the subject had clearly been caught unawares. She was in the act of eating an apple, her lips were parted, showing slightly protruding teeth confined by a dentist's plate. She wore spectacles.

Japp said :

"Plain-looking kid—but then they *are* plain at that age ! Was at my dentist's yesterday. Saw a picture in the Sketch of Marcia Gaunt, this season's beauty. *I* remember her at fifteen when I was down at the Castle over their burglary business. Spotty, awkward, teeth sticking out, hair all lank and anyhow. They grow into beauties overnight—I don't know how they do it ! It's like a miracle."

Poirot smiled.

"Women," he said, " are a miraculous sex ! What about the child's family ? Have they anything helpful to say ? "

Japp shook his head.

"Nothing that's any help. Mother's an invalid. Poor old Canon King is absolutely bowled over. He swears that the girl was frightfully keen to go to Paris—had been looking forward to it. Wanted to study painting and music—that sort of thing. Miss Pope's girls go in for Art with a capital A. As you probably know, Miss Pope's is a very well-known establishment. Lots of society girls go there. She's strict—quite a dragon—and very expensive—and extremely particular whom she takes."

Poirot sighed.

"I know the type. And Miss Burshaw who took the girls over from England?"

"Not exactly frantic with brains. Terrified that Miss Pope will say it's her fault."

Poirot said thoughtfully:

"There is no young man in the case?"

Japp gesticulated towards the snapshot.

"Does she look like it?"

"No, she does not. But notwithstanding her appearance, she may have a romantic heart. Fifteen is not so young."

"Well," said Japp. "If a romantic heart spirited her off that train, I'll take to reading lady novelists."

He looked hopefully at Poirot.

"Nothing strikes you—eh?"

Poirot shook his head slowly. He said:

"They did not, by any chance, find her shoes also by the side of the line?"

"Shoes? No. Why shoes?"

Poirot murmured:

"Just an idea. . . ."

## II

Hercule Poirot was just going down to his taxi when the telephone rang. He took off the receiver.

"Yes?"

Japp's voice spoke.

"Glad I've just caught you. It's all off, old man. Found a message at the Yard when I got back. The girl's turned up.

At the side of the main road fifteen miles from Amiens. She's dazed and they can't get any coherent story from her, doctor says she's been doped—However, she's all right. Nothing wrong with her."

Poirot said slowly :

" So you have, then, no need of my services ? "

" Afraid not ! In fact—sorrrry you have been trrrroubled."

Japp laughed at his witticism and rang off.

Hercule Poirot did not laugh. He put back the receiver slowly. His face was worried.

### III

Detective Inspector Hearn looked at Poirot curiously. He said :

" I'd no idea you'd be so interested, sir."

Poirot said :

" You had word from Chief Inspector Japp that I might consult with you over this matter ? "

Hearn nodded.

" He said you were coming over on some other business, and that you'd give us a hand with this puzzle. But I didn't expect you now it's all cleared up. I thought you'd be busy on your own job."

Hercule Poirot said :

" My own business can wait. It is this affair here that interests me. You called it a puzzle, and you say it is now ended. But the puzzle is still there, it seems."

" Well, sir, we've got the child back. And she's not hurt. That's the main thing."

" But it does not solve the problem of *how* you got her back, does it ? What does she herself say ? A doctor saw her, did he not ? What did he say ? "

" Said she'd been doped. She was still hazy with it. Apparently, she can't remember anything much after starting off from Cranchester. All later events seem to have been wiped out. Doctor thinks she might just possibly have had slight concussion. There's a bruise on the back of her head. Says that would account for a complete blackout of memory."

Poirot said :

"Which is very convenient for—someone !"

Inspector Hearn said in a doubtful voice :

"You don't think she is shamming, sir ?"

"Do you ?"

"No, I'm sure she isn't. She's a nice kid—a bit young for her age."

"No, she is not shamming." Poirot shook his head. "But I would like to know *how she got off that train.* I want to know who is responsible—and *why ?*"

"As to why, I should say it was an attempt at kidnapping, sir. They meant to hold her to ransom."

"But they didn't !"

"Lost their nerve with the hue and cry—and planted her by the road quick."

Poirot inquired sceptically :

"And what ransom were they likely to get from a Canon of Cranchester Cathedral ? English Church dignitaries are not millionaires."

Detective Inspector Hearn said cheerfully :

"Made a botch of the whole thing, sir, in my opinion."

"Ah, that's your opinion."

Hearn said, his face flushing slightly :

"What's yours, sir ?"

"I want to know *how* she was spirited off that train."

The policeman's face clouded over.

"That's a real mystery, that is. One minute she was there, sitting in the dining-car, chatting to the other girls. Five minutes later she's vanished—hey presto—like a conjuring trick."

"Precisely, like a conjuring trick ! Who else was there in the coach of the train where Miss Pope's reserved compartments were ?"

Inspector Hearn nodded.

"That's a good point, sir. That's important. It's particularly important because it was the last coach on the train and as soon as all the people were back from the restaurant car, the doors between the coaches were locked—actually so as to prevent people crowding along to the restaurant car and demanding tea before they'd had time to clear up lunch and

get ready. Winnie King came back to the coach with the others
—the school had three reserved compartments there."

" And in the other compartments of the coach ? "

Hearn pulled out his notebook.

" Miss Jordan and Miss Butters—two middle-aged spinsters
going to Switzerland. Nothing wrong with them, highly
respectable, well known in Hampshire where they come from.
Two French commercial travellers, one from Lyons, one from
Paris. Both respectable middle-aged men. A young man,
James Elliot, and his wife—flashy piece of goods *she* was.
He's got a bad reputation, suspected by the police of being
mixed up in some questionable transactions—but has never
touched kidnapping. Anyway, his compartment was searched
and there was nothing in his hand luggage to show that he was
mixed up in this. Don't see how he *could* have been. Only
other person was an American lady, Mrs. Van Suyder, travelling to Paris. Nothing known about her. Looks O.K. That's
the lot."

Hercule Poirot said :

" And it is quite definite that the train did not stop after it
left Amiens ? "

"Absolutely. It slowed down once, but not enough to let
any one jump off—not without damaging themselves pretty
severely and risking being killed."

Hercule Poirot murmured :

" That is what makes the problem so peculiarly interesting.
The schoolgirl vanishes into thin air *just outside Amiens*. She
reappears from thin air *just outside Amiens*. Where has she
been in the meantime ? "

Inspector Hearn shook his head.

" It sounds mad, put like that. Oh ! by the way, they told
me you were asking something about shoes—the girl's shoes.
She had her shoes on all right when she was found, but there
*was* a pair of shoes on the line, a signalman found them. Took
'em home with him as they seemed in good condition. Stout
black walking shoes."

" Ah," said Poirot. He looked gratified.

Inspector Hearn said curiously :

" I don't get the meaning of the shoes, sir ? Do they mean
anything ? "

" They confirm a theory," said Hercule Poirot. " A theory
of how the conjuring trick was done."

IV

Miss Pope's establishment was, like many other establish-
ments of the same kind, situated in Neuilly. Hercule Poirot,
staring up at its respectable façade, was suddenly submerged
by a flow of girls emerging from its portals.

He counted twenty-five of them, all dressed alike in dark
blue coats and skirts with uncomfortable-looking British hats
of dark blue velour on their heads, round which was tied the
distinctive purple and gold of Miss Pope's choice. They were
of ages varying from fourteen to eighteen, thick and slim, fair
and dark, awkward and graceful. At the end, walking with
one of the younger girls, was a grey-haired, fussy looking woman
whom Poirot judged to be Miss Burshaw.

Poirot stood looking after them a minute, then he rang the
bell and asked for Miss Pope.

Miss Lavinia Pope was a very different person from her
second-in-command, Miss Burshaw. Miss Pope had personality. Miss Pope was awe inspiring. Even should Miss Pope
unbend graciously to parents, she would still retain that
obvious superiority to the rest of the world which is such a
powerful asset to a schoolmistress.

Her grey hair was dressed with distinction, her costume was
severe but chic. She was competent and omniscient.

The room in which she received Poirot was the room of a
woman of culture. It had graceful furniture, flowers, some
framed, signed photographs of those of Miss Pope's pupils
who were of note in the world—many of them in their presen-
tation gowns and feathers. On the walls hung reproductions
of the world's artistic masterpieces and some good water-
colour sketches. The whole place was clean and polished to
the last degree. No speck of dust, one felt, would have the
temerity to deposit itself in such a shrine.

Miss Pope received Poirot with the competence of one whose
judgment seldom fails.

" M. Hercule Poirot? I know your name, of course. I

suppose you have come about this very unfortunate affair of
Winnie King. A most distressing incident."

Miss Pope did not look distressed. She took disaster as
it should be taken, dealing with it competently and thereby
reducing it almost to insignificance.

" Such a thing," said Miss Pope, " has never occurred
before."

" And never will again ! " her manner seemed to say.

Hercule Poirot said :

" It was the girl's first term here, was it not ? "

" It was."

" You had a preliminary interview with Winnie—and with
her parents ? "

" Not recently. Two years ago, I was staying near Cranchester—with the Bishop, as a matter of fact——"

Miss Pope's manner said :

(" Mark this, please. I am the kind of person who stays
with Bishops ! ")

" While I was there I made the acquaintance of Canon and
Mrs. King. Mrs. King, alas, is an invalid. I met Winnie then.
A very well brought up girl, with a decided taste for art. I
told Mrs. King that I should be happy to receive her here in a
year or two—when her general studies were completed. We
specialise here, M. Poirot, in Art and Music. The girls are
taken to the Opera, to the Comédie Française, they attend
lectures at the Louvre. The very best masters come here to
instruct them in music, singing, and painting. The broader
culture, that is our aim."

Miss Pope remembered suddenly that Poirot was not a
parent and added abruptly :

" What can I do for you, M. Poirot ? "

" I would be glad to know what is the present position
regarding Winnie ? "

" Canon King has come over to Amiens and is taking
Winnie back with him. The wisest thing to do after the shock
the child has sustained."

She went on :

" We do not take delicate girls here. We have no special
facilities for looking after invalids. I told the Canon that in
my opinion he would do well to take the child home with him."

Hercule Poirot asked bluntly :

" What in your opinion actually occurred, Miss Pope ? "

" I have not the slightest idea, M. Poirot. The whole thing, as reported to me, sounds quite incredible. I really cannot see that the member of my staff who was in charge of the girls was in any way to blame—except that she might, perhaps, have discovered the girl's absence sooner."

Poirot said :

" You have received a visit, perhaps, from the police ? "

A faint shiver passed over Miss Pope's aristocratic form. She said glacially :

" A Monsieur Lefarge of the Préfecture called to see me, to see if I could throw any light upon the situation. Naturally I was unable to do so. He then demanded to inspect Winnie's trunk which had, of course, arrived here with those of the other girls. I told him that that had already been called for by another member of the police. Their departments, I fancy, must overlap. I got a telephone call, shortly afterwards, insisting that I had not turned over all Winnie's possessions to them. I was extremely short with them over that. One must not submit to being bullied by officialdom."

Poirot drew a long breath. He said :

" You have a spirited nature. I admire you for it, Mademoiselle. I presume that Winnie's trunk had been unpacked on arrival ? "

Miss Pope looked a little put out of countenance.

" Routine," she said. " We live strictly by routine. The girls trunks are unpacked on arrival and their things put away in the way I expect them to be kept. Winnie's things were unpacked with those of the other girls. Naturally, they were afterwards repacked, so that her trunk was handed over exactly as it had arrived."

Poirot said : " *Exactly ?* "

He strolled over to the wall.

" Surely this is a picture of the famous Cranchester Bridge with the Cathedral showing in the distance."

" You are quite right, M. Poirot. Winnie had evidently painted that to bring to me as a surprise. It was in her trunk with a wrapper round it and ' *For Miss Pope from Winnie* ' written on it. Very charming of the child."

" Ah ! " said Poirot. " And what do you think of it—as a painting ? "

He himself had seen many pictures of Cranchester Bridge. It was a subject that could always be found represented at the Academy each year—sometimes as an oil painting—sometimes in the water-colour room. He had seen it painted well, painted in a mediocre fashion, painted boringly. But he had never seen it quite as crudely represented as in the present example.

Miss Pope was smiling indulgently.

She said :

" One must not discourage one's girls, M. Poirot. Winnie will be stimulated to do better work, of course."

Poirot said thoughtfully :

" It would have been more natural, would it not, for her to do a water-colour ? "

" Yes. I did not know she was attempting to paint in oils."

" Ah," said Hercule Poirot. " You will permit me, Mademoiselle ? "

He unhooked the picture and took it to the window. He examined it, then, looking up, he said :

" I am going to ask you, Mademoiselle, to give me this picture."

" Well, really, M. Poirot——"

" You cannot pretend that you are very attached to it. The painting is abominable."

" Oh, it has no *artistic* merit, I agree. But it is a pupil's work and——"

" I assure you, Mademoiselle, that it is a most unsuitable picture to have hanging upon your wall."

" I don't know why you should say *that*, M. Poirot."

" I will prove it to you in a moment."

He took a bottle, a sponge and some rags from his pocket. He said :

" First I am going to tell you a little story, Mademoiselle. It has a resemblance to the story of the Ugly Duckling that turned into a Swan."

He was working busily as he talked. The odour of turpentine filled the room.

" You do not perhaps go much to theatrical revues ? "

" No, indeed, they seem to me so trivial. . . ."

" Trivial, yes, but sometimes instructive. I have seen a clever revue artist change her personality in the most miraculous way. In one sketch she is a cabaret star, exquisite and glamorous. Ten minutes later, she is an undersized, anæmic child with adenoids, dressed in a gym tunic—ten minutes later still, she is a ragged gypsy telling fortunes by a caravan."

" Very possible, no doubt, but I do not see——"

" But I am showing you how the conjuring trick was worked on the train. Winnie, the schoolgirl, with her fair plaits, her spectacles, her disfiguring dental plate—goes into the *Toilette*. She emerges a quarter of an hour later as—to use the words of Detective Inspector Hearn—'a flashy piece of goods'. Sheer silk stockings, high heeled shoes—a mink coat to cover a school uniform, a daring little piece of velvet called a hat perched on her curls—and a face—oh yes, a face. Rouge, powder, lipstick, mascara ! What is the real face of that quick change *artiste* really like ? Probably only the good God knows ! But you, Mademoiselle, you yourself, you have often seen how the awkward schoolgirl changes almost miraculously into the attractive and well-groomed débutante."

Miss Pope gasped.

" Do you mean that Winnie King disguised herself as——"

" Not Winnie King—no. Winnie was kidnapped *on the way across London*. Our quick change *artiste* took her place. Miss Burshaw had never seen Winnie King—how was she to know that the schoolgirl with the lank plaits and the brace on her teeth was not Winnie King at all ? So far, so good, but the impostor could not afford actually to arrive *here*, since *you* were acquainted with the *real* Winnie. So hey presto, Winnie disappears in the *Toilette* and emerges as wife to a man called Jim Elliot whose passport includes a wife ! The fair plaits, the spectacles, the lisle thread stockings, the dental plate— all that can go into a small space. But the thick unglamorous shoes and the hat—that very unyielding British hat—have to be disposed of elsewhere—they go out of the window. Later, the real Winnie is brought across the channel—no one is looking for a sick, half-doped child being brought from *England* to *France*—and is quietly deposited from a car by the side of the main road. If she has been doped all along with scopolamine, she will remember very little of what has occurred."

Miss Pope was staring at Poirot. She demanded :

" But *why ?* What would be the *reason* of such a senseless masquerade ? "

Poirot replied gravely :

" Winnie's luggage ! These people wanted to smuggle some thing from England into France—something that every Customs man was on the look-out for—in fact, stolen goods. But what place is safer than a schoolgirl's trunk ? You are well-known, Miss Pope, your establishment is justly famous. At the Gare du Nord the trunks of Mesdemoiselles the little Pensionnaires are passed *en bloc.* It is the well-known English school of Miss Pope ! And then, after the kidnapping, what more natural than to send and collect the child's luggage—ostensibly from the Préfecture ? "

Hercule Poirot smiled.

" But fortunately, there was the school routine of unpacking trunks on arrival—and a present for you from Winnie—*but not the same present that Winnie packed at Cranchester.*"

He came towards her.

" You have given this picture to me. Observe now, you must admit that it is not suitable for your select school ! "

He held out the canvas.

As though by magic Cranchester Bridge had disappeared. Instead was a classical scene in rich, dim colourings.

Poirot said softly :

" *The Girdle of Hyppolita.* Hyppolita gives her girdle to Hercules—painted by Rubens. A great work of art—*mais tout de même* not quite suitable for your drawing-room."

Miss Pope blushed slightly.

Hyppolita's hand was on her girdle—she was wearing nothing else. . . . Hercules had a lion skin thrown lightly over one shoulder. The flesh of Rubens is rich, voluptuous flesh. . . .

Miss Pope said, regaining her poise :

" A fine work of art. . . . All the same—as you say—after all, one must consider the susceptibilities of parents. Some of them are inclined to be *narrow.* . . . if you know what I mean. . . ."

## V

It was just as Poirot was leaving the house that the on-slaught took place. He was surrounded, hemmed-in, over-whelmed by a crowd of girls, thick, thin, dark and fair.

" Mon Dieu ! " he murmured. " Here indeed is the attack by the Amazons ! "

A tall fair girl was crying out :

" A rumour has gone round——"

They surged closer. Hercule Poirot was surrounded. He disappeared in a wave of young, vigorous femininity.

Twenty-five voices arose, pitched in various keys but all uttering the same momentous phrase.

" *M. Poirot, will you write your name in my autograph book. . . . ?* "

# X

# THE FLOCK OF GERYON

## I

" I REALLY do apologise for intruding like this, M. Poirot."

Miss Carnaby clasped her hands fervently round her hand-bag and leaned forward, peering anxiously into Poirot's face. As usual, she sounded breathless.

Hercule Poirot's eyebrows rose.

She said anxiously :

" You do remember me, don't you ? "

Hercule Poirot's eyes twinkled. He said :

" I remember you as one of the most successful criminals that I have ever encountered ! "

" Oh dear me, M. Poirot, must you really say such things ? You *were* so kind to me. Emily and I often talk about you, and if we see anything about you in the paper we cut it out at once and paste it in a book. As for Augustus, we have taught him a new trick. We say, ' Die for Sherlock Holmes, die for Mr. Fortune, die for Sir Henry Merrivale, and then *die for M. Hercule Poirot* ' and he goes down and lies like a *log*—lies absolutely still without moving until we say the word ! "

" I am gratified," said Poirot. " And how is *ce cher Auguste* ? "

Miss Carnaby clasped her hands and became eloquent in praise of her Pekinese.

" Oh, M. Poirot, he's cleverer than ever. He knows *everything*. Do you know, the other day I was just admiring a baby in a pram and suddenly I felt a tug and there was Augustus trying his hardest to bite through his lead. Wasn't that clever ? "

Poirot's eyes twinkled. He said :

" It looks to me as though Augustus shared these criminal tendencies we were speaking of just now ! "

Miss Carnaby did not laugh. Instead, her nice plump face grew worried and sad. She said in a kind of gasp :

" Oh, M. Poirot, I'm so *worried*."

Poirot said kindly : " What is it ? "

" Do you know, M. Poirot, I'm afraid—I really am afraid—that I must be a *hardened criminal*—if I may use such a term. Ideas come to me ! "

" What kind of ideas ? "

" The most extraordinary ideas ! For instance, yesterday, a really most *practical* scheme for robbing a post office came into my head. I wasn't thinking about it—it just came ! And another very ingenious way for evading custom duties. . . . I feel convinced—quite convinced—that it would work."

" It probably would," said Poirot dryly. " That is the danger of your ideas."

" It has worried me, M. Poirot, very much. Having been brought up with strict principles, as I have been, it is *most* disturbing that such lawless—such really *wicked*—ideas should come to me. The trouble is partly, I think, that I have a good deal of leisure time now. I have left Lady Hoggin and I am engaged by an old lady to read to her and write her letters every day. The letters are soon done and the moment I begin reading she goes to sleep, so I am left just sitting there—with an idle mind—and we all know the use the devil has for idleness."

" Tcha, tcha," said Poirot.

" Recently I have read a book—a very modern book, translated from the German. It throws a most interesting light on criminal tendencies. One must, so I understand, *sublimate* one's impulses ! That, really, is why I came to you."

" Yes ? " said Poirot.

" You see, M. Poirot. I think that it is really not so much *wickedness* as a craving for excitement ! My life has unfortunately been very humdrum. The—er—campaign of the Pekinese dogs, I sometimes feel, was the only time I really *lived*. Very reprehensible, of course, but, as my book says, one must not turn one's back on the truth. I came to you, M. Poirot, because I hoped it might be possible to—to sublimate that craving for excitement by employing it, if I may put it that way, on the side of the angels."

" Aha," said Poirot. " It is then as a colleague that you present yourself ? "

Miss Carnaby blushed.

" It is very presumptuous of me, I know. But you were so *kind*——"

She stopped. Her eyes, faded blue eyes, had something in them of the pleading of a dog who hopes against hope that you will take him for a walk.

" It is an idea," said Hercule Poirot slowly.

" I am, of course, not at all clever," explained Miss Carnaby. " But my powers of—of dissimulation are good. They have to be—otherwise one would be discharged from the post of companion immediately. And I have always found that to appear even stupider than one is, occasionally has good results."

Hercule Poirot laughed. He said :

" You enchant me, Mademoiselle."

" Oh dear, M. Poirot, what a very kind man you are. Then you do encourage me to *hope* ? As it happens, I have just received a small legacy—a very small one, but it enables my sister and myself to keep and feed ourselves in a frugal manner so that I am not absolutely dependent on what I earn."

" I must consider," said Poirot, " where your talents may best be employed. You have no idea yourself, I suppose ? "

" You know, you must really be a thought reader, M. Poirot. I *have* been anxious lately about a friend of mine. I was going to consult you. Of course you may say it is all an old maid's fancy—just imagination. One is prone, perhaps to exaggerate, and to see *design* where there may be only *co-incidence*."

" I do not think you would exaggerate, Miss Carnaby. Tell me what is on your mind."

" Well, I have a friend, a very dear friend, though I have not seen very much of her of late years. Her name is Emmeline Clegg. She married a man in the North of England and he died a few years ago leaving her very comfortably off. She was unhappy and lonely after his death and I am afraid she is in some ways a rather foolish and perhaps credulous woman. Religion, M. Poirot, can be a great help and sustenance—but by that I mean orthodox religion."

" You refer to the Greek Church ? " asked Poirot.

Miss Carnaby looked shocked.

"Oh no, indeed. Church of England. And though I do not *approve* of Roman Catholics, they are at least *recognised*. And the Wesleyans and Congregationalists—they are all well-known respectable bodies. What I am talking about are these *odd* sects. They just spring up. They have a kind of emotional appeal but sometimes I have very grave doubts as to whether there is any true religious feeling behind them at all."

"You think your friend is being victimised by a sect of this kind?"

"I do. Oh! I certainly do. The Flock of the Shepherd, they call themselves. Their headquarters is in Devonshire— a very lovely estate by the sea. The adherents go there for what they term a Retreat. That is a period of a fortnight— with religious services and rituals. And there are three big Festivals in the year, the Coming of the Pasture, the Full Pasture, and the Reaping of the Pasture."

"Which last is stupid," said Poirot. "Because one does not reap pasture."

"The whole thing is stupid," said Miss Carnaby with warmth. "The whole sect centres round the head of the movement, the Great Shepherd, he is called. A Dr. Andersen. A very handsome-looking man, I believe, with a presence."

"Which is attractive to the women, yes?"

"I am afraid so," Miss Carnaby sighed. "My father was a very handsome man. Sometimes, it was most awkward in the parish. The rivalry in embroidering vestments—and the division of church work . . ."

She shook her head reminiscently.

"Are the members of the Great Flock mostly women?"

"At least three quarters of them, I gather. What men there are, are mostly *cranks*! It is upon the women that the success of the movement depends and—and on the *funds* they supply."

"Ah," said Poirot. "Now we come to it. Frankly, you think the whole thing is a ramp?"

"Frankly, M. Poirot, I do. And another thing worries me. I happen to know that my poor friend is so bound up in this religion that she has recently made a will leaving all her property to the movement."

Poirot said sharply:

" Was that—suggested to her ? "

" In all fairness, no. It was entirely her own idea. The Great Shepherd had shown her a new way of life—so all that she had was to go on her death to the great Cause. What really worries me is——"

" Yes—go on——"

" Several very wealthy women have been among the devotees. In the last year *three* of them, no less, have died."

" Leaving all their money to this sect ? "

" Yes."

" Their relations have made no protest ? I should have thought it likely that there might have been litigation."

" You see, M. Poirot, it is usually *lonely* women who belong to this gathering. People who have no very near relations or friends."

Poirot nodded thoughtfully. Miss Carnaby hurried on :

" Of course I've no right to suggest anything at all. From what I have been able to find out, there was nothing *wrong* about any of these deaths. One, I believe, was *pneumonia* following *influenza* and another was attributed to gastric ulcer. There were absolutely no *suspicious circumstances*, if you know what I mean, and the deaths did not take place at Green Hills Sanctuary, but at their own homes. I've no doubt it is *quite* all right, but all the same I—well—I shouldn't like anything to happen to Emmie."

She clasped her hands, her eyes appealed to Poirot.

Poirot himself was silent for some minutes. When he spoke there was a change in his voice. It was grave and deep.

He said :

" Will you give me, or will you find out for me, the names and addresses of these members of the sect who have recently died ? "

" Yes indeed, M. Poirot."

Poirot said slowly :

" Mademoiselle, I think you are a woman of great courage and determination. You have good histrionic powers. Would you be willing to undertake a piece of work that may be attended with considerable danger ? "

" I should like nothing better," said the adventurous Miss Carnaby.

Poirot said warningly :

" If there is a risk at all, it will be a grave one. You comprehend—either this is a mare's nest or else it is *serious*. To
find out which it is, it will be necessary for you yourself
to become a member of the Great Flock. I would suggest that
you exaggerate the amount of the legacy that you recently
inherited. You are now a well-to-do woman with no very
definite aim in life. You argue with your friend Emmeline
about this religion she has adopted—assure her that it is all
nonsense. She is eager to convert you. You allow yourself
to be persuaded to go down to Green Hills Sanctuary. And
there you fall a victim to the persuasive powers and magnetic
influence of Dr. Andersen. I think I can safely leave that
part to you ? "

Miss Carnaby smiled modestly. She murmured :

" I think I can manage *that* all right ! "

## II

" Well, my friend, what have you got for me ? "

Chief Inspector Japp looked thoughtfully at the little man
who asked the question. He said ruefully :

" Not at all what I'd like to have, Poirot. I hate these
long-haired, religious cranks like poison. Filling up women
with a lot of mumbo-jumbo. But this fellow's being careful.
There's nothing one can get hold of. All sounds a bit batty but
harmless."

" Have you learned anything about this Dr. Andersen ? "

" I've looked up his past history. He was a promising
chemist and got chucked out of some German University.
Seems his mother was Jewish. He was always keen on the
study of Oriental Myths and Religions, spent all his spare
time on that and has written various articles on the subject—
some of the articles sound pretty crazy to me."

" So it is possible that he is a genuine fanatic ? "

" I'm bound to say it seems quite likely ! "

" What about those names and addresses I gave you ? "

" Nothing doing there. Miss Everitt died of ulcerative
colitis. Doctor quite positive there was no hanky-panky.

Mrs. Lloyd died of broncho-pneumonia. Lady Western died of tuberculosis. Had suffered from it many years ago—before she even met this bunch. Miss Lee died of typhoid—attributed to some salad she ate somewhere in the north of England. Three of them got ill and died in their own homes, and Mrs. Lloyd died in a hotel in the south of France. As far as those deaths go, there's nothing to connect them with the Great Flock or with Andersen's place down in Devonshire. Must be pure coincidence. All absolutely O.K. and according to Cocker."

Hercule Poirot sighed. He said :

" And yet, *mon cher*, I have a feeling that this is the tenth Labour of Hercules, and that this Dr. Andersen is the Monster Geryon whom it is my mission to destroy."

Japp looked at him anxiously.

" Look here, Poirot, you haven't been reading any queer literature yourself lately, have you ? "

Poirot said with dignity :

" My remarks are, as always, apt, sound, and to the point."

" You might start a new religion yourself," said Japp, " with the creed : ' There is no one so clever as Hercule Poirot, Amen, D.C. Repeat *ad lib.*' ! "

## III

" It is the peace here that I find so wonderful," said Miss Carnaby, breathing heavily and ecstatically.

" I told you so, Amy," said Emmeline Clegg.

The two friends were sitting on the slope of a hillside overlooking a deep and lovely blue sea. The grass was vivid green, the earths and the cliffs a deep, glowing red. The little estate now known as Green Hills Sanctuary was a promontory comprising about six acres. Only a narrow neck of land joined it to the mainland so that it was almost an island.

Mrs. Clegg murmured sentimentally :

" The red land—the land of glow and promise—where threefold destiny is to be accomplished."

Miss Carnaby sighed deeply and said :

"I thought the Master put it all so beautifully at the service last night."

"Wait," said her friend, "for the festival to-night. The Full Growth of the Pasture !"

"I'm looking forward to it," said Miss Carnaby.

"You will find it a wonderful spiritual experience," her friend promised her.

Miss Carnaby had arrived at Green Hills Sanctuary a week previously. Her attitude on arrival had been : "Now what's all this nonsense ? Really, Emmie, a sensible woman like you—etc., etc."

At a preliminary interview with Dr. Andersen, she had conscientiously made her position quite clear.

"I don't want to feel that I am here under false pretences, Dr. Andersen. My father was a clergyman of the Church of England and I have never wavered in my faith. I don't hold with heathen doctrines."

The big, golden-haired man had smiled at her—a very sweet and understanding smile. He had looked indulgently at the plump, rather belligerent figure sitting so squarely in her chair.

"Dear Miss Carnaby," he said. "You are Mrs. Clegg's friend, and as such welcome. And believe me, our doctrines are not heathen. Here all religions are welcomed, and all honoured equally."

"Then they shouldn't be," said the staunch daughter of the late Reverend Thomas Carnaby.

Leaning back in his chair, the Master murmured in his rich voice : "In my Father's House are many mansions . . . Remember that, Miss Carnaby."

As they left the presence, Miss Carnaby murmured to her friend : "He really is a very handsome man."

"Yes," said Emmeline Clegg. "And so wonderfully spiritual."

Miss Carnaby agreed. It was true—she had felt it—an aura of unworldliness—of spirituality. . . .

She took a grip upon herself. She was not here to fall a prey to the fascination, spiritual or otherwise, of the Great Shepherd. She conjured up a vision of Hercule Poirot. He seemed very far away, and curiously mundane. . . .

" Amy," said Miss Carnaby to herself. " Take a grip upon yourself. Remember what you are here for. . . ."

But as the days went on, she found herself surrendering only too easily to the spell of Green Hills. The peace, the simplicity, the delicious though simple food, the beauty of the services with their chants of Love and Worship, the simple moving words of the Master, appealing to all that was best and highest in humanity—here all the strife and ugliness of the world was shut out. Here was only Peace and Love. . . .

And to-night was the great summer Festival, the Festival of the Full Pasture. And at it, she, Amy Carnaby, was to become initiated—to become one of the Flock.

The Festival took place in the white, glittering, concrete building, called by the Initiates the Sacred Fold. Here the devotees assembled just before the setting of the sun. They wore sheepskin cloaks and had sandals on their feet. Their arms were bare. In the centre of the Fold on a raised platform stood Dr. Andersen. The big man, golden-haired and blue-eyed, with his fair beard and his handsome profile had never seemed more compelling. He was dressed in a green robe and carried a shepherd's crook of gold.

He raised this aloft and a deathly silence fell on the assembly.

" Where are my sheep ? "

The answer came from the crowd.

" *We are here, O Shepherd.*"

" Lift up your hearts with joy and thanksgiving. This is the Feast of Joy."

" *The Feast of Joy and we are joyful.*"

" There shall be no more sorrow for you, no more pain. All is joy ! "

"*All is joy. . . .*"

" How many heads has the Shepherd ? "

" *Three heads, a head of gold, a head of silver, a head of sounding brass.*"

" How many bodies have the Sheep ? "

" *Three bodies, a body of flesh, a body of corruption, and a body of light.*"

" How shall you be sealed in the Flock ? "

" *By the Sacrament of Blood.*"

" Are you prepared for that Sacrament ? "

" *We are.*"

" Bind your eyes and hold forth your right arm."

The crowd obediently bound their eyes with the green scarves provided for the purpose. Miss Carnaby, like the rest held her arm out in front of her.

The Great Shepherd moved along the lines of his Flock. There were little cries, moans of either pain or ecstasy.

Miss Carnaby, to herself, said fiercely :

" Most blasphemous, the whole thing ! This kind of religious hysteria is to be deplored. I shall remain absolutely calm and observe the reactions of other people. I will *not* be carried away—I will *not*. . . ."

The Great Shepherd had come to her. She felt her arm taken, held, there was a sharp, stinging pain like the prick of a needle. The Shepherd's voice murmured :

" *The Sacrament of Blood that brings joy.* . . ."

He passed on.

Presently there came a command.

" Unveil and enjoy the pleasures of the spirit ! "

The sun was just sinking. Miss Carnaby looked round her. At one with the others, she moved slowly out of the Fold. She felt suddenly uplifted, happy. She sank down on a soft, grassy bank. Why had she ever thought she was a lonely, unwanted, middle-aged woman ? Life was wonderful —she herself was wonderful ! She had the power of thought —of dreaming. There was nothing that she could not accomplish !

A great rush of exhilaration surged through her. She observed her fellow devotees round her—they seemed suddenly to have grown to an immense stature.

" *Like trees walking* . . ." said Miss Carnaby to herself reverently.

She lifted her hand. It was a purposeful gesture—with it she could command the earth. Cæsar, Napoleon, Hitler— poor, miserable, little fellows ! They knew nothing of what she, Amy Carnaby, could do ! To-morrow she would arrange for World Peace, for International Brotherhood. There should be no more Wars—no more Poverty—no more Disease. She, Amy Carnaby, would design a New World.

But there need be no hurry. Time was infinite. . . .

Minute succeeded minute, hour succeeded hour! Miss Carnaby's limbs felt heavy, but her mind was delightfully free. It could roam at will over the whole universe. She slept— but even as she slept she dreamt . . . Great spaces . . . vast buildings . . . a new and wonderful world. . . .

Gradually the world shrank, Miss Carnaby yawned. She moved her stiff limbs. What had happened since yesterday? Last night she had dreamt . . .

There was a moon. By it, Miss Carnaby could just distinguish the figures on her watch. To her stupefaction the hands pointed to a quarter to ten. The sun, as she knew, had set at eight-ten. Only an hour and thirty-five minutes ago? Impossible. And yet——

"*Very* remarkable," said Miss Carnaby to herself.

## IV

Hercule Poirot said:

"You must obey my instructions very carefully. You understand?"

"Oh yes, Mr. Poirot. You may rely on me."

"You have spoken of your intention to benefit the cult?"

"Yes, Mr. Poirot. I spoke to the Master—excuse me, to Dr. Andersen myself. I told him very emotionally what a wonderful revelation the whole thing had been—how I had come to scoff and remained to believe. I—really it seemed quite natural to say all these things. Dr. Andersen, you know, has a lot of magnetic charm."

"So I perceive," said Hercule Poirot dryly.

"His manner was most convincing. One really feels he doesn't care about money at all. 'Give what you can,' he said smiling in that wonderful way of his, 'if you can give nothing, it does not matter. You are one of the Flock just the same.' 'Oh, Dr. Andersen,' I said, 'I am not so badly off as *that*. I have just inherited a considerable amount of money from a distant relative and though I cannot actually touch any of the money until the legal formalities are all complied with, there is one thing I want to do at once.' And then I explained that I was making a will and that I wanted to leave all I had to the Brotherhood. I explained that I had no near relatives."

"And he graciously accepted the bequest?"

"He was very detached about it. Said it would be many long years before I passed over, that he could tell I was cut out for a long life of joy and spiritual fulfilment. He really speaks most *movingly*."

"So it would seem."

Poirot's tone was dry. He went on:

"You mentioned your health?"

"Yes, Mr. Poirot. I told him that I had had lung trouble, and that it had recurred more than once, but that a final treatment in a Sanatorium some years ago had, I hoped, quite cured me."

"Excellent!"

"Though why it is necessary for me to say that I am consumptive when my lungs are as sound as a bell I really cannot see."

"Be assured it *is* necessary. You mentioned your friend?"

"Yes. I told him (strictly in confidence) that dear Emmeline, besides the fortune she had inherited from her husband, would inherit an even larger sum shortly from an aunt who was deeply attached to her."

"*Eh bien*, that ought to keep Mrs. Clegg safe for the time being!"

"Oh, Mr. Poirot, do you really think there *is* anything wrong?"

"That is what I am going to endeavour to find out. Have you met a Mr. Cole down at the Sanctuary?"

"There was a Mr. Cole there last time I went down. A most peculiar man. He wears grass-green shorts and eats nothing but cabbage. He is a very ardent believer."

"*Eh bien*, all progresses well—I make you my compliments on the work you have done—all is now set for the Autumn Festival."

V

" Miss Carnaby—just a moment."

Mr. Cole clutched at Miss Carnaby, his eyes bright and feverish.

" I have had a Vision—a most remarkable Vision. I really must tell you about it."

Miss Carnaby sighed. She was rather afraid of Mr. Cole and his Visions. There were moments when she was decidedly of the opinion that Mr. Cole was mad.

And she found these Visions of his sometimes very embarrassing. They recalled to her certain outspoken passages in that very modern German book on the Subconscious Mind which she had read before coming down to Devon.

Mr. Cole, his eyes glistening, his lips twitching, began to talk excitedly.

" I had been meditating—reflecting on the Fullness of Life, on the Supreme Joy of Oneness—and then, you know, my eyes were opened and I *saw*——"

Miss Carnaby braced herself and hoped that what Mr. Cole had seen would not be what he had seen the last time—which had been, apparently, a Ritual Marriage in ancient Sumeria between a god and goddess.

" I saw "—Mr. Cole leant towards her, breathing hard, his eyes looking (yes, really they did) *quite* mad—" the Prophet Elijah descending from Heaven in his fiery chariot."

Miss Carnaby breathed a sigh of relief. Elijah was much better, she didn't mind Elijah.

" Below," went on Mr. Cole, " were the altars of Baal—hundreds and hundreds of them. A Voice cried to me : ' Look, write and testify that which you shall see——' "

He stopped and Miss Carnaby murmured politely : " Yes ? "

" On the altars were the sacrifices, bound there, helpless, waiting for the knife. Virgins—hundreds of virgins—young beautiful, naked virgins——"

Mr. Cole smacked his lips, Miss Carnaby blushed.

" Then came the ravens, the ravens of Odin, flying from the North. They met the ravens of Elijah—together they circled in the sky—they swooped, they plucked out the eyes of the

victims—there was wailing and gnashing of teeth—and the
Voice cried : ' Behold a Sacrifice—for on this day shall
Jehovah and Odin sign blood brotherhood ! ' Then the Priests
fell upon their victims, they raised their knives—they mutilated their victims——"

Desperately Miss Carnaby broke away from her tormentor
who was now slavering at the mouth in a kind of sadistic
fervour :

" Excuse me one moment."

She hastily accosted Lipscomb, the man who occupied the
Lodge which gave admission to Green Hills and who provi-
dentially happened to be passing.

" I wonder," she said, " if you have found a brooch of mine.
I must have dropped it somewhere about the grounds."

Lipscomb, who was a man immune from the general sweet-
ness and light of Green Hills, merely growled that he hadn't
seen any brooch. It wasn't *his* work to go about looking
for things. He tried to shake off Miss Carnaby but she
accompanied him, babbling about her brooch, till she had
put a safe distance between herself and the fervour of Mr.
Cole.

At that moment, the Master himself came out of the Great
Fold and, emboldened by his benignant smile, Miss Carnaby
ventured to speak her mind to him.

Did he think that Mr. Cole was quite—was quite——

The Master laid a hand on her shoulder.

" You must cast out Fear," he said. " Perfect Love casteth
out Fear. . . ."

" But I think Mr. Cole *is* mad. Those Visions he has——"

" As yet," said the Master, " he sees Imperfectly. . . .
through the Glass of his own Carnal Nature. But the day
will come when he shall see Spiritually—Face to Face."

Miss Carnaby was abashed. Of course, put like that—
She rallied to make a smaller protest.

" And really," she said, " need Lipscomb be so abominably
rude ? "

Again the Master gave his Heavenly Smile.

" Lipscomb," he said, " is a faithful watch-dog. He is a
crude—a primitive soul—but faithful—utterly faithful."

He strode on. Miss Carnaby saw him meet Mr. Cole, pause,

put a hand on Mr. Cole's shoulder. She hoped that the
Master's influence might alter the scope of future visions.

In any case, it was only a week now to the Autumn Festival.

VI

On the afternoon preceding the Festival, Miss Carnaby met
Hercule Poirot in a small teashop in the sleepy little town of
Newton Woodbury. Miss Carnaby was flushed and even more
breathless than usual. She sat sipping tea and crumbling a
rock bun between her fingers.

Poirot asked several questions to which she replied mono-
syllabically.

Then he said :

" How many will there be at the Festival ? "

" I think a hundred and twenty. Emmeline is there, of
course, and Mr. Cole—really *he* has been *very* odd lately. He
has visions. He described some of them to me—really most
peculiar—I hope, I do hope, he is not *insane*. Then there will
be quite a lot of new members—nearly twenty."

" Good. You know what you have to do ? "

There was a moment's pause before Miss Carnaby said in
a rather odd voice :

" I know what you told me, M. Poirot. . . ."

" *Très bien !* "

Then Amy Carnaby said clearly and distinctly :

" *But I am not going to do it.*"

Hercule Poirot stared at her. Miss Carnaby rose to her
feet. Her voice came fast and hysterical.

" You sent me here to spy on Dr. Andersen. You suspected
him of all sorts of things. But he is a wonderful man—a great
Teacher. I believe in him heart and soul ! And I am not
going to do your spying work any more, M. Poirot ! I am one
of the Sheep of the Shepherd. The Master has a new message
for the World and from now on, I belong to him body and soul.
And I'll pay for my own tea, please."

With which slight anticlimax Miss Carnaby planked down
one and threepence and rushed out of the teashop.

" *Nom d'un nom d'un nom,*" said Hercule Poirot.

The waitress had to ask him twice before he realised that she was presenting the bill. He met the interested stare of a surly looking man at the next table, flushed, paid the check and got up and went out.

He was thinking furiously.

## VII

Once again the Sheep were assembled in the Great Fold. The Ritual Questions and Answers had been chanted.

" Are you prepared for the Sacrament ? "

" *We are.*"

" Bind your eyes and hold out your right arm."

The Great Shepherd, magnificent in his green robe, moved along the waiting lines. The cabbage-eating, vision-seeing Mr. Cole, next to Miss Carnaby, gave a gulp of painful ecstasy as the needle pierced his flesh.

The Great Shepherd stood by Miss Carnaby. His hands touched her arm . . .

" *No, you don't. None of that. . . .*"

Words incredible—unprecedented. A scuffle, a roar of anger. Green veils were torn from eyes—to see an unbelievable sight —the Great Shepherd struggling in the grasp of the sheep-skinned Mr. Cole aided by another devotee.

In rapid professional tones, the erstwhile Mr. Cole was saying :

"—and I have here a warrant for your arrest. I must warn you that anything you say may be used in evidence at your trial."

There were other figures now at the door of the Sheep Fold —blue uniformed figures.

Someone cried : " It's the *police*. They're taking the Master away. They're taking the Master. . . ."

Everyone was shocked—horrified. . . . To them the Great Shepherd was a martyr ; suffering, as all great teachers suffer, from the ignorance and persecution of the outside world. . . .

Meanwhile Detective Inspector Cole was carefully packing up the hypodermic syringe that had fallen from the Great Shepherd's hand.

## VIII

" My brave colleague ! "

Poirot shook Miss Carnaby warmly by the hand and introduced her to Chief Inspector Japp.

" First class work, Miss Carnaby," said Chief Inspector Japp. " We couldn't have done it without you and that's a fact."

" Oh dear ! " Miss Carnaby was fluttered. " It's so *kind* of you to say so. And I'm afraid, you know, that I've really *enjoyed* it all. The excitement, you know, and playing my part. I got quite carried away sometimes. I really felt I *was* one of those foolish women."

" That's where your success lay," said Japp. " You were the genuine article. Nothing less would have taken that gentleman in ! He's a pretty astute scoundrel."

Miss Carnaby turned to Poirot.

" That was a terrible moment in the teashop. I didn't know *what* to do. I just had to act on the spur of the moment."

" You were magnificent," said Poirot warmly. " For a moment I thought that either you or I had taken leave of our senses. I thought for one little minute that you *meant* it."

" It was such a shock," said Miss Carnaby. " Just when we had been talking confidentially. I saw in the glass that Lipscomb, who keeps the Lodge of the Sanctuary, was sitting at the table behind me. I don't know now if it was an accident or if he had actually followed me. As I say, I had to do the best I could on the spur of the minute and trust that you would understand."

Poirot smiled.

" I did understand. There was only one person sitting near enough to overhear anything we said and as soon as I left the teashop I arranged to have him followed when he came out. When he went straight back to the Sanctuary I understood that I could rely on you and that you would not let me down —but I was afraid because it increased the danger for you."

" Was—was there really danger ? What was there in the syringe ? "

Japp said :

" Will you explain, or shall I ? "

Poirot said gravely :

" Mademoiselle, this Dr. Andersen had perfected a scheme of exploitation and murder—scientific murder. Most of his life has been spent in bacteriological research. Under a different name he has a chemical laboratory in Sheffield. There he makes cultures of various bacilli. It was his practice, at the Festivals, to inject into his followers a small but sufficient dose of Cannabis Indica—which is also known by the names of Hashish or Blang. This gives delusions of grandeur and pleasurable enjoyment. It bound his devotees to him. These were the Spiritual Joys that he promised them."

" Most remarkable," said Miss Carnaby. " Really a most remarkable sensation."

Hercule Poirot nodded.

" That was his general stock in trade—a dominating personality, the power of creating mass hysteria and the reactions produced by this drug. But he had a second aim in view.

" Lonely women, in their gratitude and fervour, made wills leaving their money to the Cult. One by one, these women died. They died in their own homes and apparently of natural causes. Without being too technical I will try to explain. It is possible to make intensified cultures of certain bacteria. The bacillus Coli Communis, for instance, the cause of ulcerative colitis. Typhoid bacilli can be introduced into the system. So can the Pneumococcus. There is also what is termed Old Tuberculin which is harmless to a healthy person but which stimulates any old tubercular lesion into activity. You perceive the cleverness of the man ? These deaths would occur in different parts of the country, with different doctors attending them and without any risk of arousing suspicion. He had also, I gather, cultivated a substance which had the power of delaying but intensifying the action of the chosen bacillus."

" He's a devil, if there ever was one ! " said Chief Inspector Japp.

Poirot went on :

" By my orders, you told him that you were a tuberculous subject. There was Old Tuberculin in the syringe when Cole arrested him. Since you were a healthy person it would not have harmed you, which is why I made you lay stress on your tubercular trouble. I was terrified that even now he *might* choose some other germ, but I respected your courage and I had to let you take the risk."

"Oh, *that's* all right," said Miss Carnaby brightly. "I don't mind taking risks. I'm only frightened of bulls in fields and things like that. But have you enough evidence to *convict* this dreadful person?"

Japp grinned.

"Plenty of evidence," he said. "We've got his laboratory and his cultures and the whole layout!"

Poirot said:

"It is possible, I think, that he has committed a long line of murders. I may say that it was not because his mother was a Jewess that he was dismissed from that German University. That merely made a convenient tale to account for his arrival here and to gain sympathy for him. Actually, I fancy, he is of pure Aryan blood."

Miss Carnaby sighed.

"*Qu'est ce qu'il y a?*" asked Poirot.

"I was thinking," said Miss Carnaby, "of a marvellous dream I had at the First Festival—hashish, I suppose. I arranged the whole world so beautifully! No wars, no poverty, no ill health, no ugliness. . . ."

"It must have been a fine dream," said Japp enviously.

Miss Carnaby jumped up. She said:

"I must get home. Emily has been so anxious. And dear Augustus has been missing me terribly, I hear."

Hercule Poirot said with a smile:

"He was afraid, perhaps, that like him, you were going to 'die for Hercule Poirot'!"

# XI

# THE APPLES OF THE HESPERIDES

I

HERCULE POIROT looked thoughtfully into the face of the man behind the big mahogany desk. He noted the generous brow, the mean mouth, the rapacious line of the jaw and the piercing, visionary eyes. He understood from looking at the man why Emery Power had become the great financial force that he was.

And his eyes falling to the long delicate hands, exquisitely shaped, that lay on the desk, he understood, too, why Emery Power had attained renown as a great collector. He was known on both sides of the Atlantic as a connoisseur of works of art. His passion for the artistic went hand in hand with an equal passion for the historic. It was not enough for him that a thing should be beautiful—he demanded also that it should have a tradition behind it.

Emery Power was speaking. His voice was quiet—a small, distinct voice that was more effective than any mere volume of sound could have been.

" You do not, I know, take many cases nowadays. But I think you will take this one."

" It is, then, an affair of great moment ? "

Emery Power said :

" It is of moment to me."

Poirot remained in an enquiring attitude, his head slightly on one side. He looked like a meditative robin.

The other went on :

" It concerns the recovery of a work of art. To be exact, a gold chased goblet, dating from the Renaissance. It is said to be the goblet used by Pope Alexander VI—Roderigo Borgia. He sometimes presented it to a favoured guest to drink from. That guest, M. Poirot, usually died."

" A pretty history," Poirot murmured.

" It's career has always been associated with violence. It has been stolen more than once. Murder has been done to gain possession of it. A trail of bloodshed has followed it through the ages."

" On account of its intrinsic value or for other reasons ? "

" Its intrinsic value is certainly considerable. The workmanship is exquisite (it is said to have been made by Benvenuto Cellini). The design represents a tree round which a jewelled serpent is coiled and the apples on the tree are formed of very beautiful emeralds."

Poirot murmured with an apparent quickening of interest :

" Apples ? "

" The emeralds are particularly fine, so are the rubies in the serpent, but of course the real value of the cup is its historical associations. It was put up for sale by the Marchese di San Veratrino in 1929. Collectors bid against each other and I secured it finally for a sum equalling (at the then rate of exchange) thirty thousand pounds."

Poirot raised his eyebrows. He murmured :

" Indeed a princely sum ! The Marchese di San Veratrino was fortunate."

Emery Power said :

" When I really want a thing, I am willing to pay for it, M. Poirot."

Hercule Poirot said softly :

" You have no doubt heard the Spanish proverb : '*Take what you want—and pay for it, says God.*' "

For a moment the financier frowned—a swift light of anger showed in his eyes. He said coldly :

" You are by way of being a philosopher, M. Poirot."

" I have arrived at the age of reflection, Monsieur."

" Doubtless. But it is not reflection that will restore my goblet to me."

" You think not ? "

" I fancy action will be necessary."

Hercule Poirot nodded placidly.

" A lot of people make the same mistake. But I demand your pardon, Mr. Power, we have digressed from the matter in hand. You were saying that you had bought the cup from the Marchese di San Veratrino ? "

" Exactly. What I have now to tell you is that it was stolen before it actually came into my possession."

" How did that happen ? "

" The Marchese's Palace was broken into on the night of the sale and eight or ten pieces of considerable value were stolen, including the goblet."

" What was done in the matter ? "

Power shrugged his shoulders.

" The police, of course, took the matter in hand. The robbery was recognised to be the work of a well-known international gang of thieves. Two of their number, a Frenchman called Dublay and an Italian called Riccovetti, were caught and tried—some of the stolen goods were found in their possession."

" But not the Borgia goblet ? "

" But not the Borgia goblet. There were, as far as the police could ascertain, three men actually engaged in the robbery—the two I have just mentioned and a third, an Irishman named Patrick Casey. This last was an expert cat burglar. It was he who is said to have actually stolen the things. Dublay was the brains of the group and planned their coups ; Riccovetti drove the car and waited below for the goods to be lowered down to him."

" And the stolen goods ? Were they split up into three parts ? "

" Possibly. On the other hand, the articles that were recovered were those of least value. It seems possible that the more noteworthy and spectacular pieces had been hastily smuggled out of the country."

" What about the third man, Casey ? Was he never brought to justice ? "

" Not in the sense you mean. He was not a very young man. His muscles were stiffer than formerly. Two weeks later he fell from the fifth floor of a building and was killed instantly."

" Where was this ? "

" In Paris. He was attempting to rob the house of the millionaire banker, Duvauglier."

" And the goblet has never been seen since ? "

" Exactly."

" It has never been offered for sale ? "

" I am quite sure it has not. I may say that not only the police, but also private inquiry agents, have been on the look out for it."

" What about the money you had paid over ? "

" The Marchese, a very punctilious person, offered to refund it to me as the cup had been stolen from his house."

" But you did not accept ? "

" No."

" Why was that ? "

" Shall we say because I preferred to keep the matter in my own hands ? "

" You mean that if you had accepted the Marchese's offer, the goblet, if recovered, would be his property, whereas now it is legally yours ? "

" Exactly."

Poirot asked :

" What was there behind that attitude of yours ? "

Emery Power said with a smile :

" You appreciate that point, I see. Well, M. Poirot, it is quite simple. *I thought I knew who was actually in possession of the goblet.*"

" Very interesting. And who was it ? "

" Sir Reuben Rosenthal. He was not only a fellow collector but he was at the time a personal enemy. We had been rivals in several business deals—and on the whole I had come out the better. Our animosity culminated in this rivalry over the Borgia Goblet. Each of us was determined to possess it. It was more or less a point of honour. Our appointed representatives bid against each other at the sale."

" And your representative's final bid secured the treasure ? "

" Not precisely. I took the precaution of having a second agent—ostensibly the representative of a Paris dealer. Neither of us, you understand, would have been willing to yield to the other, but to allow a third party to acquire the cup, with the possibility of approaching that third party quietly afterwards—that was a very different matter."

" In fact, *une petite déception.*"

" Exactly."

" Which was successful—and immediately afterwards Sir Reuben discovered how he had been tricked ? "

Power smiled.

It was a revealing smile.

Poirot said : " I see the position now. You believed that Sir Reuben, determined not to be beaten, deliberately commissioned the theft ? "

Emery Power raised a hand.

" Oh no, no ! It would not be so crude as that. It amounted to this—shortly afterwards Sir Reuben would have purchased a Renaissance goblet, *provenance* unspecified."

" The description of which would have been circulated by the police ? "

" The goblet would not have been placed openly on view."

" You think it would have been sufficient for Sir Reuben to *know* that he possessed it ? "

" Yes. Moreover, if I had accepted the Marchese's offer— it would have been possible for Sir Reuben to conclude a private arrangement with him later, thus allowing the goblet to pass legally into his possession."

He paused a minute and then said :

" But by retaining the legal ownership, there were still possibilities left open to me of recovering my property."

" You mean," said Poirot bluntly, " that you could arrange for it to be stolen from Sir Reuben."

" Not *stolen*, M. Poirot. I should have been merely recovering my own property."

" But I gather that you were not successful ? "

" For a very good reason. Rosenthal has never had the goblet in his possession ! "

" How do you know ? "

" Recently there has been a merger of oil interests. Rosenthal's interests and mine now coincide. We are allies and not enemies. I spoke to him frankly on the subject and he at once assured me that the cup had never been in his possession."

" And you believe him ? "

" Yes."

Poirot said thoughtfully :

" Then for nearly ten years you have been, as they say in this country, barking up the mistaken tree ? "

The financier said bitterly :

" Yes, that is exactly what I have been doing ! "

" And now—it is all to start again from the beginning ? "

The other nodded.

" And that is where I come in ? I am the dog that you set upon the cold scent—a very cold scent."

Emery Power said dryly :

" If the affair were easy it would not have been necessary for me to send for you. Of course, if you think it impossible——"

He had found the right word. Hercule Poirot drew himself up. He said coldly :

" I do not recognise the word *impossible*, Monsieur ! I ask myself only—is this affair sufficiently interesting for me to undertake ? "

Emery Power smiled again. He said :

" It has this interest—*you may name your own fee.*"

The small man looked at the big man. He said softly :

" Do you then desire this work of art so much ? Surely not ! "

Emery Power said :

" Put it that I, like yourself, do not accept defeat."

Hercule Poirot bowed his head. He said :

" Yes—put that way—I understand. . . ."


II


Inspector Wagstaffe was interested.

" The Veratrino cup ? Yes, I remember all about it. I was in charge of the business this end. I speak a bit of Italiano, you know, and I went over and had a pow-wow with the Macaronis. It's never turned up from that day to this. Funny thing, that."

" What is your explanation ? A private sale ? "

Wagstaffe shook his head.

" I doubt it. Of course it's remotely possible. . . . No, my explanation is a good deal simpler. The stuff was cached— and the only man who knew where it was is dead."

" You mean Casey ? "

" Yes. He may have cached it somewhere in Italy, or he may have succeeded in smuggling it out of the country. But *he* hid it and wherever he hid it, there it still is."

Hercule Poirot sighed.

" It is a romantic theory.  Pearls stuffed into plaster casts
—what is the story—the *Bust of Napoleon*, is it not ?  But in
this case it is not jewels—it is a large, solid gold cup.  Not
so easy to hide that, one would think."

Wagstaffe said vaguely :

" Oh, I don't know.  It could be done, I suppose.  Under
the floor-boards—something of that kind."

" Had Casey a house of his own ? "

" Yes—in Liverpool."  He grinned.  " It wasn't under the
floor-boards there.  We made sure of that."

" What about his family ? "

" Wife was a decent sort of woman—tubercular.  Worried
to death by her husband's way of life.  She was religious—
a devout Catholic—but couldn't make up her mind to leave
him.  She died a couple of years ago.  Daughter took after her
—she became a nun.  The son was different—a chip off the old
block.  Last I heard of him he was doing time in America."

Hercule Poirot wrote in his little notebook.  *America*.  He
said :  " It is possible that Casey's son may have known the
hiding-place ? "

" Don't believe he did.  It would have come into the fences'
hands by now."

" The cup might have been melted down."

" It might.  Quite possible, I should say.  But I don't
know—its supreme value is to collectors—and there's a lot
of funny business goes on with collectors—you'd be surprised !
Sometimes," said Wagstaffe virtuously, " I think collectors
haven't any morals at all."

" Ah !  Would you be surprised if Sir Reuben Rosenthal,
for instance, were engaged in what you describe as ' funny
business ' ? "

Wagstaffe grinned.

" I wouldn't put it past him.  He's not supposed to be very
scrupulous where works of art are concerned."

" What about the other members of the gang ? "

" Ricovetti and Dublay both got stiff sentences.  I should
imagine they'll be coming out about now."

" Dublay is a Frenchman, is he not ? "

" Yes, he was the brains of the gang."

" Were there other members of it ? "

" There was a girl—Red Kate she used to be called. Took a job as lady's-maid and found out all about a crib—where stuff was kept and so on. She went to Australia, I believe, after the gang broke up."

" Anyone else ? "

" Chap called Yougouian was suspected of being in with them. He's a dealer. Headquarters in Stamboul but he has a shop in Paris. Nothing proved against him—but he's a slippery customer."

Poirot sighed. He looked at his little notebook. In it was written : America, Australia, Italy, France, Turkey. . . .

He murmured :

" *I'll put a girdle round the earth——*"

" Pardon ? " said Inspector Wagstaffe.

" I was observing," said Hercule Poirot, " that a world tour seems indicated."


## III


It was the habit of Hercule Poirot to discuss his cases with his capable valet, George. That is to say, Hercule Poirot would let drop certain observations to which George would reply with the worldly wisdom which he had acquired in the course of his career as a gentleman's gentleman.

" If you were faced, Georges," said Poirot, " with the necessity of conducting investigations in five different parts of the globe, how would you set about it ? "

" Well, sir, air travel is very quick, though some say as it upsets the stomach. I couldn't say myself."

" One asks oneself," said Hercule Poirot, " what would Hercules have done ? "

" You mean the bicycle chap, sir ? "

" Or," pursued Hercule Poirot, " one simply asks, what *did* he do ? And the answer, Georges, is that he travelled energetically. But he was forced in the end to obtain information— as some say—from Prometheus—others from Nereus."

" Indeed, sir ? " said George. " I never heard of either of those gentlemen. Are they travel agencies, sir ? "

Hercule Poirot, enjoying the sound of his own voice, went on :

" My client, Emery Power, understands only one thing—*action !* But it is useless to dispense energy by unnecessary action. There is a golden rule in life, Georges, never do anything yourself that others can do for you.

" Especially," added Hercule Poirot, rising and going to the bookshelf, " when expense is no object ! "

He took from the shelf a file labelled with the letter D and opened it at the words " Detective Agencies—Reliable ".

" The modern Prometheus," he murmured. " Be so obliging, Georges, as to copy out for me certain names and addresses. Messrs. Hankerton, New York. Messrs. Laden and Bosher, Sydney. Signor Giovanni Mezzi, Rome. M. Nahum, Stamboul. Messrs. Roget et Franconard, Paris."

He paused while George finished this. Then he said :

" And now be so kind as to look up the trains for Liverpool."

" Yes, sir, you are going to Liverpool, sir ? "

" I am afraid so. It is possible, Georges, that I may have to go even further. But not just yet."

IV

It was three months later that Hercule Poirot stood on a rocky point and surveyed the Atlantic Ocean. Gulls rose and swooped down again with long melancholy cries. The air was soft and damp.

Hercule Poirot had the feeling, not uncommon in those who come to Inishgowlen for the first time, that he had reached the end of the world. He had never in his life imagined anything so remote, so desolate, so abandoned. It had beauty, a melancholy, haunted beauty, the beauty of a remote and incredible past. Here, in the west of Ireland, the Romans had never marched, tramp, tramp, tramp : had never fortified a camp : had never built a well-ordered, sensible, useful road. It was a land where common sense and an orderly way of life were unknown.

Hercule Poirot looked down at the tips of his patent-leather shoes and sighed. He felt forlorn and very much alone. The standards by which he lived were here not appreciated.

His eyes swept slowly up and down the desolate coast line, then once more out to sea. Somewhere out there, so tradition had it, were the Isles of the Blest, the Land of Youth. . . .

He murmured to himself:

"*The Apple Tree, the Singing and the Gold. . . .*"

And suddenly, Hercule Poirot was himself again—the spell was broken, he was once more in harmony with his patent-leather shoes and natty, dark grey gent's suiting.

Not very far away he had heard the toll of a bell. He understood that bell. It was a sound he had been familiar with from early youth.

He set off briskly along the cliff. In about ten minutes he came in sight of the building on the cliff. A high wall surrounded it and a great wooden door studded with nails was set in the wall. Hercule Poirot came to this door and knocked. There was a vast iron knocker. Then he cautiously pulled at a rusty chain and a shrill little bell tinkled briskly inside the door.

A small panel in the door was pushed aside and showed a face. It was a suspicious face, framed in starched white. There was a distinct moustache on the upper lip, but the voice was the voice of a woman, it was the voice of what Hercule Poirot called a *femme formidable*.

It demanded his business.

" Is this the Convent of St. Mary and All Angels ? "

The formidable woman said with asperity :

" And what else would it be ? "

Hercule Poirot did not attempt to answer that. He said to the dragon :

" I would like to see the Mother Superior."

The dragon was unwilling, but in the end she yielded. Bars were drawn back, the door opened and Hercule Poirot was conducted to a small bare room where visitors to the Convent were received.

Presently a nun glided in, her rosary swinging at her waist.

Hercule Poirot was a Catholic by birth. He understood the atmosphere in which he found himself.

" I apologise for troubling you, *ma mère*," he said, " but you

have here, I think, a *religieuse* who was, in the world, Kate
Casey."

The Mother Superior bowed her head. She said :
" That is so. Sister Mary Ursula in religion."

Hercule Poirot said : " There is a certain wrong that
needs righting. I believe that Sister Mary Ursula could help
me. She has information that might be invaluable."

The Mother Superior shook her head. Her face was placid,
her voice calm and remote. She said :

" Sister Mary Ursula cannot help you."

" But I assure you——"

He broke off. The Mother Superior said :

" Sister Mary Ursula died two months ago."

v

In the saloon bar of Jimmy Donovan's Hotel, Hercule
Poirot sat uncomfortably against the wall. The hotel did not
come up to his ideas of what a hotel should be. His bed was
broken—so were two of the window panes in his room—
thereby admitting that night air which Hercule Poirot dis-
trusted so much. The hot water brought him had been tepid
and the meal he had eaten was producing curious and painful
sensations in his inside.

There were five men in the bar and they were all talking
politics. For the most part Hercule Poirot could not understand what they said. In any case, he did not much care.

Presently he found one of the men sitting beside him. This
was a man of slightly different class to the others. He had
the stamp of the seedy townsman upon him.

He said with immense dignity :

" I tell you, sir. I tell you—Pegeen's Pride hasn't got a
chance, not a chance. . . . bound to finish right down the
course—right down the course. You take my tip . . . everybody ought to take my tip. Know who I am, shir, do you
know, I shay ? Atlas, thatsh who I am—Atlas of the Dublin
Sun . . . been tipping winnersh all the season. . . . Didn't
I give Larry's Girl ? Twenty-five to one—twenty-five to one.
Follow Atlas and you can't go wrong."

Hercule Poirot regarded him with a strange reverence. He said, and his voice trembled :

"*Mon Dieu*, it is an omen ! "

## VI

It was some hours later. The moon showed from time to time, peeping out coquettishly from behind the clouds. Poirot and his new friend had walked some miles. The former was limping. The idea crossed his mind that there were, after all, other shoes—more suitable to country walking than patent-leather. Actually George had respectfully conveyed as much. " A nice pair of brogues," was what George had said.

Hercule Poirot had not cared for the idea. He liked his feet to look neat and well-shod. But now, tramping along this stony path, he realised that there *were* other shoes. . . .

His companion said suddenly :

" Is it the way the Priest would be after me for this ? I'll not have a mortal sin upon my conscience."

Hercule Poirot said : " You are only restoring to Cæsar the things which are Cæsar's."

They had come to the wall of the Convent. Atlas prepared to do his part.

A groan burst from him and he exclaimed in low, poignant tones that he was destroyed entirely !

Hercule Poirot spoke with authority.

" Be quiet. It is not the weight of the world that you have to support—only the weight of Hercule Poirot."

## VII

Atlas was turning over two new five pound notes.

He said hopefully :

" Maybe I'll not remember in the morning the way I earned this. I'm after worrying that Father O'Reilly will be after me."

" Forget everything, my friend. To-morrow the world is yours."

Atlas murmured :

" And what'll I put it on ? There's Working Lad, he's a grand horse, a lovely horse he is ! And there's Sheila Boyne. 7 to 1 I'd get on her."

He paused :

" Was it my fancy now or did I hear you mention the name of a heathen god ? Hercules, you said, and glory be to God, there's a Hercules running in the three-thirty to-morrow."

" My friend," said Hercule Poirot, " put your money on that horse. I tell you this, Hercules cannot fail."

And it is certainly true that on the following day Mr. Rosslyn's Hercules very unexpectedly won the Boynan Stakes, starting price 60 to 1.

<h2 style="text-align:center">VIII</h2>

Deftly Hercule Poirot unwrapped the neatly done-up parcel. First the brown paper, then the wadding, lastly the tissue paper.

On the desk in front of Emery Power he placed a gleaming golden cup. Chased on it was a tree bearing apples of green emeralds.

The financier drew a deep breath. He said :

" I congratulate you, M. Poirot."

Hercule Poirot bowed.

Emery Power stretched out a hand. He touched the rim of the goblet, drawing his finger round it. He said in a deep voice :

" Mine ! "

Hercule Poirot agreed.

" Yours ! "

The other gave a sigh. He leaned back in his chair. He said in a business-like voice :

" Where did you find it ? "

Hercule Poirot said :

" I found it on an altar."

Emery Power stared.

Poirot went on :

" Casey's daughter was a nun. She was about to take her

final vows at the time of her father's death. She was an ignorant but a devout girl. The cup was hidden in her father's house in Liverpool. She took it to the Convent wanting, I think, to atone for her father's sins. She gave it to be used to the glory of God. I do not think that the nuns themselves ever realised its value. They took it, probably, for a family heirloom. In their eyes it was a chalice and they used it as such."

Emery Power said :

" An extraordinary story ! " He added : " What made you think of going there ? "

Poirot shrugged his shoulders.

" Perhaps—a process of elimination. And then there was the extraordinary fact that no one had ever tried to dispose of the cup. That looked, you see, as though it were in a place where ordinary material values did not apply. I remembered that Patrick Casey's daughter was a nun."

Power said heartily :

" Well, as I said before, I congratulate you. Let me know your fee and I'll write you a cheque."

Hercule Poirot said:

" There is no fee."

The other stared at him.

" What do you mean ? "

" Did you ever read fairy stories when you were a child ? The King in them would say : ' Ask of me what you will ' ? "

" So you *are* asking something ? "

" Yes, but not money. Merely a simple request."

" Well, what is it ? D'you want a tip for the markets ? "

" That would be only money in another form. My request is much simpler than that."

" What is it ? "

Hercule Poirot laid his hands on the cup.

" Send this back to the Convent."

There was a pause. Then Emery Power said :

" Are you quite mad ? "

Hercule Poirot shook his head.

" No, I am not mad. See, I will show you something."

He picked up the goblet. With his finger-nail, he pressed hard into the open jaws of the snake that was coiled round the tree. Inside the cup a tiny portion of the gold chased interior slid aside leaving an aperture into the hollow handle.

Poirot said :

" You see ? This was the drinking cup of the Borgia Pope. Through this little hole the poison passed into the drink. You have said yourself that the history of this cup is evil. Violence and blood and evil passions have accompanied its possession. Evil will perhaps come to you in your turn."

" Superstition ! "

" Possibly. But why were you so anxious to possess this thing ? Not for its beauty. Not for its value. You have a hundred—a thousand perhaps—beautiful and rare things. You wanted it to sustain your pride. You were determined not to be beaten. *Eh bien*, you are not beaten. You win ! The goblet is in your possession. But now, why not make a great—a supreme gesture ? Send it back to where it has dwelt in peace for nearly ten years. Let the evil of it be purified there. It belonged to the Church once—let it return to the Church. Let it stand once more on the altar, purified and absolved as we hope that the souls of men shall be also puri-fied and absolved from their sins."

He leaned forward.

" Let me describe for you the place where I found it—the Garden of Peace, looking out over the Western Sea towards a forgotten Paradise of Youth and Eternal Beauty."

He spoke on, describing in simple words the remote charm of Inishgowlan.

Emery Power sat back, one hand over his eyes. He said at last :

" I was born on the west coast of Ireland. I left there as a boy to go to America."

Poirot said gently :

" I heard that."

The financier sat up. His eyes were shrewd again. He said, and there was a faint smile on his lips :

" You are a strange man, M. Poirot. You shall have your way. Take the goblet to the Convent as a gift in my name. A pretty costly gift. Thirty thousand pounds—and what shall I get in exchange ? "

Poirot said gravely :

" The nuns will say Masses for your soul."

The rich man's smile widened—a rapacious, hungry smile. He said :

" So, after all, it may be an investment ! Perhaps, the best one I ever made. . . ."

IX

In the little parlour of the Convent, Hercule Poirot told his story and restored the chalice to the Mother Superior.

She murmured :

" Tell him we thank him and we will pray for him."

Hercule Poirot said gently :

" He needs your prayers."

" Is he then an unhappy man ? "

Poirot said :

" So unhappy that he has forgotten what happiness means. So unhappy that he does not know he is unhappy."

The nun said softly :

" Ah, a rich man. . . ."

Hercule Poirot said nothing—for he knew there was nothing to say. . . .

# XII

# THE CAPTURE OF CERBERUS

## I

HERCULE POIROT, swaying to and fro in the tube train, thrown now against one body, now against another, thought to himself that there were too many people in the world ! Certainly there were too many people in the Underground world of London at this particular moment (6.30 p.m.) of the evening. Heat, noise, crowd, contiguity—the unwelcome pressure of hands, arms, bodies, shoulders ! Hemmed in and pressed around by strangers—and on the whole (he thought distastefully) a plain and uninteresting lot of strangers ! Humanity seen thus *en masse* was not attractive. How seldom did one see a face sparkling with intelligence, how seldom a *femme bien mise* ! What was this passion that attacked women for knitting under the most unpropitious conditions ? A woman did not look her best knitting ; the absorption, the glassy eyes, the restless, busy fingers ! One needed the agility of a wild cat, and the willpower of a Napoleon to manage to knit in a crowded tube, but women managed it ! If they succeeded in obtaining a seat, out came a miserable little strip of shrimp pink and click, click went the pins !

No repose, thought Poirot, no feminine grace ! His elderly soul revolted from the stress and hurry of the modern world. All these young women who surrounded him—so alike, so devoid of charm, so lacking in rich, alluring femininity ! He demanded a more flamboyant appeal. Ah ! to see a *femme du monde*, *chic*, sympathetic, *spirituelle*—a woman with ample curves, a woman ridiculously and extravagantly dressed ! Once there had been such women. But now—now——

The train stopped at a station ; people surged out, forcing Poirot back on to the points of knitting pins ; surged in, squeezing him into even more sardine-like proximity with his fellow passengers. The train started off again with a jerk,

Poirot was thrown against a stout woman with knobbly parcels, said " *Pardon !* " bounced off again into a long angular man whose attaché-case caught him in the small of the back. He said " *Pardon !* " again. He felt his moustaches becoming limp and uncurled. *Quel enfer !* Fortunately the next station was his !

It was also the station of what seemed to be about a hundred and fifty other people, since it happened to be Piccadilly Circus. Like a great tidal wave they flowed out on to the platform. Presently Poirot was again jammed tightly on an escalator being carried upwards towards the surface of the earth.

Up, thought Poirot, from the Infernal Regions. . . . How exquisitely painful was a suitcase rammed into one's knees from behind on an ascending escalator !

At that moment, a voice cried his name. Startled, he raised his eyes. On the opposite escalator, the one descending, his unbelieving eyes saw a vision from the past. A woman of full and flamboyant form ; her luxuriant henna red hair crowned with a small plastron of straw to which was attached a positive platoon of brilliantly feathered little birds. Exotic-looking furs dripped from her shoulders.

Her crimson mouth opened wide, her rich, foreign voice echoed resoundingly. She had good lungs.

" It *is* ! " she screamed. " But it is ! *Mon cher Hercule Poirot !* We must meet again ! I insist ! "

But Fate itself is not more inexorable than the behaviour of two escalators moving in an inverse direction. Steadily, remorselessly, Hercule Poirot was borne upward, and the Countess Vera Rossakoff was borne downwards.

Twisting himself sideways, leaning over the balustrade, Poirot cried despairingly :

" *Chère Madame*—where can I find you ? "

Her reply came to him faintly from the depths. It was unexpected, yet seemed at the moment strangely apposite.

" *In Hell. . . .*"

Hercule Poirot blinked. He blinked again. Suddenly he rocked on his feet. Unawares he had reached the top—and had neglected to step off properly. The crowd spread out round him. A little to one side a dense crowd was pressing on to the

downward escalator. Should he join them ? Had that been
the Countess's meaning ? No doubt that travelling in the
bowels of the earth at the rush hour *was* Hell. If that *had* been
the Countess's meaning, he could not agree with her more. . . .

Resolutely Poirot crossed over, sandwiched himself into the
descending crowd and was borne back into the depths. At the
foot of the escalator no sign of the Countess. Poirot was left
with a choice of blue, amber, etc. lights to follow.

Was the Countess patronising the Bakerloo or the Piccadilly
line ? Poirot visited each platform in turn. He was swept
about amongst surging crowds boarding or leaving trains,
but nowhere did he espy that flamboyant Russian figure, the
Countess Vera Rossakof.

Weary, battered, and infinitely chagrined, Hercule Poirot
once more ascended to ground level and stepped out into the
hubbub of Piccadilly Circus. He reached home in a mood of
pleasurable excitement.

It is the misfortune of small precise men to hanker after
large and flamboyant women. Poirot had never been able to
rid himself of the fatal fascination the Countess held for him.
Though it was something like twenty years since he had seen
her last the magic still held. Granted that her make-up now
resembled a scene-painter's sunset, with the woman under
the make-up well hidden from sight, to Hercule Poirot she
still represented the sumptuous and the alluring. The little
bourgeois was still thrilled by the aristocrat. The memory
of the adroit way she stole jewellery roused the old
admiration. He remembered the magnificent aplomb with
which she had admitted the fact when taxed with it. A woman
in a thousand—in a million ! And he had met her again—
and lost her !

" *In Hell*," she had said. Surely his ears had not deceived
him ? She *had* said that ?

But what had she meant by it ? *Had* she meant London's
Underground Railways ? Or were her words to be taken in a
religious sense ? Surely, even if her own way of life made Hell
the most plausible destination for her after this life, surely—
surely her Russian courtesy would not suggest that Hercule
Poirot was necessarily bound for the same place ?

No, she must have meant something quite different. She

must have meant—Hercule Poirot was brought up short
against bewilderment. What an intriguing, what an unpre-
dictable woman ! A lesser woman might have shrieked " The
Ritz " or " Claridge's ". But Vera Rossakoff had cried
poignantly and impossibly :  " Hell ! "

Poirot sighed. But he was not defeated. In his perplexity
he took the simplest and most straightforward course on the
following morning, he asked his secretary, Miss Lemon.

Miss Lemon was unbelievably ugly and incredibly efficient.
To her Poirot was nobody in particular—he was merely her
employer. She gave him excellent service. Her private
thoughts and dreams were concentrated on a new filing
system which she was slowly perfecting in the recesses of her
mind.

" Miss Lemon, may I ask you a question ? "

" Of course, M. Poirot." Miss Lemon took her fingers off the
typewriter keys and waited attentively.

" If a friend asked you to meet her—or him—in Hell, what
would you do ? "

Miss Lemon, as usual, did not pause. She knew, as the
saying goes, all the answers.

" It would be advisable, I think, to ring up for a table,"
she said.

Hercule Poirot stared at her in a stupefied fashion.

He said, *staccato*, " You—would—ring—up—for—a table ? "

Miss Lemon nodded and drew the telephone towards her.

" To-night ? " she asked, and taking assent for granted
since he did not speak, she dialled briskly.

" Temple Bar 14578 ? Is that *Hell* ?  Will you please
reserve a table for two. M. Hercule Poirot. Eleven o'clock."

She replaced the receiver and her fingers hovered over the
keys of her typewriter. A slight—a very slight look of impatience was discernible upon her face. She had done her part,
the look seemed to say, surely her employer could now leave
her to get on with what she was doing ?

But Hercule Poirot required explanations.

" What is it, then, this *Hell* ? " he demanded.

Miss Lemon looked slightly surprised.

" Oh didn't you know, M. Poirot ?  It's a night club—quite
new and very much the rage at present—run by some Russian

woman, I believe. I can fix up for you to become a member before this evening quite easily."

Whereupon, having wasted (as she made obvious) quite time enough, Miss Lemon broke into a perfect fusillade of efficient typing.

At eleven that evening Hercule Poirot passed through a doorway over which a Neon sign discreetly showed one letter at a time. A gentleman in red tails received him and took from him his coat.

A gesture directed him to a flight of wide shallow stairs leading downwards. On each step a phrase was written. The first one ran :

" *I meant well. . . .*"

The second :

" *Wipe the slate clean and start afresh. . . .*"

The third :

" *I can give it up any time I like. . . .*"

" The good intentions that pave the way to Hell," Hercule Poirot murmured appreciatively. " *C'est bien imaginé, ça !* "

He descended the stairs. At the foot was a tank of water with scarlet lilies. Spanning it was a bridge shaped like a boat. Poirot crossed by it.

On his left in a kind of marble grotto sat the largest and ugliest and blackest dog Poirot had ever seen ! It sat up very straight and gaunt and immovable. It was perhaps, he thought, (and hoped !) not *real*. But at that moment the dog turned its ferocious and ugly head and from the depths of its black body a low, rumbling growl was emitted. It was a terrifying sound.

And then Poirot noticed a decorative basket of small round dog biscuits. They were labelled, " *A sop for Cerberus !* "

It was on them that the dog's eyes were fixed. Once again the low, rumbling growl was heard. Hastily Poirot picked up a biscuit and tossed it towards the great hound.

A cavernous red mouth yawned ; then came a snap as the powerful jaws closed again. Cerberus had accepted his sop ! Poirot moved on through an open doorway.

The room was not a big one. It was dotted with little tables, a space of dancing floor in the middle. It was lighted with small red lamps, there were frescoes on the walls, and at the far end was a vast grill at which officiated chefs dressed as devils with tails and horns.

All this Poirot took in before, with all the impulsiveness of her Russian nature, Countess Vera Rossakoff, resplendent in scarlet evening dress, bore down upon him with outstretched hands.

" Ah, you have come ! My dear—my *very* dear friend ! what a joy to see you again ! After such years—so many— how many ?—— No, we will not say how many ! To me it seems but as yesterday. You have not changed—not in the least have you changed ! "

" Nor you, *chère amie*," Poirot exclaimed, bowing over her hand.

Neverthelesss he was fully conscious now that twenty years is twenty years. Countess Rossakoff might not uncharitably have been described as a ruin. But she was at least a spectacular ruin. The exuberance, the full-blooded enjoyment of life was still there, and she knew, none better, how to flatter a man.

She drew Poirot with her to a table at which two other people were sitting.

" My friend, my celebrated friend, M. Hercule Poirot," she announced. " He who is the terror of evildoers ! I was once afraid of him myself, but now I lead a life of the extreme, the most virtuous dullness. Is it not so ? "

The tall thin elderly man to whom she spoke said, " Never say dull, Countess."

" The Professor Liskeard," the Countess announced. " He who knows everything about the past and who gave me the valuable hints for the decorations here."

The Archæologist shuddered slightly.

" If I'd known what you meant to do ! " he murmured. " The result is so appalling."

Poirot observed the frescoes more closely. On the wall facing him Orpheus and his jazz band played, while Eurydice looked hopefully towards the grill. On the opposite wall Osiris and Isis seemed to be throwing an Egyptian underworld boating party. On the third wall some bright young people were enjoying mixed bathing in a state of Nature.

" The Country of the Young," explained the Countess and

added in the same breath, completing her introductions : " And this is my little Alice."

Poirot bowed to the second occupant of the table, a severe-looking girl in a check coat and skirt. She wore horn-rimmed glasses.

" She is very, *very* clever," said Countess Rossakoff. " She has a degree and she is a psychologist and she knows all the reasons why lunatics are lunatics ! It is not, as you might think, because they are mad ! No, there are all sorts of other reasons ! I find that very peculiar."

The girl called Alice smiled kindly but a little disdainfully. She asked the Professor in a firm voice if he would like to dance. He appeared flattered but dubious.

" My dear young lady, I fear I only waltz."

" This *is* a waltz," said Alice patiently.

They got up and danced. They did not dance well.

The Countess Rossakoff sighed. Following out a train of thought of her own, she murmured, " And yet she is not *really* bad-looking. . . ."

" She does not make the most of herself," said Poirot judicially.

" Frankly," cried the Countess, " I cannot understand the young people of nowadays. They do not try any more to please—always, in my youth, I tried—the colours that suited me—a little padding in the frocks—the corset laced tight round the waist—the hair, perhaps, a more interesting shade——"

She pushed back the heavy Titian tresses from her forehead —it was undeniable that she, at least, was still trying and trying hard !

" To be content with what Nature has given you, that— that is *stupid* ! It is also arrogant ! The little Alice she writes pages of long words about Sex, but how often, I ask you, does a man suggest to her that they should go to Brighton for the week-end ? It is all long words and work, and the welfare of the workers, and the future of the world. It is very worthy, but I ask you, is it *gay* ? And look, I ask you, how drab these young people have made the world ! It is all regulations and prohibitions ! Not so when I was young."

" That reminds me, how is your son, Madame ? " At the

last moment he substituted " son," for " little boy," remembering that twenty years had passed.

The Countess's face lit up with enthusiastic motherhood.

" The beloved angel ! So big now, such shoulders, so handsome ! He is in America. He builds there—bridges, banks, hotels, department stores, railways, anything the Americans want ! "

Poirot looked slightly puzzled.

" He is then an engineer ?  Or an architect ? "

" What does it matter ? " demanded the Countess. " He is adorable ! He is wrapped up in iron girders, and machinery, and things called stresses. The kind of things that I have never understood in the least. But we adore each other— always we adore each other ! And so for his sake I adore the little Alice. But yes, they are engaged. They meet on a plane or a boat or a train, and they fall in love, all in the midst of talking about the welfare of the workers. And when she comes to London she comes to see me and I take her to my heart." The Countess clasped her arms across her vast bosom, " And I say—' You and Niki love each other—so I too love you— but if you love him why do you leave him in America ? ' And she talks about her ' job ' and the book she is writing, and her career, and frankly I do not understand, but I have always said : ' One must be tolerant.' " She added all in one breath, " And what do you think, *cher ami*, of all this that I have imagined here ? "

" It is very well imagined," said Poirot, looking round him approvingly. " It is *chic* ! "

The place was full and it had about it that unmistakable air of success which cannot be counterfeited. There were languid couples in full evening dress, Bohemians in corduroy trousers, stout gentlemen in business suits. The band, dressed as devils, dispensed hot music. No doubt about it, *Hell* had caught on.

" We have all kinds here," said the Countess. " That is as it should be, is it not ?  The gates of Hell are open to all ? "

" Except, possibly, to the poor ? " Poirot suggested.

The Countess laughed.  " Are we not told that it is difficult for a rich man to enter the Kingdom of Heaven ? Naturally, then, he should have priority in Hell."

The Professor and Alice were returning to the table. The Countess got up.

" I must speak to Aristide."

She exchanged some words with the head waiter, a lean Mephistopheles, then went round from table to table, speaking to the guests.

The Professor, wiping his forehead and sipping a glass of wine, remarked :

" She is a personality, is she not ?  People feel it."

He excused himself as he went over to speak to someone at another table.  Poirot, left alone with the severe Alice, felt slightly embarrassed as he met the cold blue of her eyes.  He recognised that she was actually quite good-looking, but he found her distinctly alarming.

" I do not yet know your last name," he murmured.

" Cunningham.  Dr. Alice Cunningham.  You have known Vera in past days, I understand ? "

" Twenty years ago it must be."

" I find her a very interesting study," said Dr. Alice Cunningham.  " Naturally I am interested in her as the mother of the man I am going to marry, but I am interested in her from the professional standpoint as well.".

" Indeed ? "

" Yes.  I am writing a book on criminal psychology.  I find the night life of this place very illuminating.  We have several criminal types who come here regularly.  I have discussed their early life with some of them.  Of course you know all about Vera's criminal tendencies—I mean that she steals ? "

" Why, yes—I know that," said Poirot, slightly taken aback.

" I call it the Magpie complex myself.  She takes, you know, always *glittering* things.  Never money.  Always jewels.  I find that as a child she was petted and indulged but very much shielded.  Life was unendurably dull for her—dull and safe. Her nature demanded drama—it craved for *punishment*.  That is at the root of her indulgence in theft.  She wants the *importance*, the *notoriety* of being *punished* ! "

Poirot objected, " Her life can surely not have been safe and dull as a member of the *ancien régime* in Russia during the Revolution ? "

A look of faint amusement showed in Miss Cunningham's pale blue eyes.

"Ah," she said. "A member of the *ancien régime?* She has told you that?"

"She is undeniably an aristocrat," said Poirot staunchly, fighting back certain uneasy memories of the wildly varying accounts of her early life told him by the Countess herself.

"One believes what one wishes to believe," remarked Miss Cunningham, casting a professional eye on him.

Poirot felt alarmed. In a moment, he felt, he would be told what was *his* complex. He decided to carry the war into the enemy's camp. He enjoyed the Countess Rossakoff's society partly because of her aristocratic *provenance*, and he was not going to have his enjoyment spoiled by a spectacled little girl with boiled gooseberry eyes and a degree in psychology !

"Do you know what I find astonishing?" he asked.

Alice Cunningham did not admit in so many words that she did *not* know. She contented herself with looking bored but indulgent.

Poirot went on :

"It amazes me that *you*—who are young, and who could look pretty if you took the trouble—well, it amazes me that you do *not* take the trouble ! You wear the heavy coat and skirt with the big pockets as though you were going to play the game of golf. But it is not here the golf links, it is the underground cellar with the temperature of 71 Fahrenheit, and your nose it is hot and shines, but you do not powder it, and the lipstick you put it on your mouth without interest, without emphasising the curve of the lips ! You are a woman, but you do not draw attention to the fact of being a woman. And I say to you ' *Why not?* ' It is a pity ! "

For a moment he had the satisfaction of seeing Alice Cunningham look human. He even saw a spark of anger in her eyes. Then she regained her attitude of smiling contempt.

"My dear M. Poirot," she said, "I'm afraid you're out of touch with the modern ideology. It is *fundamentals* that matter—not the trappings."

She looked up as a dark and very beautiful young man came towards them.

"This is a most interesting type," she murmured with zest.

" Paul Varesco ! Lives on women and has strange depraved cravings ! I want him to tell me more about a nursery governess who looked after him when he was three years old."

A moment or two later she was dancing with the young man. He danced divinely. As they drifted near Poirot's table, Poirot heard her say : " And after the summer at Bognor she gave you a toy crane ? A *crane*—yes, that's very suggestive."

For a moment Poirot allowed himself to toy with the speculation that Miss Cunningham's interest in criminal types might lead one day to her mutilated body being found in a lonely wood. He did not like Alice Cunningham, but he was honest enough to realise that the reason for his dislike was the fact that she was so palpably unimpressed by Hercule Poirot ! His vanity suffered !

Then he saw something that momentarily put Alice Cunningham out of his head. At a table on the opposite side of the floor sat a fair-haired young man. He wore evening dress, his whole demeanour was that of one who lives a life of ease and pleasure. Opposite him sat the right kind of expensive girl. He was gazing at her in a fatuous and foolish manner. Any one seeing them might have murmured : " The idle rich ! " Nevertheless Poirot knew very well that the young man was neither rich nor idle. He was, in fact, Detective Inspector Charles Stevens, and it seemed probable to Poirot that Detective Inspector Stevens was here on business. . . .

On the following morning Poirot paid a visit to Scotland Yard to his old friend Chief Inspector Japp.

Japp's reception of his tentative inquiries was unexpected.

" You old fox ! " said Japp affectionately. " How you get on to these things beats me ! "

" But I assure you I know nothing—nothing at all ! It is just idle curiosity."

Japp said that Poirot could tell that to the Marines !

" You want to know all about this place *Hell* ? Well, on the surface it's just another of these things. It's caught on ! They must be making a lot of money, though of course the expenses are pretty high. There's a Russian woman ostensibly running it, calls herself the Countess Something or other——"

"I am acquainted with Countess Rossakoff," said Poirot coldly. "We are old friends."

"But she's just a dummy," Japp went on. "She didn't put up the money. It might be the head waiter chap, Aristide Papopolous—he's got an interest in it—but we don't believe it's really his show either. In fact we don't know *whose* show it is!"

"And Inspector Stevens goes there to find out?"

"Oh, you saw Stevens, did you? Lucky young dog landing a job like that at the taxpayer's expense! A fat lot he's found out so far!"

"What do you suspect there is to find out?"

"Dope! Drug racket on a large scale. And the dope's being paid for not in money, but in precious stones."

"Aha?"

"This is how it goes. Lady Blank—or the Countess of Whatnot—finds it hard to get hold of cash—and in any case doesn't want to draw large sums out of the Bank. But she's got jewels—family heirlooms sometimes! They're taken along to a place for 'cleaning' or 'resetting'—there the stones are taken out of their settings and replaced with paste. The unset stones are sold over here or on the Continent. It's all plain sailing—there's been no robbery, no hue and cry after them. Say sooner or later it's discovered that a certain tiara or necklace is a fake? Lady Blank is all innocence and dismay—can't imagine *how* or *when* the substitution can have taken place—necklace has never been out of her possession! Sends the poor, perspiring police off on wild-goose chases after dismissed maids, or doubtful butlers, or suspicious window-cleaners.

"But we're not quite so dumb as these social birds think! We had several cases come up one after another—*and we found a common factor*—all the women showed signs of dope—nerves, irritability—twitching, pupils of eyes dilated, etcetera. Question was: Where were they getting the dope from and who was running the racket?"

"And the answer, you think, is this place *Hell*?"

"We believe it's the headquarters of the whole racket. We've discovered where the work on the jewellery is done—a place called Golconda Ltd.—respectable enough on the surface, high-class imitation jewellery. There's a nasty bit of work called Paul Varesco—ah, I see you know him ? "

" I have seen him—in *Hell*."

" That's where I'd like to see him—in the real place ! He's as bad as they make 'em—but women—even decent women— eat out of his hand ! He's got some kind of connection with Golconda Ltd. and I'm pretty sure he's the man behind *Hell*. It's ideal for his purpose—everyone goes there, society women, professional crooks—it's the perfect meeting place."

" You think the exchange—jewels for dope—takes place there ? "

" Yes. We know the Golconda side of it—we want the other —the dope side. We want to know who's supplying the stuff and where it's coming from."

" And so far you have no idea ? "

" I *think* it's the Russian woman—but we've no evidence. A few weeks ago we thought we were getting somewhere. Var-esco went to the Golconda place, picked up some stones there and went straight from there to *Hell*. Stevens was watching him, but he didn't actually see him pass the stuff. When Varesco left we picked him up—*the stones weren't on him*. We raided the club, rounded up everybody ! Result, no stones, no dope ! "

" A *fiasco*, in fact ? "

Japp winced. " You're telling me ! Might have got in a bit of a jam, but luckily in the round up we got Peverel (you know, the Battersea murderer). Pure luck, he was supposed to have got away to Scotland. One of our smart sergeants spotted him from his photos. So all's well that ends well— kudos for us—terrific boost for the club—it's been more packed than ever since !"

Poirot said :

" But it does not advance the dope inquiry. There is, perhaps, a place of concealment on the premises ? "

" Must be. But we couldn't find it. Went over the place with a toothcomb. And between you and me, there's been an unofficial search as well—" he winked. " Strictly on the Q.T. Spot of breaking and entering. Not a success, our ' unofficial ' man nearly got torn to pieces by that ruddy great dog ! It sleeps on the premises."

" Aha, Cerberus ? "

" Yes. Silly name for a dog—to call it after a packet of salt."

" Cerberus," murmured Poirot thoughtfully.

" Suppose you try your hand at it, Poirot," suggested Japp. " It's a pretty problem and worth doing. I hate the drug racket, destroys people body and soul. That really *is* Hell if you like ! "

Poirot murmured meditatively: " It would round off things—yes. Do you know what the twelfth labour of Hercules was ? "

" No idea."

" *The Capture of Cerberus*. It is appropriate, is it not ? "

" Don't know what you're talking about, old man, but remember : ' *Dog eats Man* ' is news." And Japp leaned back roaring with laughter.


" I wish to speak to you with the utmost seriousness," said Poirot.

The hour was early, the Club as yet nearly empty. The Countess and Poirot sat at a small table near the doorway.

" But I do not feel serious," she protested. " *La petite Alice*, she is always serious and, *entre nous*, I find it very boring. My poor Niki, what fun will he have ? None."

" I entertain for you much affection," continued Poirot steadily. " And I do not want to see you in what is called the jam."

" But it is absurd what you say there ! I am on top of the world, the money it rolls in ! "

" You own this place ? "

The Countess's eye became slightly evasive.

" Certainly," she replied.

" But you have a partner ? "

" Who told you that ? " asked the Countess sharply.

" Is your partner Paul Varesco ? "

" Oh ! Paul Varesco ! What an idea ! "

" He has a bad—a criminal record. Do you realise that you have criminals frequenting this place ? "

The Countess burst out laughing.

" There speaks the *bon bourgeois* ! Naturally I realise ! Do you not see that that is half the attraction of this place ? These young people from Mayfair—they get tired of seeing their own kind round them in the West End. They come here, they see the criminals ; the thief, the blackmailer, the confidence trickster—perhaps, even, the murderer—the man who will be in the Sunday papers next week ! It is exciting, that—they think they are seeing life ! So does the prosperous man who all the week sells the knickers, the stockings, the corsets ! What a change from his respectable life and his respectable friends ! And then, a further thrill—there at a table, stroking his moustache, is the Inspector from Scotland Yard—an Inspector in tails ! "

" So you knew that ? " said Poirot softly.

Her eyes met his and she smiled.

" *Mon cher ami*, I am not so simple as you seem to suppose ! "

" Do you also deal in drugs here ? "

" Ah, ça no ! " The Countess spoke sharply. " That would be an abomination ! "

Poirot looked at her for a moment or two, then he sighed.

" I believe you," he said. " But in that case it is all the more necessary that you tell me who really owns this place."

" I own it," she snapped.

" On paper, yes. But there is someone behind you."

" Do you know, *mon ami*, I find you altogether too curious ? Is he not much too curious, Dou dou ? "

Her voice dropped to a coo as she spoke the last words and she threw the duck bone from her plate to the big black hound who caught it with a ferocious snap of the jaws.

" What is it that you call that animal ? " asked Poirot, diverted.

" *C'est mon petit Dou dou !* "

" But it is ridiculous, a name like that ! "

" But he is adorable ! He is a police dog ! He can do anything—anything—Wait ! "

She rose, looked round her, and suddenly snatched up a plate with a large succulent steak which had just been deposited before a diner at a nearby table. She crossed to the marble niche and put the plate down in front of the dog, at the same time uttering a few words in Russian.

Cerberus gazed in front of him. The steak might not have existed.

" You see ? And it is not just a matter of *minutes* ! No, he will remain like that for *hours* if need be ! "

Then she murmured a word and like lightning Cerberus bent his long neck and the steak disappeared as though by magic.

Vera Rossakoff flung her arms round the dog's neck and embraced him passionately, rising on tip-toe to do so.

" See how gentle he can be ! " she cried. " For me, for Alice, for his friends—they can do what they like ! But one has but to give him the word and Presto ! I can assure you he would tear a—police inspector, for instance—into little pieces ! Yes, into little pieces ! "

She burst out laughing.

" I would have but to say the word——"

Poirot interrupted hastily. He mistrusted the Countess's sense of humour. Inspector Stevens might be in real danger.

" Professor Liskeard wants to speak to you."

The Professor was standing reproachfully at her elbow.

" You took my steak," he complained. " Why did you take my steak ? It was a good steak ! "

" Thursday night, old man," said Japp. " That's when the balloon goes up. It's Andrews' pigeon, of course—Narcotic Squad—but he'll be delighted to have you horn in. No, thanks, I won't have any of your fancy *sirops*. I have to take care of my stomach. Is that whisky I see over there ? That's more the ticket ! "

Setting his glass down, he went on :

" We've solved the problem, I think. There's another way out at that Club—*and we've found it !* "

" Where ? "

" Behind the grill. Part of it swings round."

" But surely you would see——"

" No, old boy. When the raid started, the lights went out—switched off at the main—and it took us a minute or two to get them turned on again. Nobody got out the front way because it was being watched, but it's clear now that somebody could have nipped out by the secret way with the doings. We've been examining the house behind the Club—and that's how we tumbled to the trick."

" And you propose to do—what ? "

Japp winked.

" Let it go according to plan—the police appear, the lights go out—*and somebody's waiting on the other side of that secret door to see who comes through*. This time we've *got* 'em ! "

" Why Thursday ? "

Again Japp winked.

" We've got the Golconda pretty well taped now. There will be stuff going out of there on Thursday. Lady Carrington's emeralds."

" You permit," said Poirot, " that I too make one or two little arrangements ? "

Sitting at his usual small table near the entrance on Thursday night Poirot studied his surroundings. As usual *Hell* was going with a swing !

The Countess was even more flamboyantly made up than usual if that was possible. She was being very Russian to-night, clapping her hands and screaming with laughter. Paul Varesco had arrived. Sometimes he wore faultless evening dress, sometimes, as to-night, he chose to present himself in a kind of *apache* get-up, tightly-buttoned coat, scarf round the neck. He looked vicious and attractive. Detaching himself from a stout, middle-aged woman plastered with diamonds, he leaned over Alice Cunningham who was sitting at a table writing busily in a little notebook and asked her to dance. The stout woman scowled at Alice and looked at Varesco with adoring eyes.

There was no adoration in Miss Cunningham's eyes. They gleamed with pure scientific interest, and Poirot caught fragments of their conversation as they danced past him. She had progressed beyond the nursery governess and was now seeking information about the matron at Paul's preparatory school.

When the music stopped, she sat down by Poirot looking happy and excited.

" Most interesting," she said. " Varesco will be one of the most important cases in my book. The symbolism is unmistakable. Trouble about the vests for instance—for vest read *hair shirt* with all its associations—and the whole thing becomes quite plain. You may say that he's a definitely criminal type but a cure *can* be effected——"

" That she can reform a rake," said Poirot, " has always been one of woman's dearest illusions ! "

Alice Cunningham looked at him coldly.

" There is nothing *personal* about this, M. Poirot."

" There never is," said Poirot. " It is always pure disinterested altruism—but the object of it is usually an attractive member of the opposite sex. Are you interested, for instance, in where *I* went to school, or what was the attitude of the matron to *me* ? "

" You are not a criminal type," said Miss Cunningham.

" Do you know a criminal type when you see one ? "

" Certainly I do."

Professor Liskeard joined them. He sat down by Poirot.

" Are you talking about criminals ? You should study the criminal code of Hammurabi, M. Poirot. 1800 B.C. Most interesting. *The man who is caught stealing during a fire shall be thrown into the fire.*"

He stared pleasurably ahead of him towards the electric grill.

" And there are older, Summerian laws. *If a wife hateth her husband and saith unto him, ' Thou art not my husband ' they shall throw her into the river.* Cheaper and easier than the divorce court. But if a husband says that to his wife he only has to pay her a certain measure of silver. Nobody throws *him* in the river."

" The same old story," said Alice Cunningham. " One law for the man and one for the woman."

" Women, of course, have a greater appreciation of monetary value," said the Professor thoughtfully. " You know," he added, " I like this place. I come here most evenings. I don't have to pay. The Countess arranged that—very nice of her—in consideration of my having advised her about the decorations, she says. Not that they're anything to do with me really—I'd no idea what she was asking me questions for—and naturally she and the artist have got everything *quite* wrong. I hope nobody will ever know I had the remotest connection with the dreadful things. I should never live it down. But she's a wonderful woman—rather like a Babylonian, I always think. The Babylonians were good women of business, you know——"

The Professor's words were drowned in a sudden chorus. The word ' Police ' was heard—women rose to their feet, there was a babel of sound. The lights went out and so did the electric grill.

As an undertone to the turmoil the Professor's voice went on tranquilly reciting various excerpts from the laws of Hammurabi.

When the lights went on again Hercule Poirot was halfway up the wide, shallow steps. The police officers by the door saluted him, and he passed out into the street and strolled to the corner. Just round the corner, pressed against the wall was a small and odoriferous man with a red nose. He spoke in an anxious, husky whisper.

" I'm 'ere, guv'nor. Time for me to do my stuff ? "

" Yes. Go on."

" There's a nawful lot of coppers about ! "

" That is all right. They've been told about you."

" I 'ope they won't interfere, that's all ? "

" They will not interfere. You're sure you can accomplish what you have set out to do ? The animal in question is both large and fierce."

" 'E won't be fierce to me," said the little man confidently. " Not with what I've got 'ere ! Any dog'll follow me to Hell for it ! "

" In this case," murmured Hercule Poirot, " he has to follow you *out* of Hell ! "

In the small hours of the morning the telephone rang. Poirot picked up the receiver.

Japp's voice said :

" You asked me to ring you."

" Yes, indeed. *Eh bien ?* "

" No dope—we got the emeralds."

" Where ? "

" In Professor Liskeard's pocket."

" Professor Liskeard ? "

" Surprises you, too ? Frankly I don't know what to think ! He looked as astonished as a baby, stared at them, said he hadn't the faintest idea how they got in his pocket, and dammit I believe he was speaking the truth ! Varesco could have slipped them into his pocket easily enough in the black out. I can't see a man like old Liskeard being mixed up in this sort of business. He belongs to all these high-falutin' societies, why he's even connected with the British Museum! The only thing he ever spends money on is books, and musty old second-hand books at that. No, he doesn't fit. I'm beginning to think we're wrong about the whole thing—there never has been any dope in that Club."

" Oh, yes there has, my friend, it was there to-night. Tell me, did no one come out through your secret way ? "

" Yes, Prince Henry of Scandenberg and his equerry—he only arrived in England yesterday. Vitamian Evans, the Cabinet Minister (devil of a job being a Labour Minister, you have to be so careful ! Nobody minds a Tory politician spending money on riotous living because the taxpayers think it's his own money—but when it's a Labour man the public feel it's *their* money he's spending ! And so it is in a manner of speaking.) Lady Beatrice Viner was the last—she's getting married the day after to-morrow to the priggish young Duke of Leominster. I don't believe any of that lot were mixed up in this."

" You believe rightly. Nevertheless, the dope *was* in the Club and someone took it out of the Club."

" Who did ? "

" I did, *mon ami*," said Poirot softly.

He replaced the receiver, cutting off Japp's spluttering noises, as a bell trilled out. He went and opened the front door. The Countess Rossakoff sailed in.

" If it were not that we are, alas, too old, how compromising this would be ! " she exclaimed. " You see, I have come as you told me to do in your note. There is, I think, a policeman behind me, but he can stay in the street. And now, my friend, what is it ? "

Poirot gallantly relieved her of her fox furs.

" Why did you put those emeralds in Professor Liskeard's pocket ? " he demanded. " *Ce n'est pas gentille, ce que vous avez fait la !* "

The Countess's eyes opened wide.

" Naturally, it was in *your* pocket I meant to put the emeralds ! "

"Oh, in *my* pocket?"

"Certainly. I cross hurriedly to the table where you usually sit—but the lights they are out and I suppose by inadvertence I put them in the Professor's pocket."

"And why did you wish to put stolen emeralds in my pocket?"

"It seemed to me—I had to think quickly, you understand —the best thing to do!"

"Really, Vera, you are *impayable*!"

"But, dear friend, *consider*! The police arrive, the lights go out (our little private arrangement for the patrons who must not be embarrassed) *and a hand takes my bag off the table*. I snatch it back, but I feel through the velvet something hard inside. I slip my hand in, I find what I know by touch to be jewels and I comprehend at once who has put them there!"

"Oh you do?"

"Of course I do! It is that *salaud*! It is that lizard, that monster, that double-faced, double-crossing, squirming adder of a pig's son, Paul Varesco."

"The man who is your partner in *Hell*?"

"Yes, yes, it is he who owns the place, who puts up the money. Until now I do not betray him—I can keep faith, me! But now that he double-crosses me, that he tries to embroil me with the police—ah! now I will spit his name out —yes, *spit* it out!"

"Calm yourself," said Poirot, "and come with me into the next room."

He opened the door. It was a small room and seemed for a moment to be completely filled with DOG. Cerberus had looked outsize even in the spacious premises of *Hell*. In the tiny dining-room of Poirot's service flat there seemed nothing else but Cerberus in the room. There was also, however, the small and odoriferous man.

"We've turned up here according to plan, guv'nor," said the little man in a husky voice.

"Dou dou!" screamed the Countess. "My angel Dou dou!"

Cerberus beat the floor with his tail—but he did not move.

"Let me introduce you to Mr. William Higgs," shouted Poirot, above the thunder of Cerberus's tail. "A master in his profession. During the *brouhaha* to-night," went on Poirot, " Mr. Higgs induced Cerberus to follow him up out of *Hell*."

" *You* induced him ? " The Countess stared incredulously at the small rat-like figure. " But *how ? How ?* "

Mr. Higgs dropped his eyes bashfully.

" 'Ardly like to say afore a lady. But there's things no dogs won't resist. Follow me anywhere a dog will if I want 'im to. Of course you understand it won't work the same way with bitches—no, that's different, that is."

The Countess Rossakoff turned on Poirot.

" But why ? *Why ?* "

Poirot said slowly :

" A dog trained for the purpose will carry an article in his mouth until he is commanded to loose it. He will carry it if need be for hours. Will you now tell your dog to drop what he holds ? "

Vera Rossakoff stared, turned, and uttered two crisp words.

The great jaws of Cerberus opened. Then, it was really alarming, *Cerberus's tongue seemed to drop out of his mouth.* . . .

Poirot stepped forward. He picked up a small package encased in pink, spongebag rubber. He unwrapped it. Inside it was a packet of white powder.

" What is it ? " the Countess demanded sharply.

Poirot said softly :

" *Cocaine.* Such a small quantity, it would seem—but enough to be worth thousands of pounds to those willing to pay for it. . . . Enough to bring ruin and misery to several hundred people. . . ."

She caught her breath. She cried out :

" And you think that *I*—but it is not so ! I swear to you it is not so ! In the past I have amused myself with the jewels, the *bibelots*, the little curiosities—it all helps one to live, you understand. And what I feel is, why not ? Why should one person own a thing more than another ? "

" Just what I feel about dogs," Mr. Higgs chimed in.

" You have no sense of right or wrong," said Poirot sadly to the Countess.

She went on :

" But *drugs—that, no !* For there one causes misery, pain, degeneration ! I had no idea—no faintest idea—that my so charming, so innocent, so delightful little *Hell* was being used for *that* purpose ! "

" I agree with you about dope," said Mr. Higgs. " Doping of greyhounds—that's dirty, that is ! I wouldn't never have nothing to do with anything like that, and I never '*ave* 'ad ! "

" But say you believe me, my friend," implored the Countess.

" But of course I believe you ! Have I not taken time and trouble to convict the real organiser of the dope racket. Have I not performed the twelfth Labour of Hercules and brought Cerberus up from Hell to prove my case ? For I tell you this, I do not like to see my friends framed—yes, *framed*—for it was *you* who were intended to take the rap if things went wrong ! It was in *your* handbag the emeralds would have been found and if any one had been clever enough (like me) to suspect a hiding-place in the mouth of a savage dog—*eh bien*, he is *your* dog, is he not ? Even if he *has* accepted *la petite Alice* to the point of obeying her orders also ! Yes, you may well open your eyes ! From the first I did not like that young lady with her scientific jargon and her coat and skirt with the big pockets. Yes, *pockets*. Unnatural that any woman should be so disdainful of her appearance ! And what does she say to me—that it is fundamentals that count ! Aha ! what is fundamental is pockets. Pockets in which she can carry drugs and take away jewels—a little exchange easily made whilst she is dancing with her accomplice whom she pretends to regard as a psychological case. Ah, but what a cover ! No one suspects the earnest, the scientific psychologist with a medical degree and spectacles. She can smuggle in drugs, and induce her rich patients to form the habit, and put up the money for a night club and arrange that it shall be run by someone with—shall we say, a little weakness in her past ! But she despises Hercule Poirot, she thinks she can deceive him with her talk of nursery governesses and vests ! *Eh bien*, I am ready for her. The lights go off. Quickly I rise from my table and go to stand by Cerberus. In the darkness I hear her come. She opens his mouth and forces in the package, and I—delicately, unfelt by her, I snip with a tiny pair of scissors a little piece from her sleeve."

Dramatically he produced a sliver of material.

"You observe—the identical checked tweed—and I will give it to Japp to fit it back where it belongs—and make the arrest—and say how clever once more has been Scotland Yard."

The Countess Rossakoff stared at him in stupefaction. Suddenly she let out a wail like a fog-horn.

"But my Niki—my Niki. This will be terrible for him——" She paused. "Or do you think not?"

"There are a lot of other girls in America," said Hercule Poirot.

"And but for you his mother would be in prison—in *prison* —with her hair cut off—sitting in a cell—and smelling of disinfectant! Ah, but you are wonderful—*wonderful*."

Surging forward she clasped Poirot in her arms and embraced him with Slavonic fervour. Mr. Higgs looked on appreciatively. The dog Cerberus beat his tail upon the floor.

Into the midst of this scene of rejoicing came the trill of a bell.

"Japp!" exclaimed Poirot, disengaging himself from the Countess's arms.

"It would be better, perhaps, if I went into the other room," said the Countess.

She slipped through the connecting door. Poirot started towards the door to the hall.

"Guv'nor," wheezed Mr. Higgs anxiously, "better look at yourself in the glass, 'adn't you?"

Poirot did so and recoiled. Lipstick and mascara ornamented his face in a fantastic medley.

"If that's Mr. Japp from Scotland Yard, 'e'd think the worst—sure to," said Mr. Higgs.

He added, as the bell pealed again, and Poirot strove feverishly to remove crimson grease from the points of his moustache: "What do yer want *me* to do—'ook it too? What about this 'ere 'Ell 'Ound?"

"If I remember rightly," said Hercule Poirot, "Cerberus returned to Hell."

"Just as you like," said Mr. Higgs. "As a matter of fact I've taken a kind of fancy to 'im. . . . Still, 'e's not the kind I'd like to pinch—not permanent—too noticeable, if you know what I mean. And think what he'd cost me in shin of beef or 'orseflesh! Eats as much as a young lion, I expect."

"From the Nemean Lion to the Capture of Cerberus," murmured Poirot. "It is complete."

A week later Miss Lemon brought a bill to her employer.

"Excuse me, M. Poirot. Is it in order for me to pay this? *Leonora, Florist. Red Roses.* Eleven pounds, eight shillings and sixpence. Sent to Countess Vera Rossakoff, *Hell*, 13 End St., W.C.1."

As the hue of red roses, so were the cheeks of Hercule Poirot. He blushed, blushed to the eyeballs.

"Perfectly in order, Miss Lemon. A little—er, tribute—to—to an occasion. The Countess's son has just become engaged in America—to the daughter of his employer, a steel magnate. Red roses are—I seem to remember, her favourite flower."

"Quite," said Miss Lemon. "They're very expensive this time of year."

Hercule Poirot drew himself up.

"There are moments," he said, "when one does not economise."

Humming a little tune, he went out of the door. His step was light, almost sprightly. Miss Lemon stared after him. Her filing system was forgotten. All her feminine instincts were aroused.

"Good gracious," she murmured. "I wonder. . . . Really —at *his* age! . . . . Surely not. . . ."

THE END